ZACK KAPLAN

Three Graves

Copyright © 2018 by Zack Kaplan

All rights reserved. No part of this publication may be reproduced, stored or transmitted in any form or by any means, electronic, mechanical, photocopying, recording, scanning, or otherwise without written permission from the publisher. It is illegal to copy this book, post it to a website, or distribute it by any other means without permission.

This novel is entirely a work of fiction. The names, characters and incidents portrayed in it are the work of the author's imagination. Any resemblance to actual persons, living or dead, events or localities is entirely coincidental.

First edition

ISBN: 9781718177352

This book was professionally typeset on Reedsy.
Find out more at reedsy.com

Before you embark on a journey of
revenge, dig two graves.
-Confucius

Chapter 1

Hand over lighter, instant ash once the first puff is inhaled. David Campos parks cars at the Hotel Bel Air. He had to use his twin brother's identity to get the job, because he's been caught boosting cars since he was twelve. He's had his share of strikes. One more and he'll find himself in lock-up for a long stretch. This keeps him on the straight and narrow. His partner this evening, James Powell's tale, is quite the opposite. He grew up in a poor black neighborhood, his father a bus driver and his mother an assistant at UCLA's parking office. He never fell in with the wrong crowd.

David offers a cigarette; James declines. He speaks as he exhales a cloud of smoke, "I don't know how you do it, college boy. School all day, standing here at night, studying between. I barely make it here for just this shit."

James gestures excitedly with his hands as he talks. "Gotta grind. If parking these cars isn't incentive enough to one day have one, I don't know what is."

David blows smoke out of the side of his mouth while shaking his head. "For you, maybe."

A Mercedes CLS550 Coupe pulls up. James nods at David. "I got this one. You finish your smoke across the way."

"Thanks bro." David scurries off into the shadows.

The driver door pops open. Max is a beast of a man, with a buzzed head and goatee, wearing a black T-shirt under a black suit. He hands the keys to James in exchange for a valet slip and opens the back door for his boss. Colin Graves, late thirties, handsome, dapper in his bespoke suit exits buttoning his jacket as he comes to full standing. He grabs the hand of his wife, Betty, as she floats out of the car. She's angelic, with model-turned-movie-star looks, and Colin treats her that way. They walk hand in hand towards the restaurant and Max follows behind as their car pulls away. He stands outside as they dine.

The restaurant attracts sophisticated and discerning customers. Solar systems have fewer stars than this eatery, both as an arbitrary means of measurement as well as celebrities who are regular patrons. The food is of superfine quality, exceptional appeal, and much too costly. The portions are microscopic and the prices are macroscopic. Most people hope to gain weight after a meal here. At least body fat is something tangible to justify the extraordinary price per mouthful.

The place is packed. The air is filled with the sound waves of casual conversations intermingling and bouncing off one another. Ornate molding frames the walls and the ceilings are coffered. Dark-grained wood and décor in black and white gives the place a noir feel. The only color comes from the strategically placed paintings of local LA Artist, Miles Regis, who must be more connected than the Prince of Darkness. The devil himself couldn't get a painting hung in here if his bifurcated tail depended on it.

The maitre d' seats Betty and Colin, pulling out her chair. Colin shakes his hand; this isn't their first time here. While they are far from regulars, both are memorable – especially Betty. Her presence does to Colin almost what a pacemaker would to someone with a heart condition. She gives him an invincibility that's almost dangerous. The waiter approaches and pours some water into each of their glasses. He pauses, then addresses them. "Are you ready or do you need a few moments?"

"We'll each have a double-double animal style, one bloomin' onion, and the unlimited salad and breadsticks."

Betty interjects. "He's joking, we need a second."

The waiter bows, "Of course." He walks away.

"A little pushy in this joint. I wasn't even able to open my menu and,

CHAPTER 1

let's face it, it'll take a second to decide. I read on a fifth grade level with about sixty percent comprehension. You look great, by the way."

Betty playfully gives him the middle finger. "Col, they want to subtly get us in and out. It's just business. Capitalism at its finest."

"Nice to meet you, Adam Smith. Care to give me an invisible hand job?"

Betty laughs. "Crude econ joke, eh? Would you rather be dining with Karl Marx?"

"Only if we order the Duck Soup." He wiggles his eyebrows and pantomimes playing with his cigar a la Groucho Marx.

"You don't have an off button, do you?" Her laughter lines have become more pronounced since they met.

"I hear it's near my prostate?"

She cuts a piece of butter and places it on her bread. "This bread is lousy. Lukewarm bread and ice-cold butter. It is like trying to spread a brick on a foam cushion."

"That's it. I'm posting a review online. How do you spell abomination? You look great, by the way."

Betty mouths 'fuck off'. "I shouldn't be filling up on bread anyway."

"I don't know; the portions are small. Maybe fill up on lousy bread? And water." He pauses. "Wow, a hundred bucks a piece to eat like we're in jail."

"For an extra fifty they'll shank you in the bathroom."

"Oh nice." He puts up his hand and she high fives him.

The waiter interrupts their conversation. "Excuse me. Are you ready to order?"

Betty clears her throat. "In a minute or two."

The waiter politely bows. "Of course."

She takes a sip of water. "This is a celebration, right?"

"Yes it is." Colin places his hand up in the air. "At work we had a sexual harassment seminar and I'm the first in my family to pass."

"Pass or make a pass?"

"You get slapped when you pass, right?"

3

Betty smirks and shakes her head.

Colin places his hands up. "Sonny is out and I am in."

Betty's eyes light up with excitement. "Finally!" She moves her hand across her neck, "I hope it was quick."

"Like a band aid." Colin takes a braggadocio tone. "He was clinging to what worked years ago, instead of adapting to what works now. Times have changed and with most things you have to evolve. Besides, he was a huge dick. And not in a good way."

"That's gross. You're the new blood?"

"In with the new blood, like a lifesaving transfusion. Remind me of this conversation thirty years from now when I'll need to adapt or retire." He holds out his hand and she grabs his pinky with hers.

"Will do." Betty picks up her water glass and clinks it against his. Colin scans the room in a panic. "Where's that waiter, I'm starving. You look great, by the way."

She shakes her head, her big eyes gazing at him.

The two starry-eyed sweethearts, deeply in love, enjoy a blissful dinner. Course after course, they never have to share silence. Colin leans in, "You know how I know that I love you?"

"Say that three times fast," Betty purses her lips. "No, how?"

"You sing a song only I can hear."

Betty squints. "That sounds familiar. You come up with that?"

"Not exactly, and you could google it. Go on the line as the kids call it, but it articulates perfectly how I feel so I stole it."

"It's beautiful, and I love you too."

"Wait... How was your day? The big case."

"Ugh, Jake wants me to be less aggressive with the Reynold's case."

"Less aggressive? Well isn't that so 10,000 spoons when all you need is a knife. He hired you because you're like a wolverine on testosterone and angel dust."

"You know, you don't always need to be so witty."

"I don't need to obsess over the Bachelor. It makes me happy."

"I guess witty is attractive on you."

CHAPTER 1

"It was between witty and bow ties. Bow ties are impossible to get even."

As their meal ends, Colin places his napkin on his plate and arches his back with satisfaction, while Betty reapplies her lipstick using her compact.

Colin notices another table eavesdropping, "So I say, Rosa, I know you're trying to find a new home for Luc, your six-year-old daughter, but the dark web is so sketchy. Not all those guys actually have that Jared from Subway money."

Betty leans in, "You're terrible."

"How many people in here are wondering how much you're costing me, do you think?"

"I'd say a few."

"How much are you costing me?"

"Cost. Past tense. One used purse."

"That's right. I made out like a bandit."

"Yeah you did."

When the bill comes, Colin pays. "Shall we?"

Betty nods affirmatively. Colin stands up and places his hand out, helping her out of her seat. He sweetly sneaks a kiss as she rises. The two walk arm in arm towards the exit. As they approach the door, Colin's driver waits awkwardly with their coats.

"Boss," Max whispers.

"Max. What's up?"

"I need to use the bathroom before we head home."

Colin smiles. "Jeez, big guy, you could've gone any time in the last hour." Max freezes. "I'm busting your chops. I think we can get the car without incident." Max hands him the valet ticket stub and they exit.

* * *

Max enters the bathroom as two patrons shuffle out, chatting as they pass him. There are mirrors above the sink. The tiles, from floor to ceiling, are black and white, with a shine that's almost blinding. This bathroom has an attendant who is old and frail. He has gray hair and shakes a little as he stands at his post. Max makes eye contact, nods at him, and hustles towards a urinal that is filled with ice. Max looks up as he urinates, finishes, and zips up with some difficulty, as the zipper refuses to cooperate. He heads over to the sink to wash up. The attendant walks over to help him.

"Thanks. I got it though." Max attends to someone day to day, and simply can't accept the pampering.

The attendant attempts to assuage Max's unwillingness to let him do his job. "Just trying to make a living." Max reaches into his pocket and pulls out some money. The attendant places his hand up, halting the transaction. "I'm old school, my friend. A penny earned. And, I didn't earn that money. Thank you, but my pride won't let me take handouts. I'm no beggar."

"I didn't mean any disrespect, sir. I didn't imply that you were. Why don't you just give me a hand?" The attendant turns the faucet on. He squirts soap on Max's hands and when Max is done rinsing off, the attendant hands him paper towels. Max places the money in the straw basket.

* * *

Colin stands with his arm around Betty while they wait for the car. She rests her head on his chest. Colin looks up, "It feels like it's about to rain, yeah?"

"I heard it was going to be a beautiful night."

"From some sort of authority or some dipshit?"

"The KTLA weather guy."

"Oh, the latter then. I don't trust that guy. His fake tan is too dark and his bleached teeth are too white. Besides, weathermen are like slot machines. But with less personality. The one time they pay off never makes up for the thousand times they don't. Unless you can't do math. Or have a gambling problem. Or trust people with made up names like Storm and Dallas."

Betty nods. "Predicting the unpredictable is a fool's endeavor. The future is meant to be unknown and ever changing, right? If fortune cookies were on the money, I'd never eat Chinese."

"Sing it sister." Colin pats his pockets, "Shit, I think I left my wallet on the table. Which was my last fortune cookie fortune. Made no sense at the time. I'll be right back."

Before he can even finish the sentence, a white van with blacked out windows comes to a screeching halt in front of them. The couple is jarred from their previously romantic pose. Colin steps in front of Betty like a mama bear protecting her cub. His brow furrows. "What the fuck?"

The door slides open violently. Overlapping heartbeats get louder and faster. Two men in ski masks jump out, one punches Colin in the stomach. Doubled over, he searches the deepest recesses of his lungs for whatever breath he can muster. He tastes the cigarette he tried when he was fifteen. The other masked man grabs Betty; she flails and screams but cannot overpower her kidnapper. He throws her into the belly of the van. The two men then drag her winded husband into the darkness, like demons pulling a soul into hell.

The gas pedal is slammed to the floor; the rear tires smoke, and take a second to grip the road. The van fishtails, causing the side door to slide shut, before tearing off into the night.

Max, on the scene seconds too late, is washed over with panic. His heart rate instantly skyrockets. He gets the license plate number of the van as it speeds off. "No. No. No. Fuck! Fuck me!" His shaking hands can barely handle his phone.

Chapter 2

A remote, empty park has seen its share of bad things. Precipitation bloats each air molecule and the huge raindrops pelt the headlights of half a dozen cars. A faint vapor rises from the hot lights like a spirit leaving the body. The cars are lined up in a V-shape, like a flock of birds flying south for the winter. This tight pattern is a barrier or blockade. On one side there's destitution of light and on the other, crystalline spheres scare away the obscured field. Scattered brightness mixed with dark shadows provides a terrifying backdrop. There's a smell in the air. Any animals within the perimeter have long headed for the hills.

Death is breathing down Colin's neck. His hot breath is teeming with bristling hostility that makes his hair stand on end. Colin is on his knees, able to feel his spongy kneecaps. Betty is next to him. Colin looks into Betty's eyes. "Don't worry. I'm sure this is because I forgot to pay the water bill." Despite being completely wet from the rain, he can differentiate her tears from the rainwater. He whispers, "You look great, by the way."

She mouths 'fuck off' and Colin smiles.

He scans the eyes of the many unsavory henchman toting automatic weapons surrounding them. This isn't a joke and there's certainly no punch line. Betty and Colin have been caught in rains like this before and it was romantic. This lacks all of the sentiment and tenderness of those times. There will be no drying off by the fire when this is over.

Another man enters the fray. This man is no faceless silhouette securing the perimeter. Richard Pembroke holds a giant golf umbrella to avoid the monsoon rain and gale force winds. He saunters over holding a gun with villainous panache. He's handsome, manly, and well dressed. "Competition is healthy, no matter what the endeavor," rolls smoothly off Richard's tongue, dripping with evil. Betty's lip begins to quiver, like the petals of a delicate flower. "When I found out my bottom line was affected by a new kid on the block, I had to intervene."

Colin shakes his head in disbelief. He may not be able to talk himself out of this predicament. However, when being faced with an option that may not work and no other option, it's difficult to discriminate. "All due respect, I can tell by your boy band you mean business. I don't know who you think I am, but you're mistaken. It's no big deal, it happens. In fact, people think I'm Willie from *Duck Dynasty* all the time. Is that who you're after?"

Richard smirks, makes a gesture, and a shadow steps forward, slamming Colin in the face. "You're mistaken if you think I make mistakes."

Colin shakes off the punch. "That escalated quickly. How about we rewind?"

Richard pulls his hands to his chest as he talks, "Fitz, do I look incompetent?"

"Whoa, Fitz? Who the fuck is Fitz? I'm Colin. Colin Graves." He reaches for his wallet, "Fuck! My wallet is at the restaurant."

Richard pulls his gun out from his belt. "Sounds about right." He shoots Colin in the knee. Colin screams.

Betty springs up, grabbing the closest henchman's gun, who was clearly asleep with his eyes open. She points the gun at Richard and right before she can pull the trigger, the henchman grabs her hand, forcing the gunshot directly into the sky.

Richard doesn't even flinch. A Cheshire Cat smile inhabits his face as he aims his pistol. With the nonchalance of someone turning on a light switch, he empties his gun into Betty then his own guy. Betty's eyes are as big as saucers, as she feels the hot metal tear through her body.

They connect with Colin's eyes; he lets out a scream from deep in his gullet, nearly bursting his esophagus. In an instant, she collapses. The echo of Colin's heart breaking reverberates in his ears. The smell of cordite from the gunshots enters his nostrils and rips out his nose hairs. His chest tightens like a boa constrictor wrapped its powerful body around his torso and is squeezing the life out of him. He dry heaves and stands shakily. "You..."

"I sell drugs. You sell drugs. I'm the man. You want to be the man." Richard cracks his neck like a frustrated psychopath. His Id takes over; he shoots Colin in the other knee. Colin falls to the ground. Richard steps forward and places the barrel of his pistol, still warm from the shot he just squeezed off, in between Colin's eyes.

Colin breathes in deeply, "Do it! Just do it!" His hands are at his side; he has acquiesced.

Richard is mildly impressed by this guy's mustard. "Do you think you can turn over a new leaf?"

Colin tilts his head slightly. He doesn't have the heart left to play this game.

"The leaf in the expression is actually the page of a book. Just as the plot of a novel changes from page to page, people can change, right?"

"I love rhetoric, too. Truly. How about we get to the point in the story where you just kill me?"

"Oh, we're nearly there."

Richard snaps his fingers. This small, unspoken gesture is enough to change potential energy into kinetic energy. Two mammoth figures approach Colin like trained pit bulls. One grabs his arm; he swings his free hand landing a solid punch to the guy's face. He may as well have punched a wall. The beast didn't flinch, and his fist incurred most of the trauma. He wiggles away and pushes the other monster. They close in on him, suffocating his fire until it's snuffed out. Together they lock him up in a vice grip with his right arm extended.

There is 'good' on the map and this place, right now, at this time can't be further away. This is bad. Actually, bad is meat past the expiration date. This is as if you turned bad up to eleven. Colin can't even squirm. Richards tucks his gun into his belt and holds his hand out to receive. He's handed an axe. The wet blade is shiny and sharp as hell. Colin closes his eyes preparing to meet Betty soon.

Without hesitation, Richard swings the axe hitting where Colin's arm meets his shoulder, severing the connection completely. Blood spurts into the faces of the two men holding him, with some spatter making its way onto Richard. Colin's eyes roll in the back of his head and he falls limp, completely out cold. Richard spits on him. "Wise-ass motherfucker."

Within seconds, Richard's phone rings to the tune of the show *Alfred Hitchcock Presents*. He answers it and listens intently. As each second passes, Richard's pesky forehead vein begins to dance a little faster and a little harder. "What do you mean the wrong fucking guy!?" Richard places his hands on the bridge of his nose and hangs up. He thinks for a moment. He shouts to the wall of shadows behind him. "VINCE! Clean this mess up!"

Chapter 3

Richard's house is picturesque and operates like its own little entity. It's gated and set back from the road. Armed guards are strategically placed to keep out rivals. They wear suits like businessmen, but the straps of their TEC-9 automatics show when they stretch, sometimes revealing the tips of these deadly weapons. Gardeners are mowing the lawn, planting flowers, and trimming hedges. Their priority is to keep the lawn lush and dark green despite the drought. High-end luxury cars shine and glitter in the sun.

Richard rubs elbows with his underlings. This is a transparent attempt to assuage this abnormal feeling of remorse over killing an innocent couple. He fancies himself one of the guys, although at the drop of a hat he'd eliminate any one of them without a second thought. He's highly educated and has studied Machiavelli's *The Prince* as well as Marcus Aurelius' *Meditations*. He strives to instill fear, but he can't completely let go of the idea of being loved.

Muffled banter and crowd clamor emanates from the billiards room. Richard is shooting pool with the guys and he has a winning streak. The thought doesn't cross his mind that his guys throw every game.

Vincent stands beside him. He has slicked back black hair, is roughly thirty, handsome, fit, and ruthless. He's Richard's right-hand man. He never takes a drink…ever. He's always on call and realizes mistakes are costly and to be inebriated during a situation is unacceptable. He has a working girl that sees to his manly urges and he refuses to get close to anyone of the opposite sex. That type of relationship is a liability. In this game if you can't hurt someone directly, you hurt the people they care about.

Vincent speaks as he casually shoots since he's not really trying to win. "Boss, this new table is beautiful." He rubs the side. "Gorgeous."

Richard responds while chalking his stick. "This was Jackie Gleason's table." Noises of curiosity and amazement fill the room. "I bought it at auction. The story goes that in order to get the product placement in *The Hustler*, they had to give Gleason and Newman each a custom table. The Newman family still has his table. I'm assuming." Richard points to the gold coins placed around the top of the table. "Apparently, Gleason wanted these gold coins put in the table, but the cost would have been tremendous if they had used U.S. currency. These coins are Mexican. These rails aren't original either. Gleason wanted bronze but it looked like shit every time someone touched it."

One of Richard's most trusted guys, Piney, chimes in. "I bet this cost a pretty penny." Piney is solidly built, rough and tough, however his frame hides his bad eating habits. His working class British accent openly interchanges 'f's and 'th's.

Declan 'Piney' Pine was a prolific gambler in his youth. This proclivity to embrace games of chance is what landed him on Richard's crew. Back then he didn't rent an apartment or own a home. He lived in a trailer. Not a shitty trailer that trash lives in, rather a mint Airstream, pulled by his truck. It was a beautiful thing. He named it Bernadette after the song by The Four Tops. It had a generator for when he was drydocked and a satellite dish so he was able to watch his favorite football team, Liverpool. He lived the life. Piney drove minutes...hours...days to places he'd never heard of but always wanted to see.

Piney was a damn good professional gambler. Sometimes he didn't know what he was betting on, but he could always break down the math. Early on, Piney was the best backgammon player around. Some of the venues these tournaments were held at; schools, boy-scout clubs, and retirement homes made the marks easy targets. Old people, teachers, kids, and non-professionals were a great way to practice and this is how he cut his teeth.

Eventually, he moved up to the big time and found himself in the back of bars and mafia-owned clubs. People will play anything for money and backgammon was huge. Celebrities would call him up and arrange a game just so they could say they lost to Piney. Everyone who was anyone owed him money. He had markers all over town. The time had come for him to move onto something else.

Piney was a quick learner and became a master cheat at cards. One night, he was greedy and got caught during Richard's weekly game. He bet himself out of that jam and has worked for him ever since.

Richard leans on his stick. He takes a deep breath and begins to speak. "What a fucked up night. We get a solid tip about a guy that turns up soft."

Vincent takes a shot and retorts. "Don't beat yourself up over it, boss. Shit happens."

"Shit happens if you let it happen. I should've known better." Richard is bonding with his men and despite admitting he made a mistake, he doesn't tolerate the mistakes of others.

Richard's nephew, Timmy, can't keep his mouth shut. In his mid-twenties, Timmy has the wisdom of a much younger man. He's gawky and lanky. His epidermis looks simply pulled over a skeleton with little care and little emphasis on what makes one aesthetically acceptable. He compensates by having a thin, overly tidy goatee and a uniform that consists of long, ultra baggy shorts that hang low on his hips and a wife-beater over his torso. To top off the look, he wears an oversized fitted baseball cap crooked to the side.

His speech pattern is ghetto even though he'd be terrified in an actual ghetto. He's a 'wannabe.' There are people cut out to be criminals and then there's Timmy. The appeal of the life suborns this mere miscreant to be more than he's capable of handling. Timmy plays video games and reads comic books. He's a little boy among men. He never 'wacked' anybody and if he wasn't related to Richard he would be re-shelving movies at Blockbuster, if brick and mortar video stores still existed. God only knows this is all he could handle. Working the register has too many steps for him. To his credit, despite using ADD as an excuse for poor grades and an inability to concentrate, he can play hours of Halo without losing concentration.

Timmy nods as he speaks. "Uncle Rich, why don't you, like, send their family some money or something?"

Richard's demeanor suddenly changes, as he doesn't tolerate Timmy's lack of sagacity. The idea that he may share genes with Timmy causes him to shudder. He usually rationalizes Timmy's condition, as he's been known to call it, as environmental. An outside influence, whether it was mercury-based preservatives in his vaccinations or too much sun as a baby before his cranium solidified, must have caused this head shaking result. "Money? So I track down living relatives, if any, and send them random money?"

Piney interjects trying to help the young lad. "Money fixes a lot of problems, wee Timmy, but it would be difficult to place a value on what happened."

Timmy continues to press the matter. "Twenty-five G's?"

After a double take, Richard decides to toy with Timmy like a cat that has trapped a field mouse. "Twenty-five thousand dollars?"

Timmy looks up, really thinking hard, "No, fitty G's. That'd be sweet."

Richard smiles devilishly and looks in Vincent's direction. "Vince, go into the safe and get me 'fitty' G's."

Vincent walks over to the safe and begins to open it.

"Timmy, I have fifty thousand dollars and I'm going to buy your arm from you and kill your baby momma. You have a baby momma right? I'm assuming you've had sex with a woman. And neither of you would have the wherewithal to protect the world from your progeny. What do you say?"

The metallic clunk of the safe opening coincides with the end of Richard's proposition. This fat cat bats around his little mouse much to his own amusement. Timmy points to himself and then the safe and back to himself. He shrinks. "Uh, no disrespect...."

Richard cuts him off quicker than a mohel with a Ginsu knife. "Any sentence that starts off 'no disrespect' will undoubtedly be disrespectful. The qualification makes the subsequent statement less absolute."

Timmy's heart is in his stomach and he would do anything to shift the earth's rotation, turning back the hands of time. "It's just that I've been saving up for this lit Ducati and it may be tough to drive it with one arm. You feel me, right?"

Richard smiles and his sadistic side becomes even more apparent. "I feel ya. How far away are you from your purchase?" Timmy tells him he's eight thousand away and subtracting.

Richard signals to Miles, who is albino blond with pale skin. He lacks the beady red eyes found on inbred rodents. His short blond hair looks like a bad dye job, but platinum is actually his natural color. He grabs Timmy with his ghostly white hands. "Don't squirm."

Timmy begins to whine, "Never mind, I take it back." The sound of pleas for mercy is music to Richard's ears. He cannot help himself around pain, suffering, and fear. He feels the rush of endorphins like an addict as the deadly poison enters the bloodstream. "Disrespect is all around us and it really gets my goat. For example, there's no greater injustice than the disrespect directed at our first president, General George Washington. He was the measure of a man. How do we repay this forefather who freed us from the tyrannical British and laid the groundwork for the greatest country in the world? We place him on the lowest denomination bill. One dollar! A buck? This bill is shoved into G-strings all over the world. This dollar bill is wrinkled and tattered so often that soda machines don't recognize it. This dollar bill is given to bums and vagrants. This dollar bill is rolled up and used as a straw by fucking coke-heads. This bill is barely given the respect of regular worthless paper. Do you see what I'm driving at?"

Timmy can barely speak. "George Washington is great and dollar bills should be taken more seriously?" Timmy's lips are quivering and his mouth is dry.

CHAPTER 3

Richard pulls out a knife.

"Please don't. Please." Timmy squirms.

"Timmy don't squirm, it'll only make things worse." Richard uses the knife to cut Timmy's pinky off. He screams and begins to cry. "Now tell me. Should I let sleeping dogs lie with regard to last night or should I try and make up for what I did?"

Timmy just shakes his head crying. He mutters unintelligibly, "Sleeping dogs. Sleeping dogs."

Chapter 4

The sun is shining. The gloom has burned off. The early morning dew is evaporating. The park is magnificent with dogs galloping, catching frisbees, and secretly stealing moments with other dogs. People are having picnics, reading the paper, relaxing. Joggers are burning calories, listening to music, and staying fit.

It's LA. The city of angels. However, these angels have dirty faces and dirtier hands. The males are injecting steroids, hoping their square chins and chiseled abs will make them action stars. The females are going under the knife and working the casting couch, hoping their 'look' will give them careers. If they're lucky, it will.

Mick Reese wants the life. The acting bug crawled into his ear and devoured any part of his brain that would accept anything else. He's tall and thin, with a full head of dark hair. He's classically good looking, without being too pretty. He's been grinding it out for years now; audition after audition. In the same day he's been told that he's too short, too tall, too fat, and too skinny. His skin is thick and he knows that if he hangs in there long enough, his time will come.

Mick is up early staying in shape. If nothing else, the adrenaline will clear his head in case his two-bit agent finds some time to send him out. He's wearing sweat-pant shorts and a tank top. He's jogging, thinking about how cool his hair looks as he bounces, now that he has a little sweat on his brow. A cyclist loses control and Mick avoids a head-on collision by taking a detour off the beaten path. He stumbles a little on the uneven terrain, carefully coming to a halt. He turns towards the path emoting disdain like he learned in his cold reading class. "Fucker!" He walks towards the path and something catches his attention. Mesmerized by what's on the ground, like a tractor beam locked onto his eyeballs, he eventually snaps out of his daze and begins to dial furiously. He fumbles the phone, spastically regaining control. His hands cannot dial quickly enough. He takes a deep breath as he waits for an answer on the other end of the line.

The voice is calm and collected. "Police emergency."

"911! 911! I was running in the park...And this fucking biker... bicycler? Cyclist? Whatever. Anyway, I ended up off the path. I noticed on the ground." The veins in Mick's neck look like a bunch of tangled bungee cords. If his acting coach would have one critique it's that he doesn't have the adequate range for this type of scenario. He's not acting here and it's glorious. Maybe he can channel this next time he has to act like his daughter was kidnapped by terrorists.

The calm voice continues with an almost non-human tone. "Sir, what's the nature of this emergency?"

"I found a dead body in the park?" He almost doesn't believe his own words. Is this the beginning of one of the crime shows Mick has auditioned for a million times? He looks around surveying the area. Maybe this is a joke? If someone tells a joke, but there's no one around to hear it, is it a funny? He curiously pokes the dirty, bare feet with his foot.

The android voice on the other end of the line serenely asks, "What's your location?"

Mick looks around frantically, trying to get a clue to his exact location. "I don't know." He's frustrated by the scenery's similar look at every turn. "I'm surrounded by foliage."

The voice, free from disturbance, asks, "Foliage?"

"Can you ping my phone?"

"Ping your phone?"

"If you keep repeating what I say, this conversation is going to take twice as long. Can you trace my location? Pretend I'm nine years old. I don't know where I am. Do parks have addresses? There are trees and brush."

"What type of trees?"

"Are you an arborist? Because I'm not."

"So just dispatch an ambulance to 'a park somewhere with trees'?"

"I hope your supervisor listens to this call. Wait, ambulance? This guy is way past an ambulance. He is super fucking dead."

"There is a procedure in case you are mistaken."

Mick looks down at the dirty, headless, naked, male body at his feet. "I bet you a thousand dollars I'm not mistaken."

The park's secluded woods, quiet just minutes before have turned into a hive of activity. Police have secured the perimeter; both legitimate news and stringers attempt to get pictures of the violent scene. Firefighters stand around looking sexy. An ambulance is parked within the mess. The ambulance driver stands five feet from the body talking to Mick. He's short and thin, wearing a baseball-type hat that says EMT. He has a goatee and horn-rimmed glasses. He's eating an apple and spitting the juice everywhere as his lips smack with each giant bite.

After a few moments of silence Mick blurts out, "How stiff is his fucking dick?"

The EMT guy has his arms crossed and matter-of-factly retorts, "Stiff as a board. Could be bigger?"

Mick is now nervous about the subject. "I'm no cock expert."

The EMT places his hands up as he speaks, "I mean, me neither. I'm not trying to insult the guy or anything. I'm sure he made a lot of women happy... Or guys. Whatever." He crosses his arms again.

Mick crosses his arms like the EMT, as though he's studying his mannerisms. "I know that people, what's the term, rigor... rigor mortis. I was an extra on CSI."

"Yeah, everything hardens up like cement."

The coroner exits his van and slowly makes his way to the body. He hobbles over to the scene as he's in his mid-sixties, out of shape, and

CHAPTER 4

about a quart low this morning. He kneels down and all the blood rushes to his face like a dam broke. He lets out a sigh; he completely lacks flexibility.

"The coroner looks like he'll need a coroner before long."

The EMT nods, "Yup. He's pretty unhealthy and between you and me... he drinks his lunch."

"I would too if my job revolved around corpses."

A detective makes his way through the crowd, badge hanging around his neck. Dane is the epitome of everything people admire. He has blond hair and icy blue eyes. He would be Hitler's poster boy if it were 1936. His stature is impressive and his posture perfect. Strong, smart, tough, cunning. Dane doesn't take guff from anyone and people love him. He comes from a long line of cops: his grandfather, his father, his brother, all his uncles. Dane didn't always want the badge woven into the double helix of his DNA. He wrestled a demon or two. Occasionally, one of the demons would force him into submission.

***

When he was seventeen, Dane and two of his buddies committed a reprehensible crime. Something most people don't get away with. Dane was wild, brash, irascible, and never mentally conceived the notion of potential consequences. The repercussions of being a felon among a family of police never entered his bean. He didn't consider the embarrassment to his father, still active at the time. The three would-be thugs entered a liquor store with ski masks on. Dane was puerile in thinking he should bring his grandfather's service revolver to this shindig. Both friends bought pieces, cheapo Saturday night specials, from gang bangers.

The liquor store attendant decided to stand up for himself. The three teens went in tough, expecting the resistance of a cancer patient but instead found themselves in a pseudo-Mexican stand-off with an Indo-Asian Charles Bronson on PCP. The tension was palpable. Everyone was shouting and Dane was trying to calm the situation. One of his buddies was barely holding it together. When the clerk accidentally knocked over the jerky display causing a loud bang, Dane's jittery accomplice accidentally shot the clerk.

Unfortunately for the crew, the liquor store was in their neighborhood. Dane's father happened to enter the establishment after his shift, hoping to buy a bottle of Jim Beam, but instead found his son committing a crime. The three boys were standing over the body each blaming someone else when the bells on the door started ringing. Dane's father recognized his boy despite the ski mask. "Dane?"

"Dad?"

Dane's father looked the three boys right in their eyes. "Listen, guys. Calm down."

Dane's eyes drooped with sadness at his father's obvious disappointment. "Dad, I'm sor—"

Before Dane can finish his sentence, Dane's father fired two shots, killing his two friends instantly. "Listen boy, get the fuck outta here. This is your free pass. You'll become a cop or I'll put you down like I put down these scumbags." Dane ran out of the liquor store. Dane's father destroyed the video surveillance tape and received a medal for killing the two robbers.

* * *

Dane calmly walks up to the coroner. "What's up?" Dane places his hands on his hips.

The coroner wheezes a little and Dane helps him to his feet. "The loose head we have back in the fridge doesn't go with this body."

"Another decap? Well, that's not good."

The coroner finishes a swig from his special water bottle. "Yup."

Dane sniffs the coroner's bottle and shoots him a smirk. "This doesn't feel gang related or serial killer. Just feels odd. Almost familiar."

"That's your department. I'm the 'how' guy; you're the 'why' guy."

"I'm feeling the 'how' is going to be easier than the 'why.' Maybe there's some trace on the body. Update me when you get this guy back to the fridge. Try not to get aroused."

"Too late."

They both chuckle.

An officer, in uniform, walks up to Dane. He taps him on the shoulder. "Dane, the Captain wants to see you." Dane acknowledges the uniformed cop and nods.

Mick finds himself within the mist of several police officers. He stands in the center regaling them with comical stories of casting calls. "I'm in the room with the director for a callback, big-time movie guy doing a toothpaste commercial. They have me and this other guy come in, dressed in tuxedos. We are both standing there, waiting for him to connect with this woman in Peru on Skype with his iPad. It's like 2am there, and once they're connected, he brings the iPad over so the people on the other end can see each of us. Mind you, no lines, just standing there. And there's this cat. The cat gestured, purred whatever, and picked the other guy! He fucking needed the cat's opinion."

The guffaws suddenly turn to coughs and the officers either look down at the ground or walk away. Detective Ferina ruined this good time, which tends to be his modus operandi. He walks up to Mick and gets in his face. Ferina is either aggressive or passive aggressive, depending on who he's pestering. He's Cuban but refuses to permit any accent to slip out. He comes from a family of crooks, charlatans, and con artists. Both grandfathers were thieves. His father sold drugs, his brothers sell drugs, and his sisters are whores. Instead of being embarrassed about his family, Ferina embraces the fact he's extra special for not falling into the same traps. His superiority complex is a weak façade that only works on those intimidated by the badge. He's not crooked, but he does turn a blind eye when it comes to his family. As long as nobody with his last name kills anybody, he can go about his business without mixing his personal and professional lives. He's on borrowed time as it's only a matter of when; the day his two worlds will collide.

Ferina treads in no-man's-land as his family wants nothing to do with the law and he's not well liked on the force. When he was a newly promoted detective, he was partnered with a legend. This mentor begrudgingly took on this newbie whose performance up until that point was mediocre, but perseverance was enough to close the gap of passing and failing. The two were involved in a drug case that began with buy and busts that graduated to wiretapping, and after too many nights of surveillance, a solid case led to arrest warrants. Since they were the lead detectives, they had the right to bring in these dealers. During the bust, Ferina didn't frisk one of the perpetrators. The perp got the drop on Ferina's partner and Ferina froze. The legend was used as a human shield and he took a bullet behind the ear as the perp fled the scene. Ferina was cleared because the confusion created enough doubt, but his reputation was soiled like his undergarments during this faux pas. Ferina developed a defense mechanism making him more despised. He was difficult to deal with, a loner, and just a real prick.

Ferina obnoxiously waves his badge in Mick's face and speaks to the group of officers who were too cowardly to walk away. "Is this the guy? Anybody? Anybody working here or you just standing around on the city's dime?"

Mick swats lightly at the badge, practically obscuring his vision. "Take it easy, bro."

"Detective Ferina. Homicide. Don't take that tone with me. And watch your hands. I'll arrest you for assault." Ferina moves in close to Mick's face, spraying him with spittle as he speaks. "Listen, bro. You called in the body?"

Mick wipes off the spit, capturing disgust to a tee. "Correct."

"Can anyone confirm your whereabouts late last night, early this morning?"

"I don't like what you're implying."

"You don't have to like it. We need to rule everyone out."

"I called you guys. Why would I do that if I was the killer?"

"Exactly, to throw off suspicion."

Mick shakes his head in disbelief. "I was with a girl all night and this morning until I left for my run."

"What's her name?"

"What's your wife's name?"

Dane finds his way over to Mick to save him from Ferina's abuse. He hates Ferina. The two feud like sworn enemies. Although Ferina was cleared, Dane blames him for his father's death and rightfully so.

"Ferina, back off." Dane steps in front of the aspiring thespian.

Ferina moves his head to the side in order to get a view of Mick. "Mind your business."

"This is my business. I'm lead detective. Not you." Dane points towards Mick, "This guy's not the killer."

Ferina changes his posture and holds his right hand over his left wrist at below waist level, slumping his shoulders forward and bobbing his head as he speaks. "You're so smart."

Dane points at Ferina as he speaks. "This is real life. There's no unbelievable twist and there's no mastermind."

"Should I write this down?"

"We do this job. We see these things. There's no cosmic code. It's all out there. Some is sorted out and some falls through the cracks. Like a guy having a gun who was supposedly frisked."

"Again with that! I'm sorry your dad was killed, but I was cleared."

"Getting cleared and fucking up are not mutually exclusive."

"You're a disillusioned prick."

"I'm not seeing things through screens, but I ain't disillusioned neither. Every day we show up to work and tango with evil. The bitch leads and we just try not to get stepped on. Some days we do our job and some days our partner gets killed."

Ferina makes a fist and twists his head to the side. He takes a deep breath and leaves in a huff. Dane turns to Mick, "Don't mind that guy.

The chip on his shoulder is so big his neck gets sore."

Mick settles down. "It's okay. Someone needs to spike his Jamba Juice with eye of newt or some shit."

"Yeah." Dane feigns surprise. "You're an actor, right?"

Mick hates to tell people he's an actor. He only mentions it because in this town, you never know who can help you and who's in the biz. Dane's cousin could be married to Harvey Keitel for all he knows. "Isn't everybody? My favorite barista is an actor."

"You're not kidding. I need your information on the off chance we need to contact you." Dane pulls out his pad, writes down the information, and underlines Mick's name.

Chapter 5

A squirrel sits trying to remember where he buried his next meal. The sprinklers shoot on. The furry critter nearly jumps out of his skin and is up a tree within nanoseconds. The sound of water being shot through a tiny hole and redirected in a neat repeating pattern fills the air. This neighborhood is affluent to say the least. A perfectly cut and groomed landscape is of mind-numbing importance. It has less to do with pride and more to do with envy. Making people envious isn't a pastime for some people, but rather their reason for existing

Every home has a 'beware of dog' or security sign clearly visible to deter thieves. Skilled burglars aren't generally thwarted by generic security measures. They're meant to keep riff-raff out. Gates and hedges surround nearly every property to ensure privacy. Many of these houses have appeared on Star Maps sold to tourists who hope to see a house Yul Brynner may have lived in. Or Gene Kelly.

Colin's house is beautifully decorated; obviously by Betty. Her vision materialized within ten minutes of seeing the place with their real estate broker. She had to block out the overpriced staging. Lucky for the sellers, Betty could see past the look they were using to entice potential buyers.

While each room was given its own personality between the furniture, paint, and accessories, they blend perfectly. Through-out the house are pictures cataloguing Betty and Colin's time together. There are pictures of all their various adventures: trips, events and activities from swimming with dolphins and movie premieres to ice cream in front of the Eiffel Tower.

The kitchen is a piece of artwork. Stainless steel artwork. Steel in this case is not cold and distant, but rather clean and professional. The appliances all match and the room looks like it was pieced together for an advertisement. No expense was spared and everything wipes off and is impossible to break. However, Betty's culinary competency doesn't necessarily warrant the apparatus afforded her. It's not unlike the weekend golfer who shanks some of the worst shots ever with the most expensive high-tech clubs money can buy.

Colin sits with Betty at the kitchen table for dinner. He hesitates slightly as he brings the fork to his face. His hand trembles like a peon who tastes food for the king and knows it may be poisoned. "All the ingredients are new and fresh, yeah?"

Betty rolls her eyes, "You use expired chopped garlic once with this guy and it's a thing forever."

"I nearly died and if people think garlic breath is bad, garlic vomit smells like Guy Fieri doing hot yoga in a room full of his Cajun fettuccine alfredo."

"That's colorful."

"I have a vivid imagination." He closes his eyes and takes in a mouthful. There's a prayer echoing within his head, whose acoustics are fitting, as only someone with half a brain hasn't learnt from previous mistakes. He appeals to a higher power to spare his stomach. He's spent countless nights beseeching porcelain gods for forgiveness or in some instances, a quick death. "Wow. You really make this?" He shifts his tone. "Of course you made this. You look great, by the way."

Betty gives him the middle finger and squints her eyes suspiciously, "Uh-huh."

Either the food is actually good or one of her dishes had done him in and his idea of heaven is a place where Betty's meals are palatable. "This is a great day."

Betty digs in her heels for a playful altercation. "Is it? How so?"

Colin eats as he talks. "Well, I would generally describe you as the full package; smart, beautiful, funny, resourceful, strong. And to be honest, you make a good living, so you have some money, which is great, but you've always lost some points with cooking."

"Is that so?"

"To be honest, if you leaned into the fact that it's not your thing and we ordered food or maybe I cook for us – no one's perfect, no point deduction. But the trying and sucking warrants penalties. But with this," he points with his fork at his plate, "I can give you the points back."

Betty nods. "Ah, got it, so it's the same deal I've got going with your deductions when you try and fix stuff around the house."

Colin is quick to respond. "Exactly. I learned a lot from that last electrocution. I saw my childhood dog, Butters. He seems happy."

Betty picks up the dish, kisses him on the cheek and walks over to the counter. Colin stares at her as she washes dishes. The way the light is hitting her face; she looks perfect and he wants to remember this forever.

***

Colin is dreaming within a tortured, partially drug-induced sleep. Never-ending, continual nightmares are plaguing him. Flashes of Betty. Pieces of memories. He's in purgatory between asleep and awake. His subconscious is confused. He lies face up in his bed, stiff as board, like a cadaver. Next to his nightstand and lamp hangs an IV drip, connected to his remaining hand. A chair sits next to the bed facing him, with a balled up, wrinkled blanket draped over the back. Clearly someone has been spending nights watching over him.

There's a knock on the door. Colin doesn't budge. Dane enters nonetheless and sits down in the chair. These brothers have always had each other's backs. Some siblings are close. Some are not. Dane and Colin have always been thick as thieves. Colin is the older brother and Dane is self-reliant and his own man, but he's not afraid to defer to his big brother when necessary. He sits there in silence, checking emails on his phone. After about an hour, Dane has dozed off, with the blanket haphazardly covering most of his body as he awkwardly sleeps in the chair.

Colin moans, pain plastered over his face despite closed eyes. He rouses as Dane wakes. "Hey, buddy. Welcome back."

Colin is groggy. "Dane, what? Uh." His throat is dry as hell and he can only whisper, "Fuck. I feel terrible. Please tell me I had an alcohol-fueled bender and you, me, Tom Brady, and Ryan Reynolds had the times of our lives."

Dane reluctantly replies, "What's the opposite of that?"

"Probably what actually happened."

Dane shakes his head, "I tracked down her body. We'll have a private service once you're up for it."

Colin looks down, defeated; the wind taken out of his sails. He's quiet for a moment, which in itself says more about how he feels than any words would be able. His eyes bulge with panic, "Fuck. Charlie? Where's Charlie? Is Charlie okay?"

Dane places his hand up and in his most soothing voice, "Calm down. I came and got her the night it happened. I'll bring her by in the morning. I didn't want her to see you comatose."

Colin, immediately at ease, struggles to sit up, "Thank you. That would be the icing on the shittiest cake ever; like a flour-less, gluten free chocolate cake shaped like Duff Goldman's dick." Colin tastes his own mouth, making a face. "It tastes like something died in my mouth."

"Brushing your teeth was low on the priority list."

Colin touches his head, "Was brushing my hair at least on the list?" He changes the subject, "Well, we have to kill this prick." He gives him an out. "This will get messy. I understand if you don't want in. You're sorta in law enforcement."

Dane leans back. "I dabble. I'd kill this asshole without this provocation. I have my helmet on and I'm ready to play. Are we going

CHAPTER 5

in Butch Cassidy style? Guns drawn. Last man standing?"

Colin shakes his head slightly. "Nah, we'll need to come up with a plan or we'll get torn up. Anyone know what happened?"

"Only those who need to. I called Frankie. He did his thing and altered the optics."

"Good, can you pass me that water?"

Dane hands him the water bottle. "Unofficially, the police department is at our disposal."

Colin takes a swig, "How many parking tickets can we give him that won't look suspicious?"

"They're all still your friends. You leaving the force doesn't matter." Dane is glad his brother is back among the living.

"I did crush it at softball every year."

* * *

Wally Adrian finds himself in a tight spot. The hot interrogation lights are making the tiny room stifling. The stale air around him feels like a cage and the three ounces of water he was given what seems like hours ago has barely staved off his thirst. In and out the system nearly his entire existence, this is the first time that he's nervous about his immediate future. He knows he fucked up and he knows he fucked up hard. Making the suspect wait is commonplace; there are too many reasons on the spectrum of good to bad to set the mind spinning. The police could be dotting I's and crossing T's to have a tighter case so they can throw the book at him, or it could be simple psychological warfare; a means to the end of breaking him into giving them their case. This feels different though. Wally has been a relatively clever career criminal, mostly low-level stuff, and the only black guy on Little Georgie Scanavino's crew. In this case, he stepped in it bad, freelancing for his brother's gang, killing a rival from the Eight-Sixers. No way he can beat this murder wrap.

The door opens aggressively, and two men who are not run-of-the-mill detectives enter. They introduce themselves before sitting across from him. "I'm Chief of Police Dirk Scully, and this is Deputy Chief Jason Alvarez."

Both are decorated officers, Dirk starting his career in the early eighties and working practically every assignment from Rampart to Internal Affairs. He's mid-sixties and has been a wizard at reforming troubled areas by nipping corruption from the bottom of the chain of the command all the way to the top. By doing so, these racially distinct areas have had harmonic periods due to constitutional policing. Alvarez, a good police officer, worked his way up the chain, a Latin golden boy, for the higher ups to use as political ammunition in the battle in portraying a diverse department. While he knows, he's been used from time to time, he plays the political game himself, aspiring to one day be mayor.

Wally introduces himself. "You know who I am."

Alvarez takes the lead. "We do and you've found yourself between a rock and a hard place."

"Yup. However my day is looking up?"

"Is that so?"

"I've been in rooms like this since I was just a pup. And I ain't never met the police chief or his deputy dog. Which means you need something. And if you need something, you know how this works. That shit ain't free."

Alvarez nods at Scully. "I told you this guy was clever." He turns to Wally. "What if we made this murder go away and move your brother to Kern from Pelican Bay so his kids can see him more than twice a year?"

"And in return? Because I ain't no snitch."

Scully enters the conversation. "We heard that about you. To be honest, snitching makes our job easier, but we don't respect snitches. You can't ever fully trust tattletales."

"So what you need?"

"We would need you to vouch for one of our guys with Little Georgie.

32

You get him on the crew, and we're good."

Alvarez interjects, "So technically you're not snitching. Our guy does all the work and you just make an introduction."

"This is the easiest way anyone will ever beat a murder wrap and do right by his family."

Wally's gears are turning; this deal is too good to be true and in his experience, when that's the case you should run the other way. However, the alternative puts him in a cage for at least two decades. On top of that, he's not gang affiliated, he runs with wops so no one has his back in lock-down. In there, Little Georgie can't protect him, especially for something he did without his knowledge. When the Eight-Sixers get word he was the trigger man, his life would be on the clock. "I'm in."

Scully and Alvaraz stand up, shake his hand, and tell him they'll have the agreement drawn up. They exit the room and shake each other's hands smiling, glowing victorious.

"Good call Jason." Scully is happy with Alvarez.

Alvarez nods. "Thanks boss. When I got the call Wally was pulled in, I knew this would be the best play."

"Do you have someone in mind to be our guy on the inside?"

"Graves."

"Which one?"

"Colin. He's had a hard-on to get in on the organized crime unit, especially undercover."

"If he's half as much a mad dog as his father, he'll be perfect."

"I'll get him prepped and set up with Wally."

"Jason, this is your operation. I'll happily give you all the glory when we bring down Georgie, but if it takes a shit, you're on the hook."

"I wouldn't have it any other way."

* * *

Colin sits on the green and brown Goodwill hand-me-down couch in the bullpen at the police station throwing a football to Kenny, one of the guys in his unit. They toss the ball back and forth anxiously, waiting for any type of action.

Kenny passes the ball, "Bro, took this chick home Friday."

"So that amber alert was you?"

"Asshole."

"I know you're discerning, you did vote for Trump. Attractive? Super smart? A lot to offer the world?"

Kenny ignores Colin's jabbing. "Not a keeper, but fine. But dude, she didn't leave until 2pm on Saturday. We were done by midnight. Tops. I got up at nine and was like 'I'm gonna surf, make yourself at home.' Came back a quarter to two, and chick is still in bed."

"Narcoleptic? Homeless? Could be any number of reasons why she'd spend sixteen hours at your place after what I assume was mediocre sex."

Kenny laughs. "You're such a dick. I mean, my dog was happy, but I was like what the fuck, I need my 'me time' on the weekend. I thought for sure she would be gone by the time I was back. If I knew I was like in for a sixteen hour commitment, I would've foregone the companionship."

"I know, sixteen hours! The nerve. And all she did was give you the most personal thing anyone could. How selfish? And rude."

"Right?!"

"So, Prince Charming, how'd you leave it?"

"When I was letting her out, I just said, 'see ya'."

"'See ya?' I knew you were a rhetorician, but you just took my breath away."

"Yup and haven't heard from her since."

"I'm shocked. Boy am I glad I have my girl."

"Yeah, we all wish Betty was our girl. We have a lottery in place in case you die in the line of duty."

"That's fair. It's good to know the guys that have my back are waiting for me to die so they can date my wife."

CHAPTER 5

An officer knocks and enters. "Colin, Deputy Commissioner Alvarez wants to see you."

"Thanks, Dan. I'll head over there now. You thinking I should moisturize my hands or lube up my asshole?"

Dan smirks, "I'm thinking bring some knee-pads and Listerine for after."

Colin looks impressed. "Dan, I didn't think you had it in you. You're going places, kid."

Kenny throws the football to him. "Col, remember the little people."

"I'm a man of the people. Little meaning your cock, right?"

* * *

Colin waits outside the Deputy Commissioner's office. He sits patiently, on his phone texting Betty, who asked him if he wanted to go to the Rams game with her and her father. Colin texts back, "Uh, yeah. Any opportunity to watch super fit dudes all but molest each other in tight pant is an unequivocal 'yes.'"

She responds with a tears of joy emoji.

Deputy Alvarez's secretary tells Colin he can go into the office. He gets up and pockets his phone.

Alvarez stands and greets Colin with his hand out, "Colin, nice to see you."

Colin shakes his hand, "Likewise. Kids good?"

"Yeah, thanks. Keeping me and the wife busy." Alvarez signals for Colin to sit and he obliges. "I've told ya I knew your father, right? He was good police and a great man." Colin nods. Alvarez continues, "Between you and me, what happened was total bullshit, and speaking as a Latino myself, the fuck-up should have led to dismissal but we live in a new world and diversity is a thing. Which is great, but not at the expense of quality."

Colin sits back. "My brother and I have different points of view on this one. I've come to terms with what happened and knowing my father as well as I did, he'd put the whole thing on himself. If he was better, his partner's mistake wouldn't have cost him his life." Colin leans on his knees with his elbows. "Having said that, you can imagine how much of a peach he was if me or my brother disappointed him. It was like Catholic guilt on steroids without the kiddy rape."

Alvarez chuckles. "I see you have his sense of humor. But the reason you're here. We're putting you under in Little Georgie Scanavino's crew.

"I'll binge *The Sopranos* tonight. How do you spell Fahgettaboudit?"

"We flipped a guy to vouch for you. He's got skin in the game, so he's good to go." Alvarez hands him an envelope. "Here's your identity, apartment, car, social, cash; everything you need to go under."

Colin looks through the paperwork, "I guess I look like a 'Vic'." Alvarez points at the packet, "There's a burner with one number. My burner. We will liaise directly. You pick up Wally tomorrow and he'll get you vouched for. His file is in there too, so you know what you are dealing with."

Colin stands up. "Thank you for picking me. I feel like the luckiest girl at prom. Hopefully the captain of the football team rips my dress when I won't give it up that easy."

"I'm on the hook, so you're on the hook."

Colin pats him on the back, "I got this."

Chapter 6

The swishing sound of an expensive pen gliding between the margins of a ledger imbues the study. Before there were man caves filled with 4K TVs and St. Pauli Girl neon lights, there were rooms filled with leather bound books and dark grained wood furniture. They would serve as a place of solace for the head of the household. While this is antiquated in some respects, so is Richard. He sits poised above his ledger not unlike how he has imagined Al Capone would have been in his prime. There is a rhythmic knock on Richard's door and his younger brother, Jeff, walks in. Richard smiles. He has a soft spot for his brother and has been getting him out of jams for as long as he can remember. Between getting caught cheating on his SATs to drunk driving in college to an incident with strippers and his intramural lacrosse team, Richard has had his hands full.

Jeff has blond hair he fancies more than most women. He has a routine every morning of exfoliating and clipping individual unruly facial hairs. He owns tons of product, leave-in conditioners, tea tree oil based shampoos, and several pomades depending on his goals. Jeff never misses an opportunity to check himself out in whatever mirror he happens to pass. He's fairly tall, a hair over six feet, and when he walks he bops his head. Jeff is in his mid-twenties, much younger than Richard. He wasn't technically a mistake, but rather a change of life baby.

Richard looks up and smiles. "Jeffrey, did you see that joke I texted to you?"

"Fingering a minor. Terrible." They both chuckle. Jeff jokes around with his older brother, "Richy, how is it you always look busy?"

"Because I am busy."

Jeff sits up. "You seem extra pleased today. I dare say happy, but you're too serious to be happy."

"RP Zippers. I undercut YKK and nabbed a huge account. I had to cut some costs to compete, but what else is new?"

"Are you trying to tell me I almost lost my dick in my fly last week because you're selling cheap zippers?"

"That sounds like a 'your problem' to me."

"Those interlocking metal teeth are going to come back and bite you one day."

"Let 'em. I'm up to date on my tetanus shot." He changes the subject, "What are you doing tonight? You want to catch a movie?"

"Not tonight. There's nothing out I want to see. All super hero movies, man. And reboots."

"It's getting out of hand. The days of solid, original films have gone the way of the dodo. On a long enough timeline, extinction is inevitable for everyone and everything."

"That's a cheery thought. That include you?"

Richard looks up slyly, and gently shakes his head. "No, not me."

"I'm going to check out the Moon Bar. You want to come?"

Richard makes it clear that he's not interested without saying a word.

Jeff continues, "I need to get my dick wet. You should have seen this girl the other night. Twenty, hot, and all over me."

Richard warns his little brother. "You watch those young girls. They will lie their fucking asses off."

"Too bad old chicks can't lie their asses off; they'd look better in jeans. Besides, I have a sixth sense for guessing a chick's age."

"You be careful, little brother."

Jeff's phone rings. "I have to take this."

"An actual phone call? Not a text?"

"I know, crazy."

As he leaves the room, Richard's daughter, Jeff's niece, Alissa enters.

Jeff gives her a high five. She is sixteen, blonde, and a prime example of jailbait. She walks around the house very aware. Since she blossomed she would place her father's employees in awkward positions, openly flirting with them in front of her father. Over-perspiration and red cheeks would give away their utter embarrassment. Other than being the daughter of a criminal, Alissa is an average Californian kid. She shops on Robertson or at the mall depending on how much allowance she has left. She watches reality television or whatever is on the CW and has too many online friends scattered across various social media sites.

Alissa was on the soccer team at her high school, before sports became uncool. A couple of seasons ago she was chatting with another player on Facebook from a nearby school. She was actually corresponding with a pedophile. This predator, Cliff, posing as an innocent teen, had used the internet to commit fabled violations. These clever bastards are masters of getting the information out of naïve children and using it to hurt them. All he needed was the school Alissa attends and her jersey number. Once he had this, she became a viable target.

Unfortunately for Cliff, Richard is the type of parent that keeps tabs on his kid's cyberspace activity. Richard employs a hacker for business but Jonas also uses his skills to spy on Alissa. He had uncovered Cliff's full name, address, social security number, and criminal record with a couple of keystrokes. Richard dispatched Vince and Piney to pay him a visit to preemptively diffuse a tragedy.

* * *

Vincent and Piney enjoy this type of assignment. They will kill anyone if the job requires it, but killing criminals, especially pedophiles and rapists, is practically charity. As within all groups there is a hierarchy, and criminals are no different. They each shuffle into their positions between upper echelon and bottom feeders based on how they conduct their business. Cliff, to them, is clearly at the bottom and since Richard's child is family, they are not only doing the world a service, but they are also protecting one of their own. The two have an interesting work dynamic from spending so much time watching each other's backs. They're like an old married couple that bickers constantly, but when push comes to shove, there's no one each trusts more.

Piney finds the Dodger Game on the radio as they drive. "Here we go."

"Baseball? How do I not know you're a baseball guy?"

"Baseball's lovely mate. My father was a Yankees maniac. He'd cross the pond on business and be here all summer long. He taught me about the game."

"Holy shit. How do you like that."

"So the big question. Maris or Mantle?"

Vincent stops the car and throws it into park. "Maris."

Piney responds to Vincent's choice with an argumentative tone. "Roger Maris could've only been able to break the record playing for NY in Yankee Stadium. That's a fact."

Vincent furrows his brow, clearly annoyed. "No way. You're crazy."

Piney utilizes wild gesticulation in the defense of his theory. "It was short for him. Mantle would've had the record if all his home games were anywhere but Yankee Stadium. Mantle was a switch hitter and could go with the pitch. Imagine a five hundred foot hit being an out?"

"Horseshit. No way five hundred feet?"

"An easy five hundred feet in center field my friend."

"Left center, bro."

"Center... Tosser. If I'm wrong, I'll kiss your ass in Macy's window."

Vincent throws the car into drive. He pouts, and they sit in silence. Coming to his senses, he says, "Piney, you're entitled to your opinion."

"No worries, bruva, we're still mates."

Vincent points out of his window. "Here's the guy's place."

Most of the streetlights are either out or weakly flickering. He

CHAPTER 6

parks across the street from the house. The two men exit the car and nonchalantly pull out handguns.

Cliff hangs his pedophile shingle on a tiny ranch that has weathered aluminum siding and loose rain gutters. When it rains, the water flows with reckless abandon, creating craters below the four corners of the roof. There are various pieces of trash scattered on his patchy lawn and the shrubbery is full of dead leaves from past years. It's clear that Cliff has a lack of pride when it comes to his property.

They pause for a second at the front door, exchanging a non-verbal plan. Piney gives Vincent a nod. He kicks in the door. They skulk into the house with their guns drawn. Cliff's furniture looks like it belonged to his grandmother. The place is a labyrinth of shitty little rooms. However, the living room has an extremely high-tech computer set-up up with every possible do-dad and thing-a-ma-jig. Cliff, playing with himself, pops up from the captain's chair, completely taken aback by the intrusion.

Cliff flies off of the handle, hoping the annoyance in his voice will cause the two party crashers to reexamine their unlawful entry into his den of sin. "What the hell is this? Do you have a warrant? Get the fuck out of my house."

Piney answers him as Vincent confirms the house is empty by popping his head in each room. "We're not coppers, mate. We don't need permission to enter your house and kill ya."

Vincent opens the door to a little room in the back. It's decorated for a child. What differentiates this room from a run-of-the-mill kid's room is the wall-to-wall plastic on the floor and the video camera pointing towards the bed. Vincent bites his own fist in outrage and exits the room abruptly.

Piney's demeanor is laid back and in control. Cliff's heart is fluttering in his shirt, making the Hawaiian pattern move. It looks like a summer breeze is blowing the hula skirts worn by the scantily clad dancers. "Hey, fellas, what's this about? I'm a cool guy. You guys want money? I got money."

Piney tosses handcuffs in Cliff's direction. "Put these on." Cliff catches the cuffs and follows orders.

Cliff shakes his head, like he's trying to convince himself that this isn't happening. "I have no idea what this is about but I have ice cream sandwiches in the freezer. You guys want to chill, talk this out?"

Piney tilts his head to the side. "I can go for an ice cream sandwich."

Vincent bursts into the room, agitated. He whispers through a clenched jaw to Piney. "This fucker has a room set up. Plastic covering the floor. Video camera. The works."

Piney slaps Cliff across the face. "You kill the kids when you're done? Fucking lovely."

Cliff looks down at his feet. "I don't know what you're talking about."

Vincent tucks his gun into his pants and sits down next Cliff. Before Vincent speaks, he collects his thoughts and rubs his mouth with his right hand. "Cliff, there's no greater travesty than what you take from children. Do you know they classify your criminal mentality as one that escalates?" Cliff meekly shakes his head. "You probably started off thumbing through magazines and just fantasizing. Then, you hung out at playgrounds. Maybe you touched yourself or went home and did it. At first you were ashamed. The idea of being caught at the ball pit at McDonald's used to make your heart race. But, like all things, the feelings passed. You got bolder each time no one said anything to you at Disneyland. Next thing you know, you're kidnapping and killing. Pretty soon you're a serial killer with tiny bones buried in your backyard. Your hope is the random choosing of your victims will protect you. Police often don't know where to start. They look at people that come in contact with the kid. You find them on the internet and from what I am told, you are pretty good at covering your tracks. But, you screwed up. You went after Richard Pembroke's daughter."

Cliff starts to cry, "Fuck. No. No. No. No. I had no idea."

Vincent places his pointer finger against his own mouth to signal Cliff to stop speaking. "We considered cutting your balls off. Let you live in misery for the rest of your days. We discussed it and felt that your sick mind wouldn't stop thinking sick thoughts. You could still hurt kids despite having a broken dick. So, we're gonna torture you until you're dead and make the last moments of your life excruciating."

Piney smiles, "We have the perfect room for it, mate."

Vincent continues, "I bet you didn't see this coming when you were carefully putting the plastic down. You were probably humming a tune, like 'Camptown Races', completely unaware that the tracks you were covering would be to your own demise."

Vincent goes outside to the car and opens the trunk. He takes out a bag and carries it into the house. Cliff is hysterically crying on the couch and Piney is whispering in his ear. They drag him into his kill room. He struggles, to no avail. Vincent pulls out a leather awl and the first thing they do is puncture his eardrums. Blood spurts from his ears and drips down his neck. Sudden loss of hearing is terrifying. Piney grabs the awl, slowly plunging the pointy tool into one of Cliff's eyes and then the other. Cliff screams, unable to hear his own voice or see what will come next. They break all his teeth. They light his fingers on fire and smash his toes with hammers. They use a nail gun to make his genitalia unrecognizable. They give him a C-section and pull his intestines out. They pour acid into pipes shoved up his rectum. Cliff bleeds and he bleeds. They break his knees and his arms. They tie him to the same bed he has tortured countless kids on, and they light the bed on fire. He begins to slow roast like a luau pig. The excessive nature of this ritualistic killing is a way for Piney and Vincent to separate their bad deeds from Cliff's. They kill too, but it's not the same. They ruin lives and families, facilitating drug addiction and the crimes intertwined with the drug trade. However, they are somehow different than Cliff.

*　*　*

Richard is aware of what happened in that house on his orders. He feels sick thinking that it could have been his little girl in the plastic room. To this day she does not realize she was in danger. He can't decide whether or not to tell her there's no Santa Clause, no Heaven, and Hell is on Earth and the devil lives in man.

Alissa interrupts her father who's deep in thought. "Dad." Richard continues working without looking up. "Yes, honey?"

Alissa places her hand out. "Money."

"What for?"

Alissa chews her gum loudly and rolls her eyes. "You know, legal tender is, like, necessary for the exchange of goods and services. Or something."

"What have I told you about 'or something?'"

"It makes me sound stupid."

"And sarcasm is probably the least effective bargaining tactic. I was asking what you planned to use money for on a school night."

Alissa relays her intentions in a roundabout way, involving the life and death necessity for a new denim miniskirt.

Richard closes his ledger. "I'll tell you what. You go over to the bookshelf and get me the copy of *Beowulf* and I'll give you... How much?"

Alissa already knows to ask for more and negotiate down. "Fifty dollars."

Richard is well versed in this game as well. "Forty dollars? What do you need thirty dollars for?" Richard smirks at his own little joke.

"Dad jokes, really?" Alissa doesn't find his comment humorous. She stands with her right leg straight, right hand on her hip, and left leg slightly bent with her left foot pointed forty-five degrees.

Richard waves his hand as he speaks, "Please get me the book and we'll negotiate."

Alissa stomps over to the bookcase and easily locates *Beowulf*, but is only able to reach it if she gets on her tippy toes. She happens to be wearing hip-hugging jeans and a shirt that does not quite reach her navel. Therefore, as she strains to complete the task, the dragon tattoo on the small of her back is revealed to her doting anti-tattoo father. Richard glances over, not believing the message his eyes are sending to his brain. His blood begins to boil, virtually bubbling in his veins. His little girl has a tramp stamp. He pops out of his chair and bolts over to her.

"Jesus Christ. What the fuck is that?"

Alissa does not skip a beat. "What the fuck is what?"

"Watch your mouth." Richard notices something in her mouth and grabs her face. "What is this?"

Alissa's speech is garbled from her father's hand. "Tongue ring."

Richard is furious. "Are you insane? Why would you desecrate your body like this?"

"Desecrate? That's dramatic. Besides, it's cool."

"That's your answer? 'It's cool'?" Richard mocks her. Alissa facially articulates how unfair her father is acting. "What if that tattoo isn't cool in two years? How'd you pick that... dragon? And why is its tail pointing towards your... you know... your... you know."

Alissa places some space between her and her father. "It was on the wall of the tattoo place. The artist is super dope."

Richard shakes his head in disbelief. "Wait, wait, wait. You just randomly picked one off the wall? How about that nail in your tongue? What's with that?"

"It's an oral sex thing." She doesn't blush.

Richard is having a conniption. His face is red and he begins to scream insanely. "Are you kidding me? We don't have this type of relationship. I look at you and I see my little girl in Hello Kitty pajamas." He haphazardly points at the tattoo and the tongue ring. "Those things are gone and I'm going to keep a closer eye on you."

"Have you ever heard that tattoos are permanent?"

"Laser removal. It's a thing. And it's painful."

"That doesn't work. I'll just be scarred."

"Then I'll hire a tattoo artist to change it into Henry Kissinger's fucking face so when people look at it, they just think it's weird."

"Who the fuck is Henry Kissinger? He sounds ugly."

"Aren't you writing a paper on Nixon for your history class right now?"

"I didn't start yet. Its due in like two days."

"Go to your room. And I want that tongue ring out now. And you're grounded."

Alissa gets whinier, "Are you saying that I can't go out with Uncle Jeff tomorrow?"

"Damn it Alissa, you're only sixteen."

"So? I'm not a little girl."

"Are you arguing with me? You'll be lucky to be able to go out when you're twenty-five. What am I saying? You'll be lucky to make it to twenty-five. GO!"

Alissa complies because deep down inside, she fears him just like everyone else.

Chapter 7

Vincent's hands are at ten and two. He drives carefully, like they have one dead body and one almost-dead body in the back of the van. Piney sits shotgun, eating Twizzlers, chomping away at the tough licorice like he's watching a movie, unfazed by the recent brutality. Colin is in the back, bleeding to death. Betty's lifeless body is directly next to him, her arms and legs akimbo as if she was thrown into the back like garbage. Piney speaks through his mouthful, "Drive careful now, Vince, we don't want to get nipped."

Vincent smiles as he answers, "This isn't my first rodeo."

Piney peers into the back of the van, "This cunt is gonna be outta blood soon."

Vincent shakes his head. "I told Richard not to listen to Benny. That guy is a fucking idiot."

"A real bell-whacker. Between you and me, mate, this situation is bollocks."

"No shit. Killing regular citizens for no reason is not okay."

"Well bruva, with any luck, there's no karma."

"I'll take out bad guys all day and not lose a wink. But this? Fuck."

Piney nods in agreement. "No wonder the guy had no idea what Richard was talking about."

"Dude should've toned down the mouth though. No one likes a smart ass, especially Richard." Vincent glances up at his rear-view mirror. "Shit."

"What?"

"Police, lights and everything."

"You gotta be pullin' me leg. Please say you're pullin' me leg." Vincent flicks the turn signal and slowly pulls the van over to the side of the road. He and Piney take a deep breath. Piney makes the sign of the cross over his chest. Vincent rolls his eyes. "God? Really?" The police make them wait. Eventually, two police officers exit the squad car, stopping at the driver and passenger windows.

Vincent breaks the ice, already holding his license and registration, "Good evening, officers."

The officer on the driver's side raises his flashlight and shines the light into Vincent's eyes. "Get out of the van."

Vincent looks at Piney, "Yeah, sure."

Piney chimes in, "Absolutely."

The officer on the passenger side cuts him off. "Slowly."

The first officer asks Vincent and Piney to walk in front of the van and kneel with their hands on their heads. Like good little boys, the two continue to follow orders.

Piney looks at Vincent, "Lovely, we're fucked."

Vincent whispers, "No shit."

Dane exits his police cruiser parked behind the officer's car. He sneaks up to the back of the van, opening the door slowly, wincing ever so slightly, like he is diffusing a bomb. Vincent and Piney are too concerned with the officers radioing in police mumbo-jumbo to realize that they're being robbed. He first sees Betty, staring at him lifeless, her arms and legs twisted and contorted in a pile. His piercing blue eyes fill with tears of rage. Dane spots Colin within the shadows, unconscious and speaking incoherently. He manages to get Colin into his car.

As Dane re-approaches the van to get Betty's body, a car driving by gets a flat tire and pulls over in front of the van. Dane needs to leave the scene. He jumps into his car contemplating this rash, but conservative decision. He looks in the back at Colin's bloody body and he places the car into drive. He gives the signal for the officers to cut Vincent and Piney loose.

CHAPTER 7

They look at each other in utter disbelief. Piney shrugs at Vincent who can barely contain his glee. His uncontrollable smile is like when a baby sees a puppy for the first time. They enter the van and sit silently for a second and wait for their heart rates to come down. Piney breaks the silence. "Fuck me. My ticker is about to explode."

"Holy shit, man. What the fuck?"

Piney looks into the back of the van, "Vince, mate."

"What?"

"The guy... he's gone."

Vincent hits the steering wheel. "Shit. The cops are still here. We can't stick around. We need to keep this between us."

Piney pantomimes crossing his heart.

Vincent throws the van into drive, signals, and pulls out slowly like a teenager who accidentally just impregnated his girl.

＊＊＊

There is an echo in Dane's eardrum with each rapid, bass-filled drumbeat of his heart as he drives wildly for help. He can smell his own rank, stressed perspiration. He knows if Colin doesn't get medical attention soon, he'll bleed to death. But he needs to avoid hospitals. He's aware that in circumstances like this Colin will be placed under a microscope, and even the holiest of holy has something to hide. He'll have to enlist the aid of someone who will be discrete but isn't a hack. He covers Colin with his jacket to keep him warm.

"Hang in there, bro. You're going to be fine. Stay with me." There's a quiver in Dane's voice, revealing the skepticism of his own statement. He turns the sirens on, flashing lights and all, drives maniacally, recklessly weaving in and out of traffic. He talks to the cars he's narrowly missing the entire way. "Move, dammit!" He's abusing his horn. "Fucking move! Come on. Come on. Come on." He wipes the sweat dripping into his eyes with the back of his hand.

Colin mumbles incoherently from the back.

"Col, what was that? We're almost there." He sees their destination on the horizon and floors it. He hits the curb and flies onto the front of the property. It's a surgical pavilion. He parks crookedly on the lawn. Dane jumps out of the driver's seat hastily, leaving his door open. He runs to the back and opens Colin's door.

Dane is breathing heavily, "Col. Stay strong buddy. We're here."

There's blood everywhere. Colin is passed out and a cross between deathly pale and deathly purple. Dane picks him up and runs to the front door with him, where he's met by two big male nurses and doctor. The nurses guide Colin onto a gurney and wheel him inside. Dane's mouth is so dry he struggles to speak.

"Doc, it's pretty bad. He's lost a lot of blood." Dane is covered in Colin's blood.

Dr. Stavros Phillipoussis is the son of a powerful Greek shipping magnate. He has long, stringy, brown hair and he's only ever clean-shaven for court appearances. Everyone calls him Dr. Phil, partly as homage to Elvis' Dr. Nick, and partly because his name is a mouthful. He'll also brag that he's a mouthful. He's an exceptional doctor because he doesn't do it for the money. His family is beyond wealthy, so he doesn't concern himself with the financial hang-ups often related to practicing medicine. His relaxed policy with billing is also a negative. Since he doesn't care about the money, the threat of losing his license to practice isn't enough to keep him on the straight and narrow. He got jammed up nine months ago for prescribing diet pills to actresses, aspiring actresses, and just plain eating disorder Californians. Dane pulled a couple of strings and got him off the hook. Dr. Phil feels he owes Dane, but the truth of the matter is Dr. Phil put their mother out of her misery. She was terminal and in pain, so he euthanized her.

"It's not good. But Colin is a strong man. Like steel. They may get dinged up, but they're very difficult to break. And blood, eh? We have plenty of blood." Dr. Phil pulls a pill bottle out of his pocket. He opens it, offers some to Dane who shakes his head, then the doctor downs

CHAPTER 7

two big white pills without water.

"Doc, I'm going to try and find Colin's arm, I'll be right back."

Dr. Phil shakes his head, "Okay, but if I have to choose between keeping replantation a viable option and saving his life, I will choose the latter."

"I get it."

"You have about six hours before the limb is no good, less if we can't keep Colin stable."

"Then what am I doing still talking to you?" Dane rushes out.

The beeping of medical machines fills the air. A team is getting Colin prepped for the doctor. They place an IV into his arm and they intubate him to facilitate his breathing. They cut off his shirt. Dr. Phil is scrubbed-in, holding his sterile hands up while a nurse pours whiskey down his throat. He shakes his hands like he's doing the hokey-pokey, rolls his neck until it cracks, and jumps up and down three times. "Let's do this."

Beeeeeeeppppp. The familiar sound of someone flat lining is intertwined with barely distinguishable overlapping yells. Clear! Clear! Dr. Phil has the situation under control. Normal beeping commences. For now, Colin is hanging on.

* * *

Dane stands in front of one of the few remaining mom and pop hardware stores still alive and kicking despite the Home Depots, Lowes, and Orchard Hardware Stores strangling them out of existence. He goes around to the rear entrance, pauses for a second, and then kicks the door in. He grabs a shovel, a pickaxe and a big tub and places a wad of cash on the front counter at the register.

He gets in the car, checks his phone to track the van's GPS and starts his trek to recover Colin's arm. Vincent and Piney are well ahead of him, now by nearly two hours and look to be heading towards Vegas. He calls Dr. Phil's office for updates. Colin is fighting hard, as he expected.

His brother has always been tough as nails, and has been in his fair share of tussles mostly due to his smart mouth and his willingness to go toe to toe with anyone, regardless of whether he could or would win. He'd take a beating just to get the last word in, recover, and then get his revenge some other way. After about two hours of driving, Dane stops for some coffee and grabs a bunch of ice. He sees he's about an hour away as that's where the van stopped about an hour ago for whatever time it takes to bury a body – and maybe his brother's arm, with any luck. The sixty minutes pass like a kidney stone for Dane, as if his math is correct, this is going to be very close. If the limb is not at the original crime scene, making this trip moot.

He pulls up to the Mormon Rocks just west of the 15 off the 138. The area is huge and he uses some deductive reasoning to try and narrow down his search. After about forty-five minutes of wandering the dark looking for loose soil, he finds a spot that could be the dumpsite. He starts to dig carefully, so as not to accidentally cause more damage to the delicate limb. He eventually hits something and starts to use his hands. After a second, Betty's face is revealed. She's dirty but in the dim moonlight, and heavily shadowed light from the flashlight in his mouth, looks angelic. He gets her loose and picks her up and carries her to his car.

He goes back to the hole and searches and searches with no luck. He stands up, frustrated, pulls out his gun and empties the clip into the air. After the sound of the last pop has completely dissipated, he just falls to his ass defeated. He takes a second to collect himself and heads back to the car.

* * *

Dr. Phil stands outside, smoking, as Dane pulls up. As he approaches, the doctor's silhouette is relaxed and the billows of smoke sneak in and out of the little patches of light, appearing like his soul leaving his body. As Dane gets closer, he sees the doctor is completely covered in blood.

Dane shakes his head. "I couldn't find his fucking arm."

"Don't beat yourself up. I had to make the call two hours ago. He's stable. He'll live." He flicks the cigarette butt.

"Jesus Christ. One arm?"

Dr. Phil shakes his head. "At least he can still jerk off."

Dane scoffs, "With his left hand?"

"It's going to feel like a middle school hand job."

"That was the shit back in the day."

"He'll be extremely disoriented. We'll keep him on morphine and sedated for a couple of days."

"Then what?"

Dr. Phil shrugs his shoulders. "He'll learn to cope."

"Hey, not being dead is something." Dane shakes the doctor's hand. "Thanks doc. I owe you one."

Chapter 8

The good doctor saved Colin's life. He's twisted with ambivalence; he's broken physically and mentally, each compounding the other. When under duress the mind finds itself wandering in terrible places, finding ledges and abysses, hoping to get swallowed up by darkness.

Being crippled is bad enough on its own, but Betty's love gave him strength and her absence has made him vulnerable. He's essentially found that self-medicating and obsessing over exercising revenge and annihilating Richard has made life tolerable. His main two defense mechanisms have always been compartmentalization and humor. And not observational comedy. He was sarcastic before he was pissed and bitter. His mouth is now razor sharp, and even snarky people would think he's too snide. He did not realize how deeply this trauma would impact his day-to-day, and it's coming through as cutting irritability.

He's in agony from the lack of an extremity. He's been having phantom limb sensations, most of which are extremely painful. Some are just strange, like an itch on his missing arm or the feeling of trying to pick something up. Vicodin barely does the trick, and when it does it's not for very long. He's definitely been abusing the pills. The pain is so intense that it's been causing migraines. Not soccer mom 'I need a bubble bath, a glass of wine, and break from the kids' migraines, but deep, cavernous, echoing, pounding wish-for-death migraines. Blinding, behind the eyes, pulsating pain, pilfering what spirit still exists. He sits in the dark, nauseous from pain and he simply cannot sleep without the drug's dulling effects often mixed with whatever

CHAPTER 8

hard liquor is within reach. Dr. Phil assures him the pain will improve. 'Improve' is so arbitrary. There's no real unit of measurement that quantifies pain. Everybody's scale from one to ten is different, and Colin's is currently at eleven. This is his new life. From a certain point of view, Richard fathered this new version of Colin, and now he's got serious daddy issues.

*　*　*

Law enforcement has always enlisted the services of less than moral men. Usually, these snitches, more times than not, would sell their own mother down the river for a buck. They lose less sleep when they rat out the competition or someone they barely know. They're an interesting breed as both sides trust them just enough. Unbeknownst to Dane, prior to Colin's entanglement with Richard, Dane had a confidential informant that worked on Richard's crew. This snitch wasn't among the henchman that night. He is guilty, but for entirely different reasons.

Benny simply looks like scum. His face is gaunt. He has long, thinning, scraggly black hair and a wispy goatee. Despite being skinny and underdeveloped, he has a gut. Benny is the definition of a poor excuse for a human being. Perhaps it's because he's a product of his mom's prostitution. Maybe it's because his stepfather sexually abused him. Or it's because he's not too bright and he knows it. Ignorance is bliss and being just smart enough to realize that you're below average is enough to thwart anyone's ambition. He has had the same drug problem practically all his life, falling on and off the wagon more times than he can count. He always looks like he woke up in a gutter and, truthfully, his apartment is not too far off. He has a junkie ex-wife who's in and out of jail and a ten-year-old kid named Billy. His kid is the only thing keeping him from eating a gun. He's too lazy or too buried in his rut to make an effort to change, just in case there's a reward for living right.

As much as it chagrins Colin to admit, Benny is important to them. Happenstance has placed him within the inner circle. He has access to places they do not and is privy to information that they need. And, he owes them. They decide to take him out to breakfast to discuss his role. The diner is a hole in the wall and out of the way, to avoid people spotting them with him. If tragedy starts befalling Richard, it's best nobody suspects Benny. Benny's a snitch. The slightest pressure placed on him would come right back to them in a heartbeat.

This place is famous for its giant portion of pancakes. The amount of food that gets wasted at this joint is bordering on tragic. They give you about ten pancakes the size of the plate. A big, burly lumberjack would be lucky to eat four out of ten. A normal person starts to struggle around two. Benny must not have eaten in a while because he just downed five and looks to be going strong. He barely uses any syrup, which lends to the theory that he's actually a snake. He's essentially swallowing the dry pancakes whole. Benny's hands are dirty, not just figuratively. They look like he worked on a sewer pipe and despite being filthy, he still attempted to shake hands. Now Colin sits before him, mortified, watching him eat with these vile fucking hands. He picks up pieces of bacon creating a grease and dirt mixture. Vicodin is taking the edge off, otherwise Colin would probably puke.

Colin looks at Benny's filthy hands. "Not worried about germs, yeah?"

Benny's confused. "Me?" He thinks about it, "Nah, not really. Fuck it, right?"

Colin plays along, "Yeah, the flu can be a great way to lose weight."

Dane changes the subject. "How's the kid?"

Benny nods. "He's good... good kid."

Colin is unable to help himself, "I'm sure you're doing a great job. He still have both his eyes?"

Benny is unfazed. "Thanks, and totally. Both eyes and all his fingers and toes."

Dane signals Colin to tone it down with his eyes, "What's he, ten?"

CHAPTER 8

"Eleven."

Dane continues, "Lola?"

"Cunt," Benny rolls his eyes, changing the subject, "I apologize for the thing. I had no idea."

"You're lucky we need you," Dane leans in, "Otherwise, you'd be very dead right now."

"I know. I know. I got you, all day." Benny grabs the syrup and drowns his pancakes. He must be struggling to finish. He pushes away from the table and stands up. "I need to take a leak." Benny walks towards the bathroom, picking up tips left on the tables and pocketing them.

Colin turns to Dane. "I'd feel better about having Shemp help us on this one."

"Seriously, Shemp?" Dane shakes his head, "You know what they say about strange bedfellows. He's on the inside and with the proper leverage; he'll get things done. We're not asking him to come up with a plan, just follow one. They've trained chickens to play tic-tac-toe, I think we can guide him through this."

"Chickens are fucking dumb, but he may be dumber. And he's definitely not as delicious." Notwithstanding reservations, Colin trusts Dane implicitly. His leg is throbbing from the gunshot that tore ligaments, tendons, and shattered bone. He has physical therapy after this meeting. Colin sees Benny come out of the bathroom and turns to Dane, "I'm going to the bathroom. Try not to look at him and picture a chicken while you're talking. I bet you can't do it."

"Challenge accepted," Dane smirks. "I'll nail down the rest of the details so we can get outta here and get you to PT."

Colin struggles to get to his feet, wobbling a bit like a drunkard. He's starting to find having one arm is much more of a disadvantage than he could have fathomed. His limp, and the necessity of a cane occupying his only hand, exacerbate this truth. He places a few bucks on each table as he makes his way to the bathroom, to balance out Benny's theft. He finds himself in front of the men's room. It's a single serving bathroom and despite being vacant, he decides to wait for the single serving women's room. The idea of getting Benny's sloppy bathroom seconds makes him cringe.

A woman exits. Colin enters the bathroom and places his cane on the doorknob. He turns to the toilet and hobbles in front of it. He struggles to pull his zipper down. Two hands would make this tough zipper easy breezy. With no leverage, he decides to tackle his belt and go back to the zipper later. Incidentally, putting his belt on this morning was a nightmare; so much so, he may never take the belt off these pants again. He was like a dog chasing his own tail. The tiny muscles people never use are killing him. They seem to be isolated by these weird positions.

Benny shovels the rest of his breakfast down his weathered face while pointing at Dane's food. "You going to eat that?" Dane pushes his plate towards Benny, who continues, "Yo, check this. The menu here is like twenty pages long. They have all that food somewhere in the back? Like, who gets prime rib here? Or crab cakes? But they need to have it in case someone orders it, right?"

Dane rubs the left side of his upper lip, "Benny, you're on borrowed time."

Benny nervously interrupts, "Come on man, don't say that." He takes a sip of his water to wash down the mouth full of food. "We're cool. Like a couple of penguins."

"You're right. You follow the plan and you'll be fine on our end."

Benny picks at his nasty teeth with a toothpick and answers nonchalantly. "D, I can execute a plan better than anyone. You can count on me."

"I got the bill. I'll call you tomorrow."

Benny gets up. His bloated, full stomach can be seen though his ratty, tight-fitting black T-shirt. He rubs it as he arches his back. He exits the diner, mumbling, and notices a half-used cigarette on the ground outside. Without hesitation, he picks it up, places it in his mouth and goes about his business. It doesn't cross his mind that the

CHAPTER 8

person who discarded it may have been diseased. Dane looks at his watch and walks over to the women's bathroom. He knocks.

Colin answers the knock aggravated. "Occupado."

"Col, it's me. You okay?"

"Password?" He opens the door a crack. "Well, I'm trapped in my pants. I did get an email earlier that I have twenty percent off one item at Bed, Bath, and Beyond. I'm thinking they chose me specifically for this honor and no one else. Can we check out toilet brushes from here?"

Dane opens the door. He slides into the bathroom. "What do we have here?" He assesses the damage. After a little struggle, he pulls the zipper down.

"Piece of shit zipper."

Dane puts his hand up to calm Colin. "Brother, this is fucked up. I'm not going to lie to you. But there are people who haven't ever had two arms and you got to hold Betty with both of them. So, don't start feeling sorry for yourself. This isn't easy, but it will get easier. And I'm here and not going anywhere."

"Did we just have a moment?"

Dane laughs and pushes him. "Fucking dick."

* * *

Colin waits outside while Dane settles the bill. He points his face in the direction of the sun, closes his eyes, and just lets the warmth soak into his skin. He pictures one of the many times he said something that made Betty want to playfully punch him. Her cute fist and how she would adorably bite her bottom lip, jars him out of this happy memory. His eyes open like an android that was just activated. The realization that new moments with his person, that person destiny ordained, the one that takes breath away and in a room full of people is the only one, are done forever and it fills him with acrimony. He's suddenly hypersensitive to his surroundings. Jaywalkers, bums, people on their lunch break all scurrying around. A little dog catches his eye. The pup is practically choking himself to hustle down the street. A young child also notices the pup, and bolts across the street as his nanny turns her back.

Colin's brain reacts like he's able-bodied. Since he's not he stumbles, using his cane to keep his balance, awkwardly heading in the child's direction, terrified he won't make it. His limp turns into a stagger and he notices a lady in a SUV, on the phone, who doesn't see this tiny tyke.

At literally the last possible second, Colin falls into the street in front of the kid, as the lady jams on her brakes. He shelters the kid; the SUV screeches one inch from his body. Within a second, more screeching causes him to flinch, as the SUV is rear-ended. He rolls them out of the way of the SUV's new forward momentum.

Dane catches the tail end of the collision as he comes out of the diner. He waves his badge and flags down a patrol car. He turns to Colin on the ground, "Col, what the fuck?"

"Seriously?" Colin gives his brother a look he's seen a million time, "Should I have let this lady run over a toddler?"

"No, I mean," Dane helps him up, "I'm glad you're okay and obviously you did the right thing. Jesus Christ." Dane punches the hood of the SUV.

The lady flinches, "Hey, watch it!"

"Lady, you were on the phone. Automatically your fault." Dane addresses the uniformed officers as they hustle over. "Fellas, this lady was on the phone. Deal with this mess." The officers nod and continue to secure the scene. Dane picks up Colin's cane. He walks over, shaking his head. "I'm gonna have to switch to decaf."

* * *

Dane drives Colin to physical therapy. The adrenaline spike from nearly being struck by a car has worn off and his pain meds are in the driver's seat. He's comfortably numb at the moment, trying to

CHAPTER 8

picture every one of Betty's smiles he got to witness during their time together. When he thinks of her, he forgets to breathe and his chest tightens, and sometimes his heart takes so long to beat he thinks it's stopped. In those moments, he wishes it had and much to his disappointment shortly thereafter, there's a thump. Falling is one thing, getting back up is where the problem lies. That's where mettle is tested. Colin sways forward, gently caught by his seat belt. Dane throws the car into park. "I'll wait here. I've got some calls to make. You good?"

Colin nods and exits the car. He limps awkwardly towards the front door. He's feeling his previous tumble to save the toddler. The road rash on his legs, his deep knee and elbow bruises, all in addition to the slow healing wounds from the night he nearly died.

He enters the brightly-lit facility and sees all types of people being rehabilitated. There are athletes, the elderly, kids, and everyone in between. Therapists are helping people walk, setting up machines, and demonstrating exercises. The place is packed with an unsettling amount of injured people. Colin signs in with difficulty. He leans his cane against the counter and it slides down, hitting the ground with a loud smack. People turn and look in the direction of the noise, then go back to what they were doing. The pen affixed to the chain, to prevent theft, doesn't reach the line on the sign-in sheet available for Colin's John Hancock. He needs to place the pen down, move the clipboard closer and then sign in. What takes someone no time at all was three to five extra steps for him. He feels someone patiently waiting behind him and once he finishes, moves to the side to collect himself and nods to the guy behind him who slides into the spot in front of the counter. Colin quickly sizes him up, because he just has a feeling this guy will initiate a conversation he'd rather not have. Late twenties, medium height, fit yet emaciated. Huge calves, bandana, wearing super short shorts. If his nuts were bigger they'd hang out.

Displaying an exuberant tone, he breaks the ice Colin placed between them. "Hey bro, name's John. What's your name?"

Colin, in a completely serious tone, holds his hand out to shake. "Clubber Lang. Pleasure."

John touches Colin's shoulder as he speaks. "Super nice to meet you, Clubber." He changes the subject, "I'm an ultra long distance runner."

"I'm an ultra short distance runner." Colin does not move. "You missed it. Just finished a race."

John laughs. "I like you, Clubber. I did a seventy-mile run two weeks ago. A month ago, I did a two hundred and fifty mile run. I ran for three days straight without sleep."

Colin feigns inquisitiveness, "Let me ask you something. You ever think that if your parents had a do-over, they'd abort you?"

"Never. They're my biggest fans. Super good people." John puts him into a cross between a headlock and a hug, "I love you, man. But it's true, during my second night, I dozed off for who knows how long. A car horn woke me. I was sleep-running on a highway."

"So you're back on the three-day race? Got it. I really thought my subject change would take."

"Clubber, it's crazy. I was working as a lawyer, wearing my Thomas Pink shirts, driving my Benz, and eating dinner at 10 p.m. I had my corporate card, expense account, and an assistant to get my laundry. One night, I was at this restaurant with co-workers and escorts, because guys like us don't meet nice girls and can't trust girls that aren't in our pocket. I got up to take a squirt. I'm in the bathroom and I'm looking at myself. Between the job, the hours, the stress, the shitty food, the lack of exercise, the drinks with every client, I'm a heart attack waiting to happen. My middle was soft. My hair was thinning. I look at myself and I'm disgusted. I had fat under my chin and flabby tits. I run out of the restaurant and it's about to rain. It was very eerie."

"Wait, don't tell me. You buy a dilapidated zoo and shenanigans ensue as you and your family prepare for a grand reopening?"

John just continues, "I run and I run and I run. I have no idea where I am. I just kept going. I stopped seventy-five miles later. My feet were on fire. My legs ached. My pain receptors were in fucking shock, and once this subsided, this 'runner's high' took over my whole body and lasted for like a month. I had a bit of a coke problem. Some meth. A little H. But this high is way better. And it's fucking free, lasts for weeks, isn't poison. Next thing you know, I'm winning marathon after marathon." Colin tries to walk away, but John just follows, continuing, "I have a very healthy diet, day in and day out. However, while I'm racing, my body needs fuel. It wants fuel so bad it doesn't care what type. It wants chips, pizza, burgers, anything. As long as I can keep it down. Shit. I become a junk food monster. I remember my first fifty-mile race. I won that race no problem. I got home, crashed on my couch, and threw up all over myself for hours. I've never been happier."

"That amount of pain and vomit? I mean, it sounds like pure bliss."

"Totally. You want my number? Maybe we can get together and fuck."

Colin makes a face like he has to be on a hidden camera show. "No thank you?"

"Sex is a great exercise. You don't have to be a plucker. It's just like shooting hoops. Nice little workout."

"I prefer more traditional workouts. Especially ones that don't involve anal insertion. I think I could get into Pilates. Maybe spinning. If I change my mind and want to get fucked by some weird guy to burn calories, I'll definitely let you know."

John bobs his head, completely okay with his offer. There's no sign of embarrassment and he doesn't seem rejected. "I feel you."

They call Colin's name and he puts out his fist to bump, "Thanks, homie. I got to roll over there, blast my quads."

Then they call John's name before Colin can even turn away. "Cool, maybe we can partner up?"

"Sounds about right." Colin pops another Vicodin in his mouth and swallows it without water.

***

Colin throws his nearly empty bottle of beer against the bar's dumpster out back, "Fucking Kitashi." He's half-drunk, full-on angry standing with Dane outside the wake for the father of one of his brothers in blue. "Ian asked us to step in and we warned that gaggle of anuses not to touch Ian's dad and he goes and murders him? I'm mortified. Does he actually think we're going to let this slide?"

Dane calmly sips his beer. "Retaliation will be bad for us right now."

"We can't start a war. I get it. But fuck that guy. This is a bad time to show any weakness. What would Katniss Everdeen do?"

Dane shakes his head and thinks on it a second, staring at the whitewashed exposed brick. Then the graffiti on the dumpster, the always clever cock and balls fucking an ass. "Dry dive. We do it right, no one knows it us. We'll get the rest of those Yakuza fucks later."

"That's exactly what Katniss would do." Colin comes to life, his eyes flicker and his previous defeated countenance washes away. "You evil genius. I knew there was a reason I stopped teasing you when we were kids."

"I almost broke your arm with an oar."

"That was also a very Katniss move."

"How 'bout we drop the young adult pop culture references when we talk with Ian?"

"'Drop' leave them out or 'drop' like knowledge?"

"Betty is a saint."

"Yeah, she is."

They sit in the back of the now nearly empty bar with Ian who sports a brave face, but is completely shredded inside by the loss of his father. He can't believe the guy who moved here knowing zero English, worked himself to death for his kids, is gone. The guy who made sure he went to college. The guy who missed his fair share of games, recitals, and moments because of work, but would be up at crazy hours watching the video their mom took with tears in his eyes.

CHAPTER 8

Ian sits in one of the bar's beaten up wooden chairs and Colin and Dane stand in front of him.

Colin starts, "Dane and I are going to get rid of that condom full of ponzu sauce."

Ian shakes his head. "I don't know, guys. I feel badly about getting you sucked into this shit storm as it is."

Colin cuts him off. "We had umbrellas. We just didn't think we needed galoshes."

"It's not your fault. He wouldn't have paid, no matter what."

Dane steps in, "Monday morning quarterbacking won't do a goddamn thing."

Colin can't help himself, "Unless its for a Monday night game, then that's just being prepared for the next game."

Dane continues. "We're doing it tomorrow, no arrest. No trial." He looks him dead in the eyes, "But you need to come here with Pat at like 7 p.m. and stay here until closing. I want your alibi to be airtight, and your location indisputable. You'll have to start some awkward conversations with random people, anybody."

Colin continues, "The more memorable the better. Get weird with it. Reference unique things like unicorns, hemorrhoids, Katniss Everdeen."

Ian nods, "Like am I Team Peeta or Team Gale."

Colin gives him a high five. "Team Gale!"

Dane continues, "Fit the time into the conversations as much as possible. 'I can't believe its 9 p.m. already.' Or, 'It's 10 p.m., how much longer you staying?' Ask the bartender what time it is every forty-five minutes."

Colin places his hand on Ian's shoulder, "You'll be the main suspect for a hot second, but with an alibi as tight as Liberace's cape game, you'll be ruled out quicker than the Road Runner on EPO."

* * *

Kitashi spits on the ground in disgust, face bloodied, "You better kill me or cancel the rest of your lives."

Colin looks at the LA skyline from the top of a high-rise. It's close to midnight. "It's windy up here and I hate heights." He taps Dane, "Look," pointing off in the distance, "Movie premiere?"

Dane shrugs. Colin turns away from the ledge and gets close to Kitashi's face, "I think... we'll kill you. I'm looking forward to the Shamrock Shake coming back in March and I'd rather not have to cancel the rest of my life. I also hear that the szechuan sauce may also be back by popular demand and that would be dope. I'm tiny Rick!"

Kitashi shakes his head. "My people will fucking kill you."

Dane punches Kitashi in the face. "Your people are going to think you jumped."

"Never."

Dane pulls a gun out, "Remember that kid that was gunned down in your neighborhood last month?"

"I had nothing to do with that."

Dane continues, "This is the gun that fired the bullet that accidentally took her down. Between it being found on your person, and the text I just sent your mother that the guilt is eating you up inside, it'll play."

Colin steps in. "And that will be the official police conclusion after the shortest investigation in history."

Kitashi shakes his head, unable to speak.

Dane stands him up, tucking the gun into the back of Kitashi's pants. Colin grabs his other shoulder, "It's time for your close-up with the ground at 9.8 meters per second." The two brothers throw him off the building.

＊＊

Within a flash, Colin and Dane are in front of the police station. Colin dozed off in the car like a little kid. Maybe it's the Vicodin or it could

CHAPTER 8

be the tiny bottle of vodka he drank in the bathroom after rehab. He's probably not supposed to mix the two and he's definitely not supposed to operate a forklift or anything with blades.

Colin is a complete mess, and keeps his shades on to avoid too much undue attention. His goal is to be as low key as possible. In and out. Under the radar. The place is noisy with conversations and everybody is busy doing something. There's a real chance this could be painless. Then, as if some universal agency intervened and ordained an inevitable event, Colin slips and falls down the stairs. His cane hit a wet spot and he lost it. When he gets back on his feet, the whole place is looking at him. Dead silence is only broken by the thumping of his heart and the sound sweat makes when it envelops the palms. "Has anyone seen my other arm?" Light laughter fills the air previously sucked out of the room. "So, no more eggplant emoji, what a bummer!" Everyone shakes their heads, smiling and patting Colin on the shoulder and back as they walk by. Colin turns to Dane, "That was awesome."

Dane guides him out of the hallway. "You really didn't stick the landing."

"Right?! I'm pretty sure one of my testicles is just loose in my underwear."

"That would be horrifying."

Ian walks up to them, smiling. "Colin, good to see you." He puts out his hand for shaking; the wrong hand.

Colin ends up twisting his hand over to shake upside-down. "See what I did there? That's the most exercise I've had all week."

Ian waves them his way, "Guys, follow me. I have all the info."

As they walk to their destination, there are many bulletin boards plastered with official police business. There are also notices peppered throughout the station for softball games and retirement parties. The longer they walk, the less people seem to be around. There's a dingy little room tucked away in the bowels of the police station, forgotten, possibly for storage.

The fluorescent lighting flickers and half the bulbs need to be replaced. The tile floor is an ungodly color; whatever was on sale thirty or forty years ago. The walls are painted a matching equally ungodly color that gives the room an icky feeling; like if a room can violate a person.

"Fellas, sit down." Ian points to the chairs.

Colin sits down and addresses Ian immediately. "This isn't going to put you in a position, is it? Missionary? Reverse cowgirl? Is Dumbo Drop a position or just my favorite movie?"

Ian laughs, "I missed you, man. This room isn't wired and Internal Affairs, those fucks, think it's for storage. When something like this happens... Fuck by the book."

Dane interjects. "Book is just a guideline. Like a recipe."

Ian sits back in his chair. "Col, I never got to thank you man."

Colin waves it away. "That's extinct, my friend. You're making it up to me now."

Dane picks up the manila folder that Ian was holding. "This is family and all known associates?"

Ian nods. "Yeah. This guy is a player. But, he's good... he's like Teflon."

Dane hands Colin a photograph. "I think we have a place to start."

"What do we have here?" Colin's intrigued. "Daughter."

Chapter 9

Trendy clubs and bars in Los Angeles are ephemeral with the lifespan of a mayfly. These operations are so fragile, the softest breath could make one vanish. Despite all of this, usually all the same groups of people are involved in each new incarnation. Investing, hyping, cashing in, and then cashing out. The Moon Bar is trendy right now. The bar is poolside of a ritzy hotel that charges a ton for illusion. At first glance, the place seems worthy of the nightly expense. Upon further inspection, everything is a facade. The decor is all from Asian countries purchased from downtown wholesalers. Most would probably carry a Prop 65 warning if anyone cared to divulge. The furniture looks hip and chic, but is cheaply manufactured and not built to last. The dressers would likely crush a toddler if not anchored to the wall properly. However, photos of the place come off appealing, not unlike the Target outfits advertised on models that never seem to fit normal folks as good.

In addition to high tables, stools and chairs, there are beds scattered all around the pool for drunken patrons to lay on. The night-to-night crowd tends to be very European. The inside part of the bar is set back and tiki-bar themed. The music tends to be hip-hop and rap music. This is the Pied Piper's flute that draws the wealthy minorities from the main area.

Some nights seem arbitrarily busier than others. 'Cool' people seem to be privy to which nights to make an appearance and commingle with their own kind. Its doubtful promoters use enigma machines to get coded messages to this population; those who know exactly how much hair product to use and how short a cocktail dress needs to be, but word gets out nonetheless. The waitresses are provocatively dressed, have aspirations of one day becoming actresses, and are thus in the meantime wactresses. They walk around coercing drinks out of men that would normally milk just one eighteen-dollar drink for hours. Men susceptible to this type of chicanery don't want to look cheap to a beautiful woman. Wealth, and in many cases the appearance of wealth, are historically the easiest way to get one's dick wet. Between the establishment, the male patrons and the female patrons nothing is what it seems, and everything is an ignis fatuus.

Jeff is on the pulse when it comes to what's hot in town. Despite never working a real day ever, he's got access to unlimited funds and has been a playboy his entire adult life. He's extremely confident when it comes to the fairer sex. His money has given him physically satisfying nights with very attractive women because they noticed his fifty thousand dollar watch, or heard the engine of whatever super car he's driving. His inflated ego attributes his abilities to charm the opposite sex as the major factor in his success, rather than his money. While his confidence is based on faulty reasoning, it's still apparent and does close deals that lack of confidence would undoubtedly bungle. He comes here to scoop up young girls hoping to bump into a celebrity, as these women have proven easy prey in his experience. Jeff orders a cranberry juice and Grey Goose vodka, and pays the bartender. He sidles over to a blonde woman whose skimpy outfit has caught his eye.

Daniella is the epitome of a low talent woman who scores high in the aesthetic department. She is medium height and extremely thin. Her doe eyes, despite nothing behind them, sparkle and her crooked smile gives her an intangible sexiness. Jeff doesn't even try to hide the fact that he's checking her out, staring at her exposed stomach, legs, and ass. He has a look in his eye like he's sizing up a new car, but she's so oblivious that Mary Wollstonecraft is spinning in her grave. Daniella is leaning against a light post and holding a Michelob Ultra because she is carb conscious. She is completely self-absorbed and name drops as much as possible. "Can I tell you a secret?"

Jeff flirts back. "Depends. Do I in turn have to keep it a secret? If I'm waterboarded, I'll totally spill my guts."

Daniella laughs, "If someone is going to torture you, all bets are off."

Jeff nods and Daniella leans in and whispers in his ear.

He covers his mouth, "No way."

Daniella nods affirmatively, "Yup."

"You're the reason they broke up? You? They seemed so happy."

Daniella curtsies, "I slept with one of them."

"Him?"

She shakes her head.

"HER!"

She nods affirmatively.

"Amazing! She is hot."

"Yeah, she is." She switches gears, "I have a few projects coming out."

"Like what?"

"This untitled Gary Busey Project. It's some sort of VR situation. New Media."

Jeff's confused. "Gary Busey? I don't know. I threw away a sandwich at the Malibu Country Mart and he fished it out the garbage and finished it."

Daniella looks disappointed. "Ugh, that's gross. And I have to kiss him. I might throw up."

Dane has dressed incognito in a black leather jacket and baseball cap. He walks up to the bouncers, who each step to the gap between them he was going to pass through. "Easy fellas," he discreetly flashes his badge, "I need to get by." Both bouncers step away from each other and let him through with a nod.

He quickly finds Jeff and gets a couple quick pictures on his phone. One of the scantily clad wactresses, beautifully pale, with her English nose and dark mane, approaches Dane to take his order. "Can I get you something to drink?"

Dane nods, "Yes please. Uh, vodka tonic."

"You got it, hun."

She hands him his drink with a napkin and winks. Her number is written across the bottom. He smiles, nods at her, and moves over to Jeff, standing behind him with his back turned. He eavesdrops on their conversation, trying to get a sense of the enemy.

Daniella continues, "Busey is a genius."

Jeff sounds skeptical. "Genius? I'll say that's a debatable call."

"And the nudity is super tastefully done."

Jeff waves the length of her body, "Tasteful nudity? You're nude? This body here is nude?" She nods, and he shakes his head, changing his tune. "It sounds like Busey is a genius."

Daniella playfully pushes his shoulder, biting her lip at his sexist compliment.

Jeff offers a suggestion on how they can constructively spend their night. "How about I get sneak preview of this tastefully done nudity?"

Daniella shakes her head. "I'd love to, but I have an early casting call for 'The Untitled Melissa McCarthy Peter Dinklage Body Switch Film.'"

"I know Dink's psychic. I could put in a good word?"

Daniella's face lights up. "That would be so nice," she grabs his hand, and they leave.

Dane shakes his head both disappointed this joker closed the deal and that this poor gal not only fell for his bullshit, but was eating it up. The sea of people dancing catches his eye; he notices a black fedora. When its owner turns, it's a twenties hipster but for a brief moment, despite being impossible, he thought it was Jude. Jude was his godfather, best friends with his dad since they were kids, a crime scene photographer. He always wore a hat despite having a perfect head of hair. He wore a three-piece suit and his pocket watch had the Freemason symbol on it. Dane and Colin took turns holding it during visits. Dane took an interest in photography and Jude taught him everything. His death was tragic and nearly destroyed Dane.

CHAPTER 9

Nearly a decade ago the police responded to a quadruple homicide. Four brothers were selling dope out of their apartment. They were flashy and flapped their gums about how much cash and product they had on hand. This wild flake, nicknamed Casper, went in as a tweaker trying to score and absolutely massacred the siblings. The gunshots led to sirens and the perpetrator fled the scene in haste. The police didn't give a rat's ass who killed these dealers. They considered it a public service. However, optics are to be considered in crimes such as these. Neighbors and concerned citizens were peeking through the peepholes, standing in the hallway, and loitering around the building. The police put on a dog and pony show. The place was dusted, examined, and statements were taken. Jude arrived late because he was at another scene. Some teenage kid decided to end his problems by jumping off a building.

Jude was old school, preferring his Canon AE-1 to any digital camera. He was taking pictures of the scene when a Molotov cocktail was thrown through a window in a downstairs apartment. Chaos erupted and the officers on the scene helped escort people out of the building and the firefighters, upon arrival, squelched the flames. Jude was alone in the apartment, wrapping up, when Casper entered the room. In his haste, murdering the brothers, he dropped his wallet during the struggle, and it got kicked under the couch. The officers' due diligence was so superficial, it didn't yield the killer's wallet, just nearly out of plain sight. Casper had created a diversion with the Molotov cocktail, so he could reclaim his wallet, the only evidence linking him to the homicides. He took Jude by surprise and before Jude could react, he was filled with five bullets; killing him. His last crime scene had become his own. Casper grabbed his wallet and got the hell out of there.

Dane was devastated and requested the case. Usually, personal agendas would preclude his involvement, but the powers that be wanted vengeance and unleashed a rabid dog. Despite his best efforts, the investigation continued for months with little success. The killer left no evidence and the building was a mess with the people panicking, the firefighters, and the police presence. Completely frustrated, Dane broke some of his belongings, shot his gun off, and decided to develop Jude's final roll of film. He thought it would be a beneficial, cathartic exercise. Casper had busted in as Jude was taking pictures and Jude actually photographed his murderer.

Dane identified the shooter as Pedro Salazar, also known as Casper. He lived with his grandmother and his little brother Santiago in low-income housing. Dane knocked on the door late one night and Santiago answered. The police found their way to the Salazar residence regularly and Santiago, only fourteen, tipped his brother off. Dane, realizing Pedro had been signaled, smacked the boy. He chased Pedro and after some serious running and jumping caught up to him. He took Pedro to an industrial yard and cuffed him to his bumper. He drove around until Pedro looked like a dirty piece of meat. He dug a deep hole and covered Pedro with lye. He sent the family a mass card for the deceased from the police department.

Every time he takes a picture, he thinks of Jude.

* * *

Dane covertly places a listening device at school pickup. The bug has its own SIM card. All Dane has to do is text the code and his number to the device and he can listen whenever he wants, with virtually no range limit.

He's parked across the street, both listening and taking pictures. Alissa, held up a few minutes from her last class, meets up with her best friends, Courtney, Megan, and Alex to wait for their rides home. They have all been best friends since first grade. Each is a stereotypically flawed affluent teen. They have all made their school uniforms as slutty as possible. Alissa's shirt is tied in a knot revealing both her stomach and her tramp stamp.

"Yo, peeps!" She hugs each of them hello. Alissa blurts out, "My dad totally freaked."

Megan responds immediately, "Over what?"

"The tat and the tongue stud."

Alex shakes her head, "Really? Whatever. You're not a little girl. That's not okay."

Alissa nods as she answers, "I know. Totes. He's such a dick."

Courtney joins the conversation, "Your dad is at least cool though. My dad is such a dork."

Alex places her hand on Alissa's shoulder. "Yeah. Your dad is badass. He's gangsta."

Megan chimes in, "Yeah, 'Lis, he's legit."

Alissa rolls her eyes. "Ugh, you have no idea. You don't know him like I do. He wears socks with sandals just like your dads do. And his jokes? He's just as lame."

They all interrupt each other with overlapping sentiments echoing that they each have the least cool dad.

Courtney blurts out during a random silence, "At least he doesn't have a dad bod like all our dads!"

Alissa pretends to gag, "Gross. That is gross."

Dane finishes up with the pictures and disgustedly blurts out, "Fucking kids." Alissa's ride pulls up, a vintage muscle car. Dane makes a note of the time, Alissa gets in, the car pulls away, and Dane follows. He mumbles to himself, "It's Tuesday. Singing lesson then home."

Chapter 10

Richard's residence is a compound. Besides guesthouses and garages, he had a structure manufactured per his specifications. From a distance it seems ordinary, but its reinforced, bulletproof, and possibly the most secure area on the property. Access is limited and a computerized log records everyone that enters and exits. This is where he keeps weapons, files, and other important contraband. It's set back and has an underground tunnel to move items in and out practically undetected. Richard placed this structure as a separate entity on the edge of his property, in Jeff's name, through a shell corporation, just in case a search warrant was ever executed. The authorities would need a separate warrant. Between the time it would take to sort out legal search issues and the tunnel, Richard would have an opportunity to move anything illegal to another location. Vincent, Piney and Corky are in charge of keeping the ammo inventoried and the weapons oiled and clean. This seems like a bottom of the food chain type of assignment, but Vincent and Piney are control freaks and don't trust just anybody with their weapons. A half-assed cleaning job can mean a jammed gun when you need it most.

Holland 'Corky' Corkoran is a tall goon that stutters horribly. He has beady eyes and a distinct nose that makes him look bird-like. His face is red from the acne medicine that keeps his skin clear some of the time. He was on an acne pill when he was a teen, the main side effect being psychosis. Back then, right out of high school, he lived in Jersey with his parents in a sleepy shore town. He was on a rooftop mini-golf course, throwing rocks at cars, virtually out of his mind, when two rent-a-cops attempted to stop the vandalism. These walking police punchlines, in their shorts with flashlights and walkie-talkies in hand, approached the wild teen. Fisticuffs ensued, leading to the never-to-be police throwing the young lad off of the roof, lowering his IQ and giving him a nasty stutter. Despite his low intelligence, he's been extremely loyal to Richard.

The clicking sound of bullets being pushed into spring-loaded clips by the three men overlap, creating its own unique beat. They sit in otherwise virtual silence each with pursed lips and stand-offish body language. Piney breaks the silence, "Vince, mate."

Vincent refuses to take his eyes off the task at hand. "What?"

Piney shakes his head, "I apologize for snapping at you earlier. That was not cool."

Vincent looks up, "I have to admit. It came out of nowhere. I figured you were projecting on me and something else was bothering you."

Piney shakes his head. "Spot on. You nailed it, bruva. Truth be told, my weight has been stressing me out. I've entered a bad eating cycle."

Vincent nods and pats Piney on the back. "Eat to live my friend, not live to eat. Besides, I keep telling you, fast food is the fucking worst."

Piney tucks a gun into his pants, "I don't see how it's really different than anything else. A chicken sandwich is a chicken sandwich, yes?"

Corky shrugs his shoulders. "A ch-chicken sandwich is a ch-chicken sandwich."

Vincent stands up and walks over to a metal closet, opens the door and pulls out more clips. "You're missing the point entirely. There are two major reasons why McDonalds, Burger King, all fast food for that matter, are bad for you."

Corky directs his question at Vincent. "How about In and Out B-b-burger? I like to get my meals animal ss-tt-yle.."

Piney isn't familiar with this American slang, "Come again?"

Corky is struggling to get through his thought, "Nnn-ext time, just order a double-double an-n-imal st-style, you'll thank me."

Piney nods, "Double-double? You stuttering? Or did you mean

double-double?"

"N-n-ott C-c-ool."

Vincent focuses on the two guys, "He means double-double. It's fucking good. But fucking bad for you. All fast food chains are bad. Last thing I need is one of you fucks having a heart attack when we're in a situation."

Piney is skeptical, "Your knickers are in a twist over this fast food? What's your evidence?"

Vincent takes a seat and addresses them like he's given this a lot of thought. "For starters, everything is stored in bulk and has to last a long time on the shelf."

Corky, as so often, is unable to read between the lines. "So?"

"You ever get a dozen bagels and by the next day they're stale as hell? Why do you think bakeries give homeless people day-old shit for nothing?"

Piney crosses his arms. "Tax write-off. Kindness. PR."

Vincent slowly shakes his head from side to side. "Maybe. But mostly because it's bad. No preservatives. Stale. Those hamburger buns you eat have to last a long time, so they are full of chemicals and shit that makes you fat."

The hamster in Corky's head has just woken up. The wheel begins turning. "That dd-does make sense. I n-n-never get a burger that has a st-tale bun, but I'll try and make a m-m-meatball sub at home. Jeez. B-b-breads tougher than a t-t-turkey's ass."

Vincent nods in agreement. "Piney, your old lady makes a hell of a fish and chips, right?"

Piney doesn't hesitate, "The best by far. It's lovely, pure heaven, mate."

Vincent chooses his words carefully. "I'm a fan, but word around the campfire is some of the guys think it could be better."

Piney gets angry. "Bollocks. Those ungrateful fucks. How could they stab me in the heart like that? Fuck it, more for me."

Vincent wants to prove his point but doesn't want to start a big thing.

CHAPTER 10

"Relax, it all goes back to what I was saying. The fish and chips, in your opinion, our opinion, is top notch, but one of the other guys could think his mother's is better because that's the one he grew up on."

Corky pipes up. "I l-l-love my m-m-mother's chicken picatta, and when I go to L-l-lugosi's I can't get it because it don't t-t-taste right to me."

Vincent continues. "Exactly. Therefore, how is it that everyone likes how a Big Mac tastes? Or any fast food for that matter? What is in it, that makes it appealing to ninety-nine billion served?"

Piney takes a deep breath. "Beautiful. You just blew my mind. That shit's like quantum physics."

Corky adds his two cents, which ain't worth sticker price. "No. M-m-meta-ph-physics."

Benny opens the door suddenly and the three guys flinch a little. "Fellas. What up?" Benny doesn't give them a chance to answer. "Vince, my man, you stood me up the other day."

Vincent squints as though he has no clue what Benny is talking about. "What?"

"We were gonna take a ride up to Carmel and check out some of the classics, but you stood me up."

Vincent is confused, "No way. What are you talking about?"

"Dude it was like the third time we were gonna hang but you were a no show. Do you have a problem with me?"

Vincent is apologetic. "No. I mean. I don't know what you are talking about. Seriously?"

Benny gets concerned. "We've talked about your memory two other times, do you remember that?"

Vincent is floored. "What? My memory?"

Piney interrupts, "I hate to be a pain in the ass, but you were supposed to help me move some shit around last week."

"We were sup-p-posed to c-c-catch a movie."

Vincent is freaked out. "Are you guys fucking with me? I have no recollection of any of this whatsoever. I guess I have taken my share of blows to the head."

"Like those NFL motherfuckers."

Piney gets a call. He nods to Corky to follow and they both leave the shed.

Benny takes Vincent aside. "Bro, I have the name of this doctor, he's really good. You should check him out."

"Alright. If you guys are for real, I guess I'll make an appointment."

"Let's go now."

"Now?"

"What else you gotta do today? And what's more important than your health?"

* * *

Benny planted the seed in Vincent's head that his memory was failing. He recommended a doctor, Dr. Phil. The good doc was more than happy to help when he found out Vincent played a big role in Betty's demise. He loved Betty like his own daughter. Benny offered to chauffeur and Vincent jumped at the free ride and company, albeit scumbag company. He was concerned because the idea of memory loss is terrifying for anybody, especially a young man. He didn't want to believe his ability to retain information was compromised and he needed to know for sure.

They enter the office like fish out of water, looking at each other, unsure of the proper protocol. After shoulder shrugs and blank stares, they shuffle to the chairs and sit.

Benny points to the reception area. "Vince, man, go sign in and shit. Tell them you're here."

Vince shakes his head in disbelief. "Man, I don't know what I'm thinking. I totally forgot."

"Bro, that's why we're here. You haven't been yourself and this guy will get down to the bottom of it."

Vincent stands up, maneuvers around the table where the magazines

CHAPTER 10

are displayed, and walks over to the receptionist's window. He looks at his watch, signs his name on the first available line, and places the pencil back into the cup. His eyes lock with the receptionist who is unexpectedly attractive and he does a double take. "Hi, I have a one o'clock."

The receptionist smiles, bats her eyelashes, and grabs the sign-in sheet. She hands a clipboard to Vincent. "Okay, fill this out and we'll call you when the doctor is ready."

Vincent plops down next to Benny, letting out a huge sigh. He leans over to Vincent and shows him the magazine that he's thumbing through with a half-naked girl on the cover. "How hot is this chick, Vince? I'm gonna spring wood."

Vincent is too concerned about his own health to humor Benny. "Yeah. Nice." Vincent begins filling out his information sheet.

"What's crazy is this magazine doesn't have to struggle to find chicks that are willing to strip for the camera, man. They can fill these pages all day! The irony is if I bump into one of these gals at like a pool or someplace, they'd probably cover up and get all bashful, not thinking I've been wacking at home to their magazine pic."

"That's great, Benny." Vincent pulls out his wallet and takes out his insurance card. "Does the policy number include the three letters that are first?"

"You have insurance?" Benny places the magazine on his lap.

"Yeah. Richard gets it for me through one of the businesses."

"I was never offered any insurance benefits. I have a kid that requires expensive medical care from time to time."

Vincent continues to read the form he's filling out. "Who has secondary insurance?"

Benny's eyes bug out. "People have two insurances? I don't have any, but some people have two?"

Vincent turns to the page denoting his medical history. "Jesus, this is depressing. Check the ones that apply. Cancer... No. Chemotherapy... No. Heart disease... No. Man, this list goes on."

81

"That's not depressing, bro. You don't have any of that. You should be stoked."

"It's only a matter of time before we're all checking off some of these."

Benny turns to Vincent. "That's half empty. Negativity is bad for your health."

Vincent nods, "You're right."

"Besides, in our line, we're more likely to get capped than die of old age."

The nurse opens the door, looks at her clipboard, and calls Vincent's name. He follows the nurse out of the waiting room and Benny leans over and stares at her ass for as long as he can, nearly falling off his chair. Benny picks up the magazine he was reading, gets up, and snakes to the bathroom.

The nurse ushers Vince to the examination room and she pulls the deli paper covering the examination table down and then tears off the excess. The nurse points like she is showcasing this luxurious table. "Have a seat."

Vincent sits down and she instructs him to roll up his sleeve so she can take his blood pressure. She places the cuff around his arm, pumps it up, and places the stethoscope halfway under the cuff right below the bicep muscle. She looks at the watch, deflates the cuff, and writes something in Vincent's chart.

Vincent is unnerved by this whole experience. "How was it?"

"What?" The nurse has moved onto her next checks.

"My blood pressure. Was it good?"

"It was in normal range. You're probably a little tense."

"That's an understatement."

The nurse asks Vincent to come over to the scale where she weighs him and measures his height.

"I feel like a little kid."

The nurse answers coldly, "The doctor will be in soon," and exits.

Vincent sits, shoes off, with his wallet, phone and keys on a little

CHAPTER 10

chair in the corner. He fidgets, looks at the posters depicting anatomy, and runs his hands through his hair. A wave of boredom crashes over him and he decides to check out the room in more detail. He begins opening and closing drawers. He touches the tongue depressors and the otoscope. As he inspects the doctor's tools, Dr. Phil saunters into the room, practically giving Vincent a heart attack.

"It's okay, man, all the patients check out my scopes."

"I'm normally not this jumpy."

Vincent isn't exaggerating. He's abnormally calm. His demeanor lends to murder. Most killers have to get accustomed to taking a life. Each kill tends to make the subsequent kills easier to deal with mentally. While Vincent's first kill came easily and without mental strife, it was sloppy.

* * *

Vincent had heard some dealers were sitting on tons of cash. He clearly had little respect for them being able to defend their spoils, but he didn't just rush in. He watched the apartment for several days, studying patterns, before making his move. He decided to strike when he saw that only one of the dealers was in the apartment watching the money and the stash. Vincent didn't have a gun or the scratch to procure one, so he brought two bricks with him and knocked on the door. When the dealer let him in, he smashed him in the head with one of the bricks.

Much to Vincent's surprise, a second occupant of Herculean stature exited the bathroom to see his compadre's brains on the ground. Apparently, this giant of a man never leaves the place and his only job is to guard, not unlike Cerberus. He went for the gun tucked into his belt, but before he could fully brandish the weapon Vincent threw a brick into his face. Before Hercules could comprehend what had just happened, Vincent was on top of him. Hercules pointed his gun at Vincent and they struggled at a complete stalemate for several seconds.

The adrenaline pumping through Vincent's veins fueled this deadlock, but he knew that the bigger man usually wins when brute strength is the only factor. Vincent grabbed the brick he had thrown earlier, which was within arm's reach, and with one smashing movement had stunned Hercules. Several blows later, the giant was no more. Vincent got up, wiped his face, and straightened out his clothes. He took a deep breath, filled up a bag and exited as though nothing had happened.

Ironically, this is how he came to be employed by Richard, who was supplying these dealers with the product they were selling. So, technically, Vincent had stolen from Richard. The ability for bad guys to find people far exceeds that of law enforcement. A gangster can find a witness, a thief, or a snitch when law enforcement has a tough time finding its own dick to take a piss. Law enforcement has rules and regulations preventing many of the most effective methods. He easily found Vincent and was impressed with him, seeing only raw potential. These dealers were getting high on his dime and it was only a matter of when they would slip up. Richard utilized the Vincent incident as an excuse to kill the remaining dealers within that group. Within months, Vincent was his number one man.

* * *

Vincent jarred back from his daydream. "What seems to be the problem?" Dr. Phil pulls out a new patient chart and begins to take notes on the conversation.

At first Vincent cannot concentrate on what he's saying to the doctor because the scribbling keeps distracting him. He's very choppy, and both Dr. Phil and Vincent start and stop repeatedly because Vincent is so incoherent. Dr. Phil decides to put his chart down and just listen.

"I feel pretty good, but I am having a tough time remembering things. I don't even remember I was supposed to remember something. But not all the time."

"Have you been doing many drugs lately? Drug use and memory

CHAPTER 10

loss..."

Vincent shakes his head, "No, doc, I don't do drugs."

"Maybe you should?"

"What?" Vincent is confused.

Dr. Phil smiles, "I'm just pulling your leg. Did you sustain any blows to your head recently?"

"Not recently, but I have, over the years. Occupational hazard."

"We're going to do a full blood panel and I'll order an MRI, spinal fluid test, and electroencephalogram."

"Sounds intense."

"We just want to be thorough. Get down to the bottom of why you are having this symptom so we can treat it effectively."

"I appreciate that, doc." Vincent places his hand out.

Dr. Phil shakes, "My pleasure."

Chapter 11

Colin intentionally drank a little too much last night, to look authentically worse for wear. Undercover work is real life method acting. He'd never verbalize that he's a little too handsome to be a degenerate scumbag, but he'll sure as hell think it. He stumbles to his car in torn jeans, a ratty T-shirt, and beat-up leather jacket. He's wearing shades and holding a coffee cup when he enters Wally's building. The apartment complex is old, not terribly ramshackle but one would be hard-pressed to find a spoiled USC kid living there. Colin walks up the steps, comes to apartment 4 and knocks. After a beat, Wally opens the door a crack. "Who dat?"

"Vic. You're expecting me."

Wally sounds squirrelly, "Is that your real name or cover name?"

"Say it louder, genius." Colin pushes the door, "Let me in."

Wally's foot prevents the crack from widening. He thinks for a second then opens the door. Colin enters and closes the door behind him. He pulls a recorder and microphone out of his pocket.

Wally bugs out, "What the fuck is that?"

"Bucket of dildos... bicycle... tire iron? What's it look it?" Colin takes a step towards him, "I got to mic you up, homie."

Wally steps back with his hands up, "No one said nothing about no mic."

"That's a lot of negatives in that sentence. LA Unified Public School, yeah? 9th grade, tops?"

"Fuck you, man. Your bedside manner is bullshit."

"I'm normally a regular Florence Nightingale, but time being of the

CHAPTER 11

essence, I'm more of an angel of mercy. We need the intro on tape. Shows you cooperated so you get your deal. Besides, they know you and won't check you. They will pat me down as sure as you don't know how to sail."

Wally shakes his head. "This is some last minute add-on bullshit. My cell phone is supposed to be $40 a month, but extra for this, fees for that and of course taxes. Shit ends up costing double."

"And yet, you still bend over and take it because you have no choice. Same goes here. Let's get you lubed up because we are going to be late. Like baby-momma late." Colin wiggles his eyebrows. "You know what I'm talking about."

"You best be this tough when in the shit, because these cats are the real deal." Wally unbuttons the flannel that's intentionally several sizes too big. He may feel like an extra large but he's a medium at most.

"Thanks for the heads up. I thought I was infiltrating a gang of Amish encyclopedia salesmen." Colin untangles the wire. "You killed Wags, yeah?"

Wally watches him tape the wire on. "You asking questions you know the answers to?"

"Wags was one of my CI's. Just wanted you to know."

"I liked Wags, but the powers that be decided he needed to go. If it wasn't me, it would have been some other nigga. That's for sure. He didn't feel nothing. Didn't even see that shit coming. Best way to go."

"That was super sweet. You should write greeting cards." Colin finishes up the job. "You're all set. Put your giant shirt on and let's roll."

***

Colin has been channeling Elvis' upper and downer balancing act. Between painkillers, anxiety medicine to sleep, and amphetamines to wake up, his heartbeat is never regular, just fast or slow. His mouth is always dry, his equilibrium is off, and most of the time he's looking through blurry eyes. He can manage to focus when he has to, but the more he relies on pills, the harder it is to concentrate.

He wakes up, stumbles to the bathroom, takes a handful of something with his bottled water (cap always off because once it's off, he's not putting it back on). He looks in the mirror and his reflection is Picasso-esque, a version of his himself he doesn't quite recognize. He pumps some soap into his hand, turns on the water and tries to wash his face with his one hand and weak soap distribution. This simple task is a chore as cupping water with one hand is inefficient, ineffective, and frustrating. A bit of residual soap lingers near the outside of his right eyebrow and below his left jawbone. He dries his face, despite not doing a stellar job. Colin limps down the stairs, making his way to the kitchen and is startled to see Dane. "Jesus." He dramatically grabs his chest.

Dane's eating a turkey sandwich. "Sorry, man. I figured you heard me down here."

"Nope. You're like a ninja. If ninjas broke into places and made sandwiches."

Dane wipes some mayonnaise away from his face with the napkin he keeps in his left hand as he eats. "How you feeling?"

"I'd say as good as I look." Colin pulls a loose pill from his pocket and takes it dry.

"You look good." Dane tries to sound convincing. Colin shoots him a 'come on' look. Dane shrugs. "Improved?"

Colin ignores him, "The 'Life Sucks' playlist on Spotify has been a godsend. It makes me both so sad I want to kill myself, and too sad to kill myself."

Dane shakes his head, "No more sad stuff." He makes a sign of the horns, "Rock out to some Five Finger Death Punch."

"Maybe snort some ants and bite the head off a live bat."

"Ozzy urban legends," Dane nods gently, squinting and pursing his lips. "Well, he probably did both." He pulls out a manila envelope and

CHAPTER 11

hands it to Colin. "I've been following family."

Colin grabs its and tears the top open with his teeth. He places the envelope on the counter and uses gravity to free the papers inside. He quickly scans the contents. Dane talks with his mouth full, "Brother and daughter. Both easy. Both clueless."

Colin looks at Alissa's picture, "Singing lessons."

"Yeah, and acting, but all these kids today are so fucked up, man." Dane takes another bite of his sandwich.

"From the guy that tried to rob a convenience store with two numbnuts at the same age."

"I was mixed up. I got away with so much shit, I figured what the hell. But seriously, these kids today. Maniacs. Fucking smartphones and social media. They're living in an alternate reality. You'd think I'd be desensitized but I'm just worn from it."

"You're sounding old. The constant waves of human bullshit are eroding your shore."

Dane nods, "You just come up with that?"

"I may have read it in a fortune cookie."

"They curse in fortune cookies now?"

Colin slams down a picture on the counter. "Here we go."

Dane lifts his eyebrows. "Jeff Pembroke. He's a major poon hound."

"Like John Gage?"

"Are you referencing *Indecent Proposal*? Who's sounding old now?"

"I.P. holds up."

Dane shakes his head.

"Agree to disagree." Colin holds his finger up and sifts through one of the folders they got from the police. "Here. The thing with Laura Pembroke. I got it." Colin points to the picture of Alissa, smiles, and quickly takes another pill in celebration of his grand idea.

Dane looks at Colin, "What was that? You just took a painkiller like two minutes ago."

"Did I? I must not know what I'm doing. When you finish Pharmacy School, I put you in charge."

Dane smiles, "Asshole."

"Anyway, we need a look-like." He points at the picture of Alissa again.

"I got a C.I. that could be her sister. She'll do it."

"Drug addict or hooker? Or hooker-drug-addict? Or drug-addict-hooker?"

"Depends. She's currently clean...ish."

"So she's not saving up for med school?"

Dane laughs, "No. Failed actress."

"She'll do it for the cash or because you're fucking her?"

"A little from column A and little from column B."

"Your dick is like catnip."

"What can I say? It's a good dick."

"Apparently. Having a sex worker wrapped around it, is like getting an Uber driver to beg you to let them take you the airport for free."

Dane smirks and shrugs.

* * *

Dane exits his bathroom, wearing boxers only. He looks perfect in clothes, but looks like a statue when he not wearing a shirt. The perfect combination of muscular and lean. Despite his blond hair, his skin is more olive than pale, accentuating his physique. He's that guy in every romance novel that the readers picture while they're fucking their pear-shaped insurance broker husbands. Sometimes he's a vampire and sometimes he's a vampire-hunter. Maybe a werewolf or shape-shifter. For men, he's like Tyler Durden. If they were going to come up with an alter ego that embodies all the traits and attitudes they wished they could have, it would be him. He doesn't even have to try when it comes to the opposite sex. The lack of effort only makes it easier.

In his bed is a half-naked, equally attractive, female in her early twenties, Ingrid Barclay. She is still sweaty with effort and practically unable to move from each powerful orgasm he let her experience. Out

CHAPTER 11

of breath and experiencing the euphoria of each little aftershock, she lays periodically quivering. Ingrid not only waves her fee just to have him inside her, she can't get enough. Good luck getting a free massage if dating a masseuse.

Her story is quite stereotypical. She grew up in Idaho. She was doted on by her father and protected by her two football-playing, straw-chewing, farmer brothers. The acting bug bit her at sixteen when she won the lead in her school's production of *The Wizard of Oz*. When she was eighteen she didn't want to attend community college and then marry a farmer, so she hopped a bus to LA with two hundred bucks, some clean clothes, her lucky Dorothy costume, and her parents' blessing. She grinned ear to ear the whole ride.

Within days of her arrival, it hit her like a shovel to the face, that she was now a teeny-tiny fish in a ginormous pond; and everyone has sharp, pointy teeth but her. She had a panic attack. Her heart was in her stomach. She was embarrassed like when you ask a lady when the baby is due and it turns out she's just fat. She quickly realized her money wasn't going to get her far. She set up camp at the Vagabond Motel. She got a job slinging lattes and after a few months had a celebrity encounter. Skeet Ulrich brought a lady friend to the Vagabond the third Thursday of every month. He was always incognito with black shades, a hat, and all black clothes head to toe, which made him stand out more than if he'd dressed normal. She never had the guts to go up to him. Making coffee for people at minimum wage got old super fast. A couple of friends convinced her to be an escort, as they were doing quite well, and she was steadfast in not crossing the line from being a date to prostitution. Like all things, it's gradually escalated from hand-jobs to blowjobs to sex. She could now afford things that she never could before; her parents were good people but lower class. Over a long enough period, even the most careful criminals whether dealers, hookers, thieves, killers, eventually get arrested. Ingrid was fortunate that Dane was working a joint case with Vice. She was small potatoes and Dane, instantly smitten, got her off the hook.

Dane sips his water. "I need you to do something for me."

"Didn't I just do something for you?"

"Mathematically... you benefited five to six times more than I did. Last I counted, at least."

"Oh, is that how it works?"

"If we're keeping score."

"I guess I'll leave some money on the nightstand for ya."

"On days when we do this and you have a client at night, if they take you to o-town, you know that was all me from earlier in the day, yeah?"

"Most of my clients are gross and not very good, so you have nothing to worry about. And just because I couldn't make it as an actress doesn't mean I'm not good at acting."

"I just wouldn't want anyone getting credit for opening the pickle jar, when I loosened it."

"Pickle jar, huh? Poetic."

Dane turns serious. "You'll get more than your normal C.I. rate because it's off the books. And a little dangerous."

"But it's for you, right? And danger is my middle... my middle name is Ruth."

"When the job is done, you'll have a pretty penny. You can reevaluate things, if you like."

"That sounds judgy," Ingrid says playfully.

"If you're hearing judgy, that's on you. You in?"

"I'm in. Now come here. Open my pickle jar."

"It's a good thing I ate my Wheaties."

Ingrid looks confused. "The cereal? I don't get it."

"I think I need to check your ID."

* * *

Colin and Dane set up a meeting with another piece of the puzzle at a different diner. Diners tend to be a decent spot to conduct certain business, because the regulars tend to be an unsophisticated group and don't give a shit about what's going on around them. The place is practically empty this time of day. Less eyes means less witnesses. The only time the place is packed is at two in the morning and six in the morning. The establishment has been going strong for something like seventy years. As they enter, they are greeted by Louise who may have been working here since the doors opened. She has freckles, fire engine red hair from a box, and a full face of practically clown make-up. She somehow gets every make-up particle into all the wrinkles and crevices that haunt her face. She looks like a Stan Winston creation, only scarier.

She greets them pleasantly. "Dane, long time, no see."

Dane places his hand on her shoulder as he speaks. "Louise, has it been that long?"

"Don't worry, hun, I got my period."

Colin does a double take. "I like her."

Dane smiles, "I was pretty sure I pulled out in time."

Colin places his hand on Dane's shoulder. "Pre-ejaculate. It's like carbon monoxide. You don't know it's there and then you're dead." Colin gestures to Dane, pointing at Louise's privates, "Carpet match the drapes?"

"Not for years." Louise's laugh intermingles with a smoker's wheeze, snowballing into a full-on whooping cough, "Don't worry, fellas. When I aborted Nixon's love child, I had my tubes tied."

Dane gives her a high five. "Tricky Dick for the win." He runs to the bathroom and Colin limps over to the only occupied table. He stops and places his hand out to shake. "Mick?"

Mick stands up for some reason and then shakes his hand like he wants to take his daughter out. "Hi, sir."

Colin sits down, but Mick continues standing. "Mick, relax. Everyone is weirded out by the arm. It's like Yo-Yo Ma playing the banjo. Not ideal, but better than that retarded kid from *Deliverance*."

"That shit was intense."

"Imagine being so hard up you'd rape Ned Beatty? I think his anus would actually try and eat your dick." Mick spits up the water he was sipping. "Dane tells me that you found a headless body, yeah? That's something you'll never forget, like your first kiss or the mole on your priest's privates."

"Dude. It was terrible. Whoever did that is a maniac."

Dane makes his way over to the table and sits down. "Mick, how ya been?"

"Really good. I've been going on a lot of auditions."

"Any bookings?" Dane quips.

"Nope. Apparently 'time's up' for regular white guy actors. I just sent my DNA to 23andMe. God willing one of my ancestors was ethnic. I'll take anything... even Serbian."

Louise brings each of them a cup of coffee then walks away. Mick is nervous. "So, what's this, like, police business?"

Dane turns on the charm. "We're conducting a sting-op. You familiar?"

Mick's eyes light up like the Christmas tree at Rockefeller Center. He nods, "Yeah, sting-op. Of course. I'm down with all the lingo. I've read for tons of cop shows."

Dane continues, "We need a chameleon for one aspect of this mission."

Mick leans in, "That sounds dope. I'm method so I take this shit seriously. I booked this McDonald's commercial last year. Ate nothing but McDonald's the two weeks prior to the shoot."

Colin nods, "That dedication, have I seen it maybe?"

Mick back-peddles, "Actually, I showed up to set too heavy, gained like fifteen pounds and fainted during the fitting, so they replaced me with the guy who's been doing all the commercials since. He's made like a million dollars. Then because of the weight gain, I lost out to be the Busch Beer guy to my buddy Gerry."

"That's rough," Dane winces. He whispers something into his brother's ear. It's nothing, really, but they're hustling him. Mick's interest is piqued. "Yeah, I see it."

Mick is dying to be let in on the secret. "What? See what?"

Colin points. "I see a little James Dean."

Dane pipes in, "Not 'Rebel' Dean, but 'Giant' Dean."

Mick smiles, "I love 'Giant' Dean. 'Rebel' Dean is good too."

Colin continues, "Shame about that car accident. That's just shitty driving... If Dean did 23andMe, he'd probably find out he's at least half Asian... or a female."

Dane shakes his head. "We have connections in entertainment. Besides paying you, we'll make sure you get some theatrical work." He holds up his coffee cup and hollers over to Louise. "More Joe over here."

Louise coughs, "Dane. I'm gonna expect 25%."

Dane turns to the guys, "I was going to leave 30%."

Louise walks over with the half-empty pot, "I'm no spring chicken. I came out here hoping to star in a movie with Carey Grant. Apparently you have to be good-looking to be a movie star."

Dane doesn't miss a beat. "Tell that to Boris Karloff."

"I went on a date with Karloff and he tried to take my anal virginity."

The group nearly spits their coffee all over the table. Colin points at Louise as she walks away, "I like her."

Dane turns to Mickey, "Your help for ours. What do you say?"

"Are you serious? This is how it works, man. You never watch E! and someone's rise to stardom is boring. It's always some amazing story. This is so fuckin' cool. Do I need a gun? What's my motivation? Should I grow a mustache?"

Dane throws down a twenty and gets up, "Don't worry, we'll prep you."

Colin turns to Mickey, "Definitely grow a mustache. A little one, like Hitler."

"Really?"

Dane playfully hits Colin, "No little mustache."

Chapter 12

Alissa's bodyguard picks her up from school and escorts her home. She'd be able to drive herself around if she hadn't failed the written test and decided driving was lame. She's been dressing provocatively since she blossomed, flaunting her body, both at home and school. She openly flirts with her father's employees, of course when he's not around, as much as possible. She loves the attention and is learning how easy it can be to manipulate most men when you're attractive. The majority have caught on and have begun to avoid her like the plague. She's the type of fire they know not to play with. No good can come from getting tangled up with this evil temptress. As they have begun to pull back, she's upped the anti, sunbathing in what barely passes as a bathing suit or practicing yoga out in the open in the tiniest sports bra and the shortest shorts. This mini-succubus is in training and will be torturing men for the next couple of decades.

Tony Stone had been her bodyguard since she was five years old until recently. He is half black and half Samoan, embodying the best of both worlds. He's big, handsome, with light brown skin and green eyes. He would've been in the NFL if an after-the-whistle, cheap shot in the National Championship hadn't ruined his professional aspirations. After missing his opportunity for greatness, Tony decided he needed a career, so he applied to the LAPD. He knew he'd be perfect and was excited about the opportunity, but he was disqualified when he failed the psych test. It was a mystery to him that they'd place so much value on the MMPI, initially developed in the 1930's. The appeals process

CHAPTER 12

was a joke and he didn't have the money to hire his own shrink, so he gave up.

After bouncing around, Tony became a lifeguard in Malibu. He was a real-life Mitch Buchannon. He would patrol the beach and occasionally play second fiddle to the police when a crime had been committed in his jurisdiction. He was relatively content. Early one morning, he was getting ready for work when he came across a dead body buried in the sand. A ten-year-old boy had been sodomized and suffocated. Tony called the police; since the kid had idolized Tony and followed him around like a lost dog, the police focused on Tony for no real reason. They had no probable cause and the rapist wore a condom. Nevertheless, politics intervened and Tony was no longer working the beach. Out of options, and coming off a kiddy murder/rape investigation, he became a low-level enforcer for his brother Trick's boss, Cedric Bones.

Cedric was a lunatic. One of those loose cannons whose unpredictability made even his friends uneasy. Fear of losing an eye around this guy was just commonplace. He threw his cat out the window for missing the litter box. The prostitutes he ran were scared to have sex with him, even though they had no choice, because half the time he would beat them for no reason.

He was funneled his drugs through a middle man: heroine, cocaine and meth. Since he was in distribution, he'd have to send a huge cut up the food chain, even though his crew was doing what he thought was the heavy lifting. He eventually decided he was tired of paying for product and planned on ripping off a major rival, Pembroke. His plan was to cut the head off of Richard's organization and waltz in, seizing everything that he owned.

Cedric, Tony, and Trick waited in the shadows around the corner from the restaurant Richard was dining at with his family. Cedric was tweaked out of his mind. He was in rare form, even for him. Tony was reluctant to move forward but Trick sheepishly followed Cedric's lead. Cedric aggressively approached the family with his gun drawn and screamed for the family to get on their knees, instantly eliciting a wailing cry from Alissa. Tony grabbed Cedric's shoulder, pulling him back, and tried to talk him down. He knew this play was misguided and quite frankly fucked up. Cedric pulled away from Tony more determined to stay the course. Richard, the entire time, stayed silent and knelt there with a stone-cold expression on his face.

Cedric placed the barrel of the gun to Alissa's head. She just looked up at him with big beautiful eyes, flooding with tears not quite ready to run down her face. He was going to shoot Alissa first, so the last thing Richard saw was his dead kid. Tony, unable to stand by this travesty, stepped in front of her and would not allow him to kill this little girl. Cedric, despite his crazed state of mind, was lucid enough to permit his fear of Tony to alter his ill-conceived plan. He changed his target to Richard, placing the barrel of his gun between his eyes. Before he could pull the trigger, Cedric's brain matter was all over Richard. No one was able to even flinch. Once Trick's brain registered what had happened, he turned tail, tripping all the way down the street.

Vincent had been waiting, perched with a sniper rifle, as Richard instructed. Cedric had talked so much shit about killing him that word got back. Richard pays good money for reliable information. The cash incentive aside, this was also an opportunity to have someone extremely powerful owe a debt. Ironically, Richard had been the one supplying Cedric. He used the middleman because he couldn't trust this loose cannon, albeit effective dealer, with his identity. Cedric had no idea who he was working for and his short-sighted plan got him killed. Richard was impressed with Tony's gumption and he became Alissa's bodyguard. Richard figured if he was willing to die for his little girl without knowing her, once he did, he would keep anything from happening to her.

Tony watched her and protected her for the next decade and Richard rewarded him by giving him a more lucrative post in Bolivia. Tony would handle administrative dealings for Richard. He oversaw the manufacturing of product, kept the government off of their backs, and made sure no new competition threatened their position in this lucrative South American country. Tony also made sure Richard always had the product he needed coming from his post. Trick took over as Alissa's bodyguard.

Trick and Tony have the same parents but couldn't be more different. While Tony is the embodiment of the best of his parents, Trick is the amalgamation of the worst. He's a walking, talking bag of recessive genes. He's small, frail, way darker than Tony, with too much belly, and not enough upstairs.

He essentially babysits Alissa from a distance and is content shadowing a teenager around. He gets to the school pick-up an hour early and reads the daily racing form. His phone rings, he sees it's Tony, places the paper down and answers. "How's Bolivia, bro?"

Tony's amped. "Fucking great. The food, the women, business. All fantastic."

Trick clicks his mouth, "I can't believe Richard has you handle that whole operation."

"I can't believe you can't believe it."

"You know what I mean."

"I'm just breaking your balls. How's Alissa?"

"Good. She's good. She's in deep shit with the boss."

"What did she do?"

"Got a tattoo and a tongue ring."

"What the fuck? She's a minor. She played Jeff, didn't she?"

"Yup." He'd never admit to his brother that the tattoo was him getting played.

"Jesus, bro, it's not your fault, but the difference between doing that job well and not well is making sure that shit doesn't happen."

"I know. I know."

"Stay on top of her. She's precious cargo when she's with you. And not just to her father. I vouched for you and you know how much she means to me."

"I know."

Tony knows his brother is 'yessing' him, "Okay brother, I gotta run. We'll talk this weekend." They hang up.

Dane needs to neutralize Trick and dispose of him properly. He walks up to the passenger side of Trick's car, wearing a ball cap and sunglasses, and gloves, then opens the door and gets in.

Trick looks surprised, "Who the fuck are you?"

Dane is pointing a gun at him discreetly. "If you want you to live past today, turn the car on slowly and let's get moving."

"You a cop?"

"Not today, compadre." Trick turns the car on and pulls out of the school, "Make a left, then a right." Dane guides him to a parking garage and has him park on the top level. This time of day, the roof is empty.

Trick places the car in park, "What the fuck is this?"

Dane shoots him to the right of his face from an upward angle, killing him instantly. He's wearing gloves, and places the gun in Trick's right hand leaving a betting slip for the Santa Anita Race Track that lost $20,000 the day before. He sends a text from Trick's phone, goes down to the second level and gets in the car he stole the night before, exiting the garage.

Alissa is dismissed from school and she and her friends stroll over to pick-up; most of her clique is greeted by nannies or housekeepers. They say their goodbyes and Alissa stands there alone, baffled that Trick, while not as good as Tony, has never been late. She pulls out her phone to see what's going on.

Before she can turn her head, Mick pulls up in a convertible Mercedes Benz. He's dressed extremely sharp, with fancy shades, and his hair slicked back. Mick points to Alissa, "Alissa!!! What up?"

Alissa replies with attitude, "Who the fuck are you?"

"Ben Vogel. I'm a producer. Your father said you were beautiful, but come on, aren't fathers supposed to say that?"

Alissa roles her eyes, "Whatever. Are you really this cheesy?"

Mickey senses she's no nonsense. "Your father wanted me to meet

CHAPTER 12

with you on this project I'm working on."

Alissa glances over to where Trick's car should be parked.

"Really? You drove out here to get me? A real producer for a legitimate project is picking me up, a nobody, from school, for an audition?"

"Your father can be very persuasive." Alissa backs off a bit. Mick continues, "I got in some trouble with some bad guys, he extricated me from the pickle for a favor to be named later."

Alissa's phone dings with a text from Trick, "Hey kiddo, your dad arranged for a producer to pick you up for some big audition. I'll pick you up from the studio later today. Good luck!" Alissa can't believe her eyes. She throws caution to the wind, and hops into the car against her better judgment.

During the car ride, Mick begins to butter her up like corn on the cob. "You got a little J-Law thing going on."

Alissa blushes, "Oh please. She's a gorgeous movie star."

Mick shakes his head, "I know my stuff and you got 'it.'" He continues counting on his fingers, "Listen, I produced *Perfectly Imperfect*, *Moby Richard*, *The C-Sectioned Heart*, and *Victor's Secret*. I have worked with Joe Estevez, Rob Belushi, Rocky Carroll's nanny, and Terry O'Quinn's kid. I'm blanking on his name. Talented guy. I know my shit. Excuse me, if there's one thing that I learned from Philip Michael Thomas, Philip Baker Hall, and Philip Seymour Hoffman, rest in peace, is that it isn't polite to cuss in front of a lady."

Alissa was caught up in his energy. "It's okay. I've heard it all."

"I did this special on the internet in Uganda that won a Boxletter Award and two Trammies. I'm not telling you this to be braggadocios or to strum my own horn, I'm telling you this because when I give you a compliment it gosh darn means something."

"No, I'm sorry. I didn't mean to imply you didn't. It's just too nice. So thank you."

"You're welcome." Mick brings the car to a stop in front of a state of the art studio. Alissa's eyes become wider with each passing second as this seems more and more legit as time ticks. Mick exits the car, throws his keys to the valet, "Keep it close!" Alissa sits in her seat, mesmerized. He opens her door and helps her out of the car. "Follow me, little lady." He extends his elbow out and escorts her inside like a gentleman.

Mick struts into the building and the security guards open the door for him, calling him Mr. Vogel. Posters of movies and shows plaster the walls as they walk down a long corridor. "You see, Alissa, this is the type of place where a lot of magic happens. This is a high-tech world that we live in and technology is the wave of the future. Jimmy Cameron has this unbelievable sci-fi movie slated for the summer of 2025, maybe 2026. Gonna make *Avatar* looks like a High School diorama. He thought of that son-of-a-bitch ten years ago but kept it in the back of his desk until now because he needed to wait until technology could catch up to his vision. And he got a little sidetracked with that whole undersea exploration obsession. Jimbo and I came up with the premise while drinking ice wine and smoking cigars as we celebrated the *Titanic* re-release."

"I love *Titanic*."

"Between you and me, little lady, that's not my type of flick. Too Hollywood for me. I'm an indie guy. Me and Bill Paxton used to competitive indoor row. Rest in peace. Love him." He does the sign of the cross. "Unexpected shit comes up in this business so much so, we should expect shit to happen. I was shooting a nice little picture starring none other than Dolph Lundgren and Nia Van Peebles. We got halfway through filming when my DP had a meth-induced psychotic break, shattering Dolph's eye socket with sock full of nickels. That was it for *Tread Lightly: The Story of Ballet's First Assassin*."

Colin is on the phone as Mickey and Alissa enter the sound stage. He hangs up, placing the phone in a fanny pack. "This must be the little star. Alissa, my name is Colin. Super nice to meet you."

She stares at his missing arm.

Colin notices. "I'm not sure what's worse, the fact I'm missing my arm or that I have to wear this unsightly fanny pack to carry my shit around."

Alissa confidently replied, "I'd say fanny pack."

Colin responds enthusiastically, "Right?! Good news is it matches nothing."

Alissa is curious. "What happened?"

"A walking, talking pile of scrotal veins with an axe chopped it off for no reason."

Mick looks at him, unsure if that's true. Alissa's eyes bug out, "Seriously?"

Colin elaborates, "Yeah, total dick. Thought I was someone else."

Mick turns to him, "That's unbelievable."

Colin continues, "I know!"

Alissa shakes her head, "I hope they caught the guy."

Colin place his hand on her shoulder. "Nope. He totally got away with it. I'm working on tracking him down and getting revenge."

Alissa grabs his hand, "Good luck with that. What an awful thing."

Colin squeezes her hand softly, "Appreciate that. You feel more relaxed now, yeah? Can we get you anything before we put you on tape?"

"Water? If it's not too much trouble."

"Water is easy. Now if you wanted a Tab, that would be a problem."

Alissa looks unsure. "Tab?"

Mick echoes her confusion, "Tab?"

"That's right. I'm ancient, and Tab existed when dinosaurs roamed the planet. Probably led to their extinction. Check it out on Wikipedia. Interesting read. Especially the part about bladder cancer and rats."

Colin finds himself in front of the vending machine. He pulls out his bi-fold wallet from his fanny pack. He flips it open from the bottom with one hand and uses his thumb and forefinger to open it up, pinching all of the money and wiggling the cash out. He holds the bill with his lips, quite aware of its filthiness. A bead of sweat percolates along his hairline as he gets winded trying to procure a bottled water.

He places his wallet back into his fanny pack. He grabs the money from his mouth, locates a one-dollar bill, and uses his teeth to extract that bill from the pile, jamming the wad of money into his back pocket. He places the bill into the slot and the machine sucks it in and then shoots it out. "Come on." He tries again. "What the fuck." No dice. One more time. It shoots it out faster. "What in the ass." He grabs the bill and examines it, running his thumb and pointer finger on opposite sides of the bill to unfold a corner. He places the bill in the machine again. "Please. For the love of sweet Jesus." Rejected. Multiple beads of sweat have accumulated now and are racing down his forehead. He pulls out his money again and chooses another bill with his mouth. He speeds up the process. The bill gets sucked in. There is a pause. He waits focused like the meaning of life will reveal itself. The machine takes this bill, "Victory!" He presses his choice and the water drops. It fell funny and is wedged in the shoot. "That's disappointing," he reaches in but is unable to free it with one hand. An actor walks by and Colin gets his attention, "Hey, Mexican Butch Patrick, can you help me with my water? It's stuck and God hates me."

The actor beelines over, "Sure dude. Who's Butch Patrick?"

Colin realizes he's made a minor faux pas, "Sorry ma'am, I forgot my glasses."

She frees his water and continues on. Colin makes his way back to Alissa and Mick, handing her the water, "Here you go shorty, don't say I never did anything for ya." Her hand touches his as she grabs the water and their eyes lock. She stares at him a little too long, realizing then turning away quickly and awkwardly.

Mick unintentionally interrupts, "Okay, you ready? Let's get you mic'd up." He clips the microphone to her collar, dropping the lavalier unit down the back of her shirt, clipping it to the waistband of her skirt. He mumbles what he's actually doing during the whole process, each step of the way.

Alissa looks at Colin. "So this is like a cold read?"

"Exactly."

CHAPTER 12

Mick finishes up the mic job, "We don't want it to sound too rehearsed."

Alissa closes her eyes and takes a deep breath. "I get it. I'm good to go."

Mick and Colin get behind the camera and he pantomimes director-like movement and screams, "Action!"

Alissa looks into the camera, "Daddy, help me. Uncle Bobby said he's going to kill me if I tell you what he makes me do."

Mick turns the camera off and they begin clapping. Alissa's face lights up. "Bravo!" Mick screams. "That's talent."

Alissa looks flattered, "Really? I just said it like I thought I'd say it if it were true."

"That's legit." Colin continues, "Do you actually have any uncles?"

Alissa nods affirmatively. "I have an Uncle Jeff."

Mick touches his chin, "I have an idea. This is going to be perfect. Scratch out Bobby and say Jeff instead. I want to see the emotion you can evoke. This needs to be raw." He turns to Colin, "What do you think, Col?"

Colin is verbally dancing with Mick, "Genius. It's like someone took the comfort of Crocs and style of Louboutin to make some sort of super shoe."

Alissa smiles at Colin, "That would be pretty awesome. My Uncle Jeff's cool though."

"I'm sure he's a regular Fonzi." Colin's not missing a beat.

Alissa looks confused. "Fonzi?"

"You're so mature I keep forgetting how old you are. I'm sure he's a regular Nick Jonas." He looks at Mick, "He's the cool one, yeah?"

Mick shrugs.

Alissa nods, "I get what you're saying, and all those Jonas' are sorta lame."

"Beautiful and discerning, you got it all."

Alissa blushes at Colin's words. "I got it. Let's go again."

Mick screams action and Alissa pauses before saying her line per-

105

fectly. "Daddy, help me. Uncle Jeff said he's going to kill me if I tell you what he makes me do." She pauses. "How was that?"

They tell her she's flawless.

She stands up, "So, I'm going to text my ride and you'll call me or something?"

Mick walks towards her. "Yeah, one sec, let's get the mic. Col, help me here." Mick goes to unhook the lavalier with Colin right behind. "Watch her hair," Colin sticks a needle in her neck.

Alissa flinches, then passes out immediately.

Chapter 13

It's a beautiful night and Dr. Phil's long, stringy, thinning hair blows in the wind as his Ferrari speeds down winding streets. The growl of the engine is as seductive as the smell of the buttery leather seats. Operating a vehicle like this is more like intercourse than merely controlling the speed and direction of a motor vehicle. Half the enjoyment is finding that place where you can't tell if the car is driving or being driven. The ultimate connection between man and machine. He comes to a stop in front of Colin's house. As he gets out and closes his door, the neighborhood hears the sound of the door locking into position; a perfect, masterful fit. He's holding the medical bag he's had for his whole career; vintage with each nick and scratch telling a different story. The latches still work, although maybe worse for wear. He catches his distorted reflection as he closes the trunk, both buzzed and high, and shakes off his fleeting disappointment. He pauses at the front door, a bead of sweat dropping from his hairline down the side of this face. He cracks his neck and rings the doorbell.

Dane answers with Colin behind him, "Chick is going apeshit."

"I have just the thing."

Colin greets him. "She's downstairs. A hundred pounds of vile fury. Like my first grade teacher, Mrs. Lebaron. She was eighty years old, cursed like a sailor, and could drink us all under the table. Well, us now. Anyone can drink a six year old under the table."

Dane and Dr. Phil follow Colin down the stairs to the basement.

Colin grabs the railing and limps, step by step, until they are at the bottom. Dane steps in front of the group and unlocks the door. They enter the makeshift prison. The room is comfortable, with a small bed but very little else. Its void of anything that could be used as a weapon or used to escape.

Alissa springs to her feet, "Let me go, motherfuckers! What did you give me? My head is killing me."

Dr. Phil turns to Dane, "You were right. She's ape crazy." He approaches her holding a syringe, cautious as she's acting like a wild, unpredictable animal.

"Get away from me, faggot!"

Colin looks at Dane, smirking. He knows full well this won't go over well, and mutters under his breath, "She clearly didn't get the memo that 'faggot' is unacceptable nomenclature in today's PC climate. She should've went with ass pirate."

Dane rolls his eyes, shaking his head.

Colin still under his breath, "She doesn't even know he's Greek. And we both know Greeks are known for pornographic knick-knacks and to a lesser extent, big fat weddings... and man-boy love."

Dr. Phil pauses, clearly offended. "Whoa. I ain't no fag. You hear me, princess? I fuck women; three at a time if I like."

"Screw you, dick!"

Dr. Phil shakes his head. "Let's get this bitch sedated. Get her."

Colin signals for Dane to go ahead.

Dane grabs her with ease, manhandling her as she squirms. Dr. Phil holds up the syringe.

Alissa's eyes are huge with fear. "Wait. Stop. Is that a needle? I'm scared of needles. HELP! HELP!" She wiggles and writhes to no avail as Dane has her locked up tight.

Dr. Phil sticks her and plunges the syringe. The medicine kicks in and Alissa goes limp in Dane's arms. He places her down gently on the cot. Dr. Phil looks at Dane as he draws blood from Alissa's arm, "I don't love needles, either. Crazy bitch." He plucks some hair from her head.

"How long will she be out?" Colin asks. "I think we can go for a

CHAPTER 13

Cheerio stacking record."

Dr. Phil is unfamiliar with the reference. "What?" Off of Dane's look, he moves past Colin's nonsense. "A few hours. Here's some more sedative in case you need to calm her down again."

Dane grabs it, "Thanks Doc. As usual, we appreciate everything."

Dr. Phil puts a hand on each brother's shoulder. "You know I'm always up for this type of thing. It keeps life interesting." He grabs his bag, "I have to run. I have a couple of naked chicks waiting on me."

Colin pats him on the shoulder, "You're such a romantic. It is National Tap That Ass Day. Godspeed." Within seconds of closing the front door, they hear the roar of his Ferrari then the sound of an aggressive exit from the neighborhood. "Does his Oldsmobile Cutlass Supreme sound different to you?"

A significant prong of their attack on Richard is scheduled for later this evening. The brothers tighten up some nuts and bolts and time ticks by quickly. Dane looks at his watch, "Oh shit, its nearly time."

Colin points to the monitor, "She hasn't moved a muscle in hours." He notices his hand shakes a bit as he points, so he shoves it in his pocket so Dane doesn't see the tremor.

"I'm sure its normal."

"Hopefully Doc didn't Michael Jackson her." His vision goes in and out of focus.

"Either way."

"I hope not. I was hoping we could paint each other's nails and talk about boys while you were out tonight." A little cold sweat starts to accumulate on his forehead.

"You okay? You look a little pale."

Colin tries to cover, "You say pale, I say flawless."

"I'll pick you up when we're done with Jeff."

"Yup." Colin points to the monitor, "I'll, uh, watch the most boring show on TV. Well, besides everything on ABC."

"Don't go in there until I'm back. She's crazy."

"Come on. You never let me do anything." Colin whines.

"You're doing the phone thing. That's fun."

"Really?!" At 11pm on the dot, one of their guys will turn on a Shoghi jammer outside Richard's compound, blocking all cell signals. Colin will then call Richard from Alissa's phone; it'll go straight to voicemail and they'll play the audition tape implying Jeff's inappropriate behavior.

Dane shakes his head, smiling, and Colin closes the door behind him. He leans on the door, closes his eyes, and takes a deep breath. In a relatively short period of time, he went from comfortable to the opposite. He's already withdrawing and his body is screaming at him. These periods of comfort are getting shorter and shorter as his body acclimatizes to the dosage. Upping the dosage and frequency will do the trick but for only so long. He struggles to his medicine cabinet, nearly zombie-walking the whole way like a spaced-out mess. He pops a couple of pills, uses his hand as a cup, and drinks from the bathroom sink. He glances up at himself in the mirror as the water he haphazardly douched all over his face drips down. He wipes his mouth with his hand, runs it under the faucet, and rubs his eyes. Simply ingesting the pills have pushed back most of the side effects as his brain is fucking with him. He grabs a bottle of whiskey, walks over to the monitor and plops down in the chair. He tears the cork out with his teeth, spits it on the floor, and takes a big swig, not even feeling the alcohol burn the back of this throat.

As focused as he is on the plan, and maybe because it's in its infancy and it doesn't quite feel real yet, his mind can't stop going to that place; that terrible place people go when they look around and can't understand how they even got where they've suddenly found themselves. Things will never be the same. Even trying to move on is terrifying because it's impossible to have the confidence that shit won't happen again. This residual side effect is ever-present in everything, with everyone, and often leads to a self-fulfilling prophecy – a defense mechanism to avoid the pain and torture previously endured.

CHAPTER 13

Colin sits back, shaking his head and doing everything in his power not to scream at the top of his lungs. Each time he has a moment like this, he does some internal self-mutilation, carving out pieces that existed before Betty was taken from him. Those places deep down inside that make him human; if he can just cover them over with scar tissue he will survive this, but not for the better.

∗ ∗ ∗

Across town, Dane holds his position for the next phase of the plan. He has a team ready, strategically placed. Dane had scouted each vantage point and picked guys he can trust for this tactical mission. No blood will be shed yet, but this was adroitly planned and all shooting will be done with high-end cameras. In battle, as with most things, perception is as an important a weapon as any gun or tank or exploding doodad. Wars are won and lost with more than simply body count. Goading your adversary into an uncharacteristic response may be enough to turn a tide. Dane checks in with his team via tactical communication gear; each is good to go. A smile washes over his faces as Jeff's car pulls into valet.

Jeff is as predictable as a wasp on speed. He's a fixture at this trendy yet stale scene, clearly due to The Moon Bar's gravitational pull. He stands by the bar and patiently waits until someone catches his eye. He's never stalked his prey as a pack animal, because of his insecurity of not being the pack's most desirable member. The idea of being bested by one of his compadres for the affections of someone he's set his sights on would be more than he can bear. He's the epitome of an essentially only child with a much older brother who is more of father than sibling. A *Psych 101* joke.

One navel-bearing waitress walks up to him and he orders a beer. He gives her a twenty and tells her to keep the change. This gesture is far from generous; in case he doesn't find someone better to bed, she'll do as back-up. As soon as she turns, Ingrid enters his line of sight and

Jeff is struck directly in his genitals by Cupid's arrow. Her perfect bare stomach; dressed extremely sexily. She flips her hair and smiles, and like a tractor beam Jeff is compelled to minimize the distance between them. She is a giant magnet and he's a hunk of metal.

"Hey, I haven't seen you here before. I mean, I don't come here much. But those few occasions, you weren't here?" He just baffled himself.

Ingrid's in character and her motivation is to make Jeff think she's into him. "I've never been here before, but it seems pretty chill. Ingrid."

Jeff points at her as he talks, "Ingrid, pretty name. Yeah, very chill." His tone turns abrupt, "What do you do? I mean, sorry, what do you do? For work?" He shakes his head; his nervous energy is getting the best of him. He feels like he's blowing it, but little does he know, that's not possible. It's been scripted. He just doesn't know his lines or how his story line will unfold.

Ingrid awkwardly nods when she speaks, consistent with two strangers conversing for the first time. "And your name? Or should I just make one up?"

"Fuck, yeah, uh, I've talked to people before, I swear. Jeff. My name is Jeff."

"Well, Jeff, I'm a party planner. How about you?"

"Partier." Jeff touches his hand to his head, "I'm sorry, I don't know why I said that. That's not funny or charming... You're very pretty." His phone rings. He sees it's Richard and sends the call to voicemail, then silences the phone so he can focus on Ingrid.

"Thank you. That's sweet."

The two chat and as the conversation ages, Ingrid becomes more liberal about where she places her hands. At first she brushes his shoulder when he says something funny, then she grabs his upper arm, and eventually she places her hand on his. He's being manipulated but as Jeff looks into her eyes and at her cleavage, he can't see the ruse. Everyone has had the wool pulled over their eyes at one point or another. There's not a guy that hasn't been played, and Jeff is being worked like a circus monkey. Not only is he unaware it's happening, he's loving it. Dane's team is getting all the angles covered with photographs. Jeff orders another round. The waitress is now annoyed that not only is his focus solely on Ingrid, but his tips have decreased significantly. Twenty bucks has become the change left over from two drinks, maybe a few dollars. Jeff doesn't look her in the face when he orders, picks up his drink, or pays. He even senses her aggravation. This waitress is the stereotypical girl about town and has delusions of grandeur. As she walks away in a huff, Jeff points in her direction with his thumb, "I'll tell you, there's not a girl in this town that's not some sort of prostitute."

Ingrid stays in character. "Is that right?"

"Sorry, I'm jaded. Been out here my whole life and seen the same shit over and over. And I have money so I never know who's just looking to move to easy street."

"Easy Street? Is that off Laurel Canyon?"

Jeff laughs, "You're funny. And my goodness, I could look at you all day. I import and export cardboard, by the way. Fucking cardboard."

Ingrid touches the rim of her beer bottle with her right pointer finger. "That sounds interesting."

"I wouldn't say 'interesting.'" Jeff takes a deep breath and begins a little speech he has prepared for this type of scenario. "Smart? Maybe. Lucative? Yes. Did I get into it at the right time? Seems that way. People love having everything sent to them through the mail. People buy toilet paper online. How do you ship everything? In cardboard boxes. Definitely a 'right place at the right time' type situation." Every time he says it, it comes out more and more rehearsed.

"Somebody had to get lucky."

"I'll remind you of that later."

She forces a plausible laugh.

Jeff continues, "Do I feel like I'm chained to my desk sometimes? Absolutely." Jeff does have a desk at his house, but the only thing he's ever done on it is his housekeeper and her daughter. "That's why I need to blow off steam and meet cool people."

Ingrid looks him dead in the eyes. "Enough of this bullshit. Why don't we go check out your car?" Ingrid grabs his hand and yanks him out of the bar, much to his delight. The annoyed waitress got beat out of the first twenty, from earlier in the night. As Ingrid and Jeff leave the bar, the photo-documenting continues. Jeff slip the valet some cash to give him his keys. He's done this a million times before. He grabs her hand and leads her to his car. Every angle and every possible picture is captured.

Jeff is bursting inside at how easily all this is unfolding. His confidence is off the charts. He grabs Ingrid, spins her around, and gets her into his car. She unbuckles his pants, closes her eyes, and tries to think happy thoughts as he pushes her head down. Within a short period of time, nearly too short, Jeff becomes all that he can be and like a true gentleman, offers her a ride home. "Can I give you a ride home or you want an Uber or something?"

"A ride would be great. I live off Melrose."

Jeff is convinced Ingrid enjoyed the dirty little deed. As he begins to drive, he places his hand on the side of Ingrid's head and shoots her his million-dollar smile. The one he practices in the mirror. He then points to the corner of his own mouth, "You have a little..." Ingrid wipes her face with a tissue and places it in her purse.

Suddenly, there's the whoop of a siren and Jeff looks in his rear-view mirror to see squad car lights behind him. "What the...?" Jeff pulls the car over. "Just relax. This is no big deal. I didn't do anything. If you have Tourette's or some shit, just bite your fuckin' tongue. I don't need any headaches."

Ingrid mutters under her breath, "Dick."

Jeff rolls down his window and waits for the police officer to make his way to the car. The police officer is making Jeff sweat a little by taking his time. "What car are we in?"

"I don't know. This is your car, right?"

"Yeah, I mean, did you see the license plate on the way in?"

"No."

"I have a few of these and one may have some parking tickets or something. That's it. That's probably the deal."

The police officer finally makes his way over. He sports shaggy blond hair, has a friendly but serious face, and a calm demeanor. He points his flashlight at the steering wheel in Jeff's car. Jeff attempts to lean out of the window to talk to the officer, so he can charm him. The police officer places his right index finger on the button snap of his holster. "Place you hand on the steering wheel or I will pull my firearm."

"Jesus Christ, fucking relax." Jeff places his hands shakily on the steering wheel. "I didn't do anything. So take it easy. And I'm white, so chill the fuck out." Jeff looks down as he speaks and refuses to turn his head.

"Don't make me pull my firearm." The officer's partner is on Ingrid's side of the car, poised with hand on holster. Jeff throws his hands on the wheel; they're shaking like leaves. The officer's voice is stern. "Did you just come from the Moon Bar?"

Jeff refuses to turn his head. "Yes. I did. I'm not drunk. I'll take a Breathalyzer."

"I'm not concerned with your level of intoxication, sir, however what does concern me is that you were seen partaking in lewd behavior."

"Come on, bro. You know how it is," Jeff smiles at the police officer who remains stoic. "Okay then, maybe you don't?"

The police officer leans into the car and looks at Ingrid, "Ma'am how old are you?"

Ingrid's head is in her hands. She's breathing heavy, which turns into breathing slowly. This turns into not being able to breathe at all and a high-pitched whine blossoms into full-blown hysterical crying. "Sixteen. I'm sorry. He bought me a bunch of drinks. I think I'm drunk. Or he put something in there to make me feel weird. And he made me suck his...you know."

Jeff turns to her, "What the fuck? Are you kidding me?"

The police officer speaks sternly, "Hold it right there, do not move a muscle." He signals to his partner to get Ingrid out of the car. Her shaking hand grabs his, and he escorts her back to the squad car. He then calls for back-up in order to transport them in separate cars back to the station.

"Sir, get out of the car. Place your hands on the hood. You have the right to remain silent..."

"Hey, spare me. I know my rights; we've all seen *Cagney & Lacey*. I want my attorney."

* * *

Richard sits in his cushy chair, in front of his Macbook Air, making a laundry list of how to launder his dirty money; hunting and pecking at his keyboard desperately trying to stay relevant with each overly pressed keystroke, when a picture of Alissa catches his eye. It's been on his desk for years but today it sucks him in and takes him back to the day this image was forever frozen in time, captured for posterity. He's completely lost in thought; that deep place where the brain is so locked in, his eyes are out of focus. For whatever reason, her life flashes in his mind's eye; he smiles as her light has been the only beacon within the darkness that has ensconced his adulthood. He's completely unaware of how the day's events are going to impact him, but at this moment, he can't be more happy or grateful. This is the calm before his personal storm.

He's snapped out of his stroll down memory lane when Vincent enters the room. Succumbing to his vanity, he takes off his reading glasses and tosses them in his desk drawer. Richard inquires about the doctor's appointment in a non-intrusive manner. If there's one thing that has kept Richard on top for this long, it's the little things. Powerful people that rely on life or death loyalty need to implement various techniques to cement this allegiance. In most cases, it doesn't take much. He knows the names of all his guys, new and low end.

CHAPTER 13

He asks how wives, girlfriends, and kids are doing. Making everyone feel like they're important, even if they're not, plays to anyone's ego. Richard is a good leader because he inspires followership.

Vincent shrugs his shoulders as he answers. "It went okay. I guess. The guy couldn't tell me anything by just looking at me. They took some blood and some fancy X-rays. I'll know in a few days."

"It's probably nothing. I'm sure it's just stress. It's no small task carrying out what needs to be done on my behalf." Richard looks Vincent dead in the eyes as his tone changes. "If you need time off, you just let me know." A portion of this generous gesture is out of concern for Vincent, the rest stems from the potential repercussions of having someone off their game in charge of important aspects of his business.

"Thanks, but right now, I'm good."

Richard closes his laptop and nonchalantly poses a question. "Have you seen Alissa?"

"I have not. I did get a text from Trick that she's going somewhere with Jeff tonight?"

Richard shakes his head, "After I told her she wasn't allowed!" He isn't pleased with being blatantly disobeyed. "She's dead." I'm going to call her right now. He grabs his phone and squints at the screen, "Vince, do I not have a signal?" He holds the phone towards Vincent.

"Looks that way," Vincent takes his phone out. "Shit, me neither. Fucking technology."

Richard, out of frustration, opens his top desk drawer, throws his phone in and slams the drawer shut. "I'll ground her when she's home."

Chapter 14

"Rick!" The coffee chain barista calls out some mocha frappuccino concoction. Betty waits in line, casually looking on her phone as to not make eye contact with the creeps that constantly hit on her. Colin walks in, takes off his sunglasses and hangs them from his shirt. He steps in line behind Betty completely struck by her incredible beauty. He collects his thoughts for a moment, unsure of his next move. He's never lacked confidence, but he's completely intimidated. However, if he doesn't talk to her, he'll regret it forever. He takes a deep breath and musters up the courage to engage. Betty orders a skinny vanilla latte, pays and waits at the end of the counter. Under normal circumstances, Colin would get a regular coffee, but he calls an audible so he can stand and wait for his drink by her. He orders an americano with room for cream. He moves into position right next to her and smiles. She politely returns the smile but immediately goes back to her phone.

He leans over into her line of vision, "Hey, I'm Colin."

She displays some frustration, "I mean this in the nicest possible way. Fuck off. Please."

"Please huh, that does soften the aggressive 'fuck off.' You must work with kids, yeah?"

Betty fights a smile and smirks.

"So. Dinner?"

She shakes her head, "Sorry. I don't get picked up in coffee shops or date cops. Let alone both."

Colin puffs his chest, "Detective."

CHAPTER 14

"Same thing. Maybe worse."

"Ouch. It's not just a coffee shop; this place has tons of food options." He picks up a banana. "Look at this super-brown banana that a homeless person would pass on. And that brownie with forty thousand calories that's somehow gluten free."

"Answer is still 'no.'"

"Betty!" The barista screams out her name.

"Betty? Awesome name. Colin and Betty, sounds like a power couple."

She grabs her coffee and starts walking out. The barista shouts out, "Colin!"

Colin grabs his drink and hustles after her. Once outside, a random dirtbag runs by, grabs Betty's purse and knocks her drink out of her hand."

"Fucking jerk! Help!"

Colin hands her his coffee, "I got this." He darts down the street after the purse snatcher who turns down an alley. Betty stands there for a couple of minutes, waiting for him to return. Eventually, he turns the corner, a little disheveled, and a little sweaty but holding her purse. "Everyone hates cops until they need one."

Betty is humbled, "Thank you. Where is he?"

"Oh, I shot him. It's too hot to run and I'm not a foot pursuit kinda guy without the proper motivation. You're lucky you're cute. If you were an old lady, I woulda been in my car like five minutes ago."

"You did not."

"He's handcuffed to a dumpster a couple blocks from here. Some uniform cops will take it from here."

"Ugh. Okay. Dinner. One time. And I'm telling you right now, your odds are really bad, even though you saved today."

"I thrive under that type of pressure. Like the 1986 Boston Red Sox."

"Bob Stanley or Bill Buckner?"

"Oh, I think I love you."

"I feel sorry for you. You'll know me much better after the date. I'm not just a pretty face." She points to her head. "This here, is not just for hats."

"I can tell. Headbands. Headphones. Hats. Wait, you said not just hats. What's a burka? Is that technically a hat?"

"I'm going to hate you, aren't I?"

"You look great, by the way."

She gives him the middle finger. He smiles.

* * *

Little Georgie is a stereotype. If humans had litters of children, he'd have been the runt. He's a combination of his parents' worse physical qualities, even those that had skipped generations. Average height, skinny with a big nose, beady eyes, and a uni-brow, he lacks intelligence and temperament. The worst guy to have in charge of this type of organization but his father's sudden heart attack, perhaps from too much ricotta over a lifetime, opened a door and he stepped through. He's super sloppy and quick to act without considering consequences.

Big Georgie was a legitimate Mafioso who rose up the ranks of his family to eventually be boss. He was 'made' in his early twenties getting his bones, taking out a major rival for his capo. Shortly thereafter, he proved his obedience to omerta when, due to someone's major fuck up, he ended up pinched with his feet to the fire, keeping his mouth shut, getting a nickel upstate. He was released after eighteen months for good behavior and once out, he never went back in again. Until his death, he ran the business out of the back of a restaurant. He bankrolled a washed-up boxer, a local hero, and paid for the restaurant, a front, with the arrangement that he'd have the back to conduct his business. Once he passed, Little Georgie, in classic poser move, relocated the operation to the back of a sketchy strip club. Needless to say, he does all the interviewing of potential strippers.

His father's loyal guys have been conflicted since his ascendance to power. They know full well he's bad for business, but to whack the boss,

CHAPTER 14

especially the kid of their revered previous leader has been difficult to get behind. Despite being a complete fuck head, they watched him grow up. However, he does not listen to these experienced men who served his father, and has surrounded himself with his friends, preferring 'yes men' to wise advisors. The old guard plays cards all day while Georgie and his friends talk shit about sexual conquests and video games.

Colin and Wally are at the door of the strip club when the giant bouncer stops them. Wally's agitated, "What the fuck, Dom?"

"I don't know him."

"If you had a dime for everything you didn't know... Of course you don't know him. He's here to meet Georgie. Check, you dumb motherfucker."

He talks into his earpiece, waits for a response and waves them by with his head. They walk through the strip club, practically empty at midday, with the least talented girls dancing for the worst kind of degenerates. They enter the back, Georgie at an enormously gauche desk flanked by his guys with the old guard in the corner playing cards. Wally waves to the underlings, "Yo, Georgie. This is Vic, the guy I been telling you about." He plops down, putting one leg over the arm of the chair.

"Georgie," Colin places his hand out, "Nice sweatpants. They really go well with the tank top and gold chain."

Georgie looks unimpressed, "Vic, Wally has been jerking you off to me so hard he may break his arm."

"Just you verbalizing Wally jerking me off made my dick head for the hills. But Wally's mom... that's a different story. She's hot in a disgusting way; an example of why they don't call it a teethbrush."

Georgie laughs, "Wally's mom is nasty."

"Fuck you both." Wally is not amused.

"So, Vic," Georgie emphasizes the 'ck.' "Why do I need you?"

"Why do you need me? That's a good question." Colin turns his back, quickly pulling his gun and shooting Wally several times in the head. He flies back off the chair, dead before he hits the ground.

Everyone stands up, drawing their guns. Colin places his hands up, dropping the weapon. "Take it easy. That guy is working with the cops. He's a snitch."

Georgie keeps his men from acting, "Everyone stand down. No fucking way, Wally?"

"I got this side bitch that works at the D.A.'s office, saw his name on some immunity deal." Colin walks over and leans into Wally's exploded head, whispering, "That was for Wags." He rips his shirt open revealing the wire. "This is why you need me. That and I'll teach all the gals here how to knot a cherry stem with their tongues."

Georgie walks over to Colin and places his hands on his face, bringing him in for a hug, "I love this guy! Fucking maniac."

* * *

Colin sits in the chair, fast asleep. His neck hangs to the side and his arm dangles. A few belts of Jameson mixed with his painkillers put him out like a baby. He's jarred from this dead sleep; another nightmare. A key hits the lock and Dane enters. "Were you sleeping?"

"Nah," Colin grabs his neck. "I was just checking my eyelids for holes."

"Is that right?"

Colin changes the subject. "Well?"

"Oh, we're good to go. He's at the station as we speak and Manny will have his car within the hour."

Colin stands up slowly, trying to get his numb legs under him. The blood that pooled in his lower extremities shoots up into his brain. The head rush is dizzying and without two arms to balance, he practically falls to the ground. He braces the chair as the spell passes. "Did that look as awkward as it felt?"

"How awkward did it feel? It looked pretty awkward. Like the first few steps a newborn horse takes after it falls out of its mother."

CHAPTER 14

Colin shakes his head. "At least I'm not covered in after-birth."

"Thank goodness for small favors," Dane points towards the monitor. "She still out?"

Colin looks at the monitor. Alissa is a lump clearly out cold. "You tell me Columbo, she look up and about?"

Dane smirks, "I see how it is. Well, I hope the doc didn't kill her."

* * *

Dane and Colin make their way over to the Police Impound Lot, the current location of Jeff's towed car. They walk over to the little office housing their contact, Manny. Dane spots him and screams across the lot, "Yo, pinche!"

Manny was in his own little world, watching a video on his phone, when he was shaken from his trance, nearly jumping out of his skin, "DUDE. What the fuck? You startled me." Manny is a friend, very Mexican, with super thick black hair and extremely dark skin. The contrast between his skin and blue-white teeth is almost as distracting as his Californian accent. He looks like he should sound like the Taco Bell dog, but instead has a surfer-esque accent.

"What up, Panch?" Dane shouts as he gives Manny a complicated handshake like they're in a secret club. "Do we need to call ICE?"

"Fucking Dane. You racist motherfucker. I'm from Glendale, homie."

Dane laughs, "I'm just fucking with you."

"The car just came in, my man." He turns to Colin, "Hey man, glad you're up and about. That shit was fucked up."

Colin fist bumps Manny, "I know, right?! If T-Swift loses another one of her squad, I'll begin to think maybe she's the problem."

Manny chuckles, "I took my daughter to see her at Staples Center."

Dane's interest picks up. "How was it?"

Colin squints, shocked that his brother is asking about a Taylor Swift concert.

"We were comfortable, but couldn't see anything."

Colin can't help himself, "That how Stevie Wonder lives every day; comfortable but can't see anything."

Manny laughs, "Same, Colin."

Colin notices the keys hanging from Manny's belt. "Whoa, that's an ass load of keys." He waves his hands over his fanny pack like Vanna White, "You may want to invest in one of these sexy things. It's like a nut sack but for other things, that hovers above your pockets like an unsightly growth."

Manny plays along, "You should consider a career in sales, because I want an unsightly nut sack for sure."

"Another unsightly nut sack, because I've seen yours and it looks a fleshy caruncle filled with misshapen marbles."

Dane focuses the group, "How 'bout you guys talk about belted satchels maybe later? We sorta have a bit of a time table."

Manny hands Dane the keys, "For plausible deniability reasons, I'm gonna take a walk."

Dane fist bumps him, "We owe you one." He opens the trunk, examining the canvas they have to work with. The space is essentially empty. Just jumper cables and a roadside kit.

Colin pulls a plastic bag out of his fanny pack and hands it to Dane. "I talk a lot of shit about this thing, but it's as convenient as fuck."

"I think you look great."

"Dick."

Dane tucks Alissa's necklace into one of the seams. He places her iPhone under the roadside kit, then sprinkles Alissa's blood that Dr. Phil collect all around the trunk, peppering in her hair.

Jeff's trunk is now a crime scene.

* * *

Two officers drag a drunken disorderly through the station to booking. He's making it as difficult for them as possible. He could be some celebrity's kid, maybe an internet personality whose claim to fame is impressing young kids with shenanigans; or just someone who drank too much and couldn't control himself. He's one of many finding his way through the police station this evening. Like anything, each station is subject to lulls and periods of high activity. The ying and the yang. The ebb and the flow. Criminals don't adhere to strict hours of operation, nor do they coordinate their schedules. Every day is different and most officers agree that quiet is good thing. Others like action. They feel alive when adrenaline is pumping through their veins while chasing a robbery suspect down a crowded street. Those with a penchant for the thrill either mellow out or end up dead.

Tonight is one of those nights where the police check to see if there's a full moon. Jeff sits in the police station, cuffed to a chair, clearly agitated. His clothing is disheveled and his hair is messy. Directly across from him is a black man who appears to be homeless. The indigent individual has graying hair and a friendly face, but crazy eyes. He taunts Jeff, smiling devilishly by holding his hands up to demonstrate he's not shackled. "Name's Al, Cracker Jack. You must've gone and done something fuckin' nuts for the police to have your ass cuffed."

Jeff ignores him for a second, but despite an effort that can be seen all over his face, he answers back. "Mind your own business."

"Are you one of thems serial killers? You a crazy motherfucker?"

Jeff leans in. "It's a misunderstanding. I'll be thinking about you in your refrigerator box when I'm at home in my own bed tonight." He then directs his attention to an officer walking by, "Officer, you need to handcuff this guy, too. It's discrimination."

Al stands up, "You get me cuffed, I'll bite you."

The officer gestures for Al to sit down, and his tough guy act turns subservient. "Yes, officer. Sorry, officer. I didn't mean nothing by it." The officer turns away and Al growls at Jeff.

Jeff shouts, "Hey, can somebody help me over here? This is all a huge mistake." Several officers look up, smile, and continue going about their business. "Can I at least talk to the girl?" Before Jeff can turn his head in the opposite direction from his whiny plea, Dane is standing within his blind side.

"Mr. Pembroke, you're in some trouble. Do you have someone you can call? Lawyer?"

"Yeah, my brother's attorney, Harvey Benoit." Dane takes the cuffs off of Jeff, who rubs his wrists, then walks him over to the telephone.

Defense attorneys do indeed deserve kudos from time to time. The good ones are as wealthy as the people that can afford them. Yet at the drop of a hat one of the shrewdest, most successful defense attorneys hops out of bed or leaves whatever engagement that was occupying his or her leisure time and speeds to the police station. They wipe the sleep out of their eyes and spring one of Marlon Brando's children from the clink for driving intoxicated, wearing a blindfold, with underage hookers in the trunk.

Harvey Benoit just looks like a defense attorney. His portly body doesn't show in his face and his graying beard matches his thick, neatly cut hair. Within a jiffy, Harvey is at the station in two shakes. He knows his way around the place and walks over to the main desk where Dane pretends to look busy. "Hello, I'm looking for my client, Jeff Pembroke."

Dane's back is turned to the attorney. He hones his acting chops and places his pointer finger in the air to signal, 'one moment.' Dane then places a file alphabetically within a pile of other documents. He turns and his countenance is friendly. "I'm Detective Graves. Mr. Pembroke is over there. Follow me."

Harvey looks to where Dane points to see Jeff sitting cuffed to the chair. He waves to Harvey with his cuffs on and makes an exasperated face. Harvey waves back. "Are cuffs necessary?"

"In general?"

"I mean for Mr. Pembroke."

Dane leans in, "Apparently, your client made a *Cagney & Lacey* joke when he was being arrested and the officers felt he needed a little lesson." Dane places his finger to his lips, "That's between you and me."

"Are you charging my client?"

"Truth be told, the girl Jeff was seen partaking a lewd act with gave us the slip before we could I.D. her. We were going to get her over to the rape treatment center, but she went to the bathroom and snuck out of the building. She was very broken up. She told us she was underage, but since we don't even know who she is, kinda tough to make that stick. We checked his car for blood, hair, and other evidence that could link him to any crimes that could be related. It was clean. We aren't too interested in a public lewdness charge, so your client is free to go."

Harvey pulls out his phone, pulls up a picture, and waves Dane in closer as he shows it to him. "Is this the girl?"

Dane looks at the picture of Alissa. "Yes. That's her. You obviously know her or you wouldn't have her picture. Family?"

Harvey doesn't answer the question.

Dane continues, "Most cases of sexual abuse are relatives."

"I'm sure it's a misunderstanding and there's no way her father would press charges, so…"

Dane points at Jeff. "He's all yours." He walks him over to Jeff and unlocks the handcuffs.

Jeff hugs Harvey. "Harvey! Am I glad to see you!"

"My pleasure, Jeffrey."

Jeff becomes overly smug, "Detective, thank you for your hospitality. We should do this again."

Dane smiles, "Give us a good Yelp review."

Jeff and Harvey walk towards the exit, one glowing victorious, and the other ambivalent. Jeff places his arm around Harvey, who is visibly unnerved. "Man, you're good." Harvey's skin crawls.

The client and his attorney part ways at the entrance. Harvey gets into his black Mercedes Benz. He exhales deeply and looks at himself in the rear-view mirror. Episodes like this deepen his crow's feet and laugh lines, or grimace lines in his case. There's nothing funny about how he feels. Twenty years ago, something like this would roll off his back like he was coated in turtle wax. Two daughters later, and grandchildren on the horizon, Harvey has lost his stomach for the disgusting aspects of his job. Some days he wishes he didn't love his sports car or his apartment in Manhattan. He wishes he didn't love buying his wife pricey jewelry and spoiling his kids. As he contemplates his decisions, he notices a rival defense attorney walking into the station, clearly summoned by client. He's a young buck that reminds him of how he was at that age. Then it hits him. If he hangs up his spurs, the only one who would suffer is his family. Until something changes, he needs to grab what he can while he's still able.

Harvey picks up his phone and dials Richard. "Rich. It's me, Harv. I got some troubling news. Jeff was seen engaged in sexual relations with a minor in his car. I showed one of the detectives a picture of Alissa and he made a positive identification."

Richard is silent on the other end. His heart is in his stomach and even though one may argue that he's heartless, he isn't when it comes to his little girl.

"Rich?"

"Harv, is she there?"

"The cops were getting ready to transport her to the rape treatment center, but she got spooked and made a run for it. They aren't gonna lock up a victim. Apparently, she was distraught and said she needed to go to the bathroom and snuck out."

"Any evidence he hurt her other than the obvious?"

"They impounded his car, checked it for blood, DNA, weapons and found nothing. He's on his way home."

"Harv, thanks."

"Rich... I'm sorry."

* * *

Jeff walks to the impound lot with a bounce in his step. As far as he's

CHAPTER 14

concerned, being hauled in for having a barely underage girl polish his nob is a great story. Not only is he not embarrassed, he's proud of himself. Manny is standing there at his post texting and ignores Jeff who obnoxiously looks at the chunk of keys dangling from Manny's belt, "Nice keys bro, here's my ticket, fetch my ride will ya, hombre."

Manny continues to text, "This isn't valet, chief."

"Well, boss. Isn't your job getting me my car?"

Manny draws a line in the sand and leans harder on the post previously propping him up.

Jeff shouts angrily, "Dude, get my fuckin' car. I'll have my lawyer on your ass."

"I'd ask me nicely, otherwise we may not be able to find your car for like a month."

"Goddammit." Jeff throws his hands in the air and regains his composure. "Could I please have my car? I've been through a lot and I truly appreciate your due diligence in this matter."

Manny grabs his clipboard, looks it over and searches for the car keys hanging inside his shack. He grabs Jeff's set. "Be right back."

He hobbles towards the sea of cars off in the distance. With his back turned to Jeff, Manny devilishly smirks, because if he felt one iota of guilt over setting this asshole up, that minuscule measurement has evaporated. He pulls up right in front of Jeff and exits the car.

As Jeff drives away, Manny holds one of his keys to the door, waving goodbye to him as the entire driver's side gets a brand new, deep scratch. Manny shakes his head, whispering 'prick' under his breath.

∗ ∗ ∗

Colin lets out a piercing cry as Alissa's teeth sink deep into his neck. When he returned home for the night from the impound lot, he checked the monitor and the lump had not moved since the doctor put her out. He decided to confirm that she was still breathing, against Dane's warning to not go in alone. He unlocked the latch and entered the room. The bed was empty and before he could process anything, she was on his back with her teeth tearing at his trap. The adrenaline rush from being viciously bitten triggers his reflexes and he throws her to the ground. She hits the basement floor with a thud; stunned. He quickly cuffs her to the bed. She springs to her feet and lunges at him like an animal that doesn't realize they've been contained.

He grabs his neck. "You maniac. You bit me."

"Let me go, you freak!" Alissa pulls on the cuffed arm.

"'Freak' is a little harsh, don't you think? Because I'm missing my arm, or because I'm holding you hostage in my basement? One is politically incorrect and one is, well, justifiable."

"You have me locked down here like some sort of serial killer or something."

"I have you locked down here like some sort of serial killer or like a serial killer would have you locked down here? You've misplaced a modifier like a complete moron. And also 'or something' makes you sound stupid. Well, more stupid."

"Huh?" She doesn't follow.

"I'm not a serial killer."

"Then, how much is my ransom, 'not a serial killer?'"

Colin smiles, "Ransom? This is amazing."

"This is my third kidnapping. I'll have you know that my dad pays, then the kidnappers pay. If you know what I mean."

"Kidnapped three times? Your father needs some parenting classes."

"If you try and sell me as a slave or something, my dad will find you and kill you."

"'As a slave' is fine by itself. No need for 'or something.'"

"So you <u>are</u> selling me as a slave?"

"No. I was correcting your grammar. You're like a 'C' student, I'm assuming?"

She ignores his comment. "If you force yourself on me I'll bite your penis."

"There will be no penis-biting 'or something.' You're just a pawn. I

CHAPTER 14

came down here to make sure the doctor didn't accidentally kill you, and now I need to wash this bite out with hydrogen peroxide." Colin's dog, Charlie, barks in the distance.

Alissa gets excited, "Dog? Is that a dog? Do you have a dog?"

"No, my refrigerator barks when it's hungry. It's the weirdest thing."

Her tone changes. "Can I play with him?"

"Are you serious? You just attacked me and threatened to bite my penis. And you think I'll let you play with my adorable dog?"

"You said you're not going to hurt me. I wasn't sure what was going on."

"Her. It's a she. Try and calm down and let me think on it."

She nods.

Colin limps up the steps holding his wound, shaking his head. He's not thrilled that he'll have to explain this incident to Dane who won't say 'I told you so,' but he'll sure as hell think it. Before he knows it he's in front of his bathroom mirror, once again looking at someone he barely recognizes. His missing limb is off-putting; something he'll never get used to. More than that, he can't stop thinking of the girl he'll never see again. That pain is worse than any of the physical pain he's been forced to endure. He has that feeling in that space between his heart and his gut that makes a deep breath impossible. He wants to scream to release this unrelenting pressure, but can't because he's so angry. The two emotions are feeding each other and his torso feels like a pressure cooker that's barely hanging onto its lid. He thinks, 'fuck it,' his new mantra, takes a belt of whiskey, a couple of painkillers, then places a towel soaked with hydrogen peroxide on his bite. The sting causes his eyes to water like he's chopping onions, but temporarily shakes him out of his funk. His hearts beats faster, and he hobbles to the chair he's recently been calling home.

He plops down, grabbing the blanket slung over the arm of the chair and a photo album on the ground. The impulse when depressed to do more depressing things is inherently human. He begins to leaf through the pages. Many of the faces are long gone; whispers from a different time. He turns the page to one of his favorite pictures of Betty. She was gorgeous, a striking beauty that never took a bad picture. However, this picture he took at the gym. She wasn't expecting it; no make-up, in workout clothes, half-turning towards the camera mid-picture, and her face says, 'are you fucking kidding me?' so perfectly that he adores it. He feels his heart literally stop. He closes his eyes and prays that it just stays permanently on pause. A second or two later there's a thump. He whispers out loud, telling Betty he will see her soon and that he's sorry he cannot bring himself to be there sooner. He feels like a coward sticking around without her. It's no easy task to blindly leap into oblivion.

An old photo of his grandfather drops to the ground. He was murdered. He was a parole officer versus police, preferring the hours and the low expectations placed on him. Criminals are expected to find their way back to prison; no parole officer has the ability to stop the inevitable.

The day he was killed was his perfect morning. The sprinklers didn't soak his newspaper. His bagel came out perfectly toasted. There was one glass of OJ left just for him, and his coffee tasted like heaven. When he got to work, he had gotten the best parking spot. Just one of those days. Then the file hit his desk and when he saw who it was, his heart dropped into his stomach. Another parole officer walking by tripped and spilled his coffee on him right then. That omen in itself should have made him take the day off, but that just wasn't him. If something did happen to someone else because he evaded his responsibility he wouldn't have been able to live with himself, whether a bullet was dodged or not.

He needed to send this bad guy back to jail for violating his parole and knew this would have to be done cautiously. He decided to take a beat and do it after lunch. Before he even had the opportunity to come up with a proper plan, this repeat offender hunted him down, knowing full well he was in violation, and jumped him during his lunch break.

CHAPTER 14

This guy was on all types of illegal ingestibles and injectibles, including a big dose of acid. Colin's grandfather pleaded with this psychopath, but this crazed criminal was someplace else. He had snapped. He cuffed him and placed him in the trunk of his own car. This jittery drug addict who was going back to jail for both dirty urine and consorting with criminals drove the car into the Hollywood Reservoir. Colin's grandfather drowned. The parolee literally overheated and cooked his brain. He never recovered normal neural function.

Dane and Colin were little, but they remember their mother lost it when it happened. She made each of them a necklace in his memory. She also made them promise never to take them off and they both still wear them to this day. Colin stares at the picture. He closes his eyes and tries to sleep.

Colin sleeps the exact duration that the narcotics and alcohol impact his system. Once they wear off, sometimes after a few hours, sometimes just an hour or two, he awakes to a pounding headache, dry mouth, and overall shitty feeling. It's clearly been too long without painkillers and is now the middle of the night. The brain's reaction to narcotics certainly lends to addiction. He'd do just about anything to get rid of the pain from behind his eyes. He limps to his kitchen and downs a couple of Vicodin. Almost every room has a few painkillers scattered about so he doesn't have to go too far. Not unlike a squirrel, he's hiding his nuts everywhere but often can't remember exactly where.

He slides into the chair in front of his laptop in the kitchen and starts to research Alissa through her social media. He will learn what he can about her to gain her trust. He's compiling a list for both verbal interactions and a list of things to buy. Favorite movies, books, and music should do the trick to start. This manipulation technique is commonly attributed to pedophiles, but there are very few adults who have not implemented this type of chicanery to seduce the opposite sex. Boiled down, pretending to have things in common is the simplest plan to create moments that could eventually lead to attraction and even affection. Colin composes an email to one of his guys to pick up these items first thing in the morning so he can begin.

He spaces out for second, staring, but not seeing anything clearly beyond his own nose, like he is trying to unscramble 3D art, sipping on bottled water. When he rises to his feet, his head begins to throb. His brain is pounding and the pain is blinding. He falls to his knees and throws up everywhere. The Vicodin he just took are in his watery, mucousy upchuck. He picks up the pills, crawling over to the table with his water. He places the semi-digested pills in his mouth and they taste vile. He lays on the floor in the fetal position waiting for the pain to subside.

He closes his eyes and prays that an earthquake centralizes itself directly on his property and the chasm created swallows him whole. He opens his eyes; under the stove is filthy. He's appalled by the dust bunnies that have accumulated. They seem to multiply like regular bunnies. He spots something else under the stove and crawls on his stomach to retrieve the mystery object, assuming it's a take-out menu. It's a postcard he mailed back home the last day he and Betty were in Italy as a little surprise for when they got back. *To Betty, This trip was like* Die Hard 2 *but in an office building. Love Colin.* He turns the card over and it may be the Vicodin, but he's back in Italy with beautiful wife.

Before that trip, he'd never been out of the country. When he was younger, his family exclusively went to Florida with the occasional deviation to New York city. He found out later the trips to NYC were business for his father. The LAPD and NYPD had an exchange program. Confiscated cash would disappear from evidence and an 'out-of-towner' executed the contract. Police murder for hire. This was exclusively for violent criminals who slipped through the system. His dad would do the job and the family would leave town and be 3,000 miles away when the 'investigation' would occur. The cases were closed with little effort by the home team.

Dane enters the kitchen and interrupts Colin's flashback, "Col, are you okay?" He notices the watery puke on the floor.

"Question: at what point does food cease being food and transition into being throw up?"

"I'm no scientist, but I'd say once it passes through the esophagus it's no longer food."

"Okay then. This is all puke," pointing to the ground, "Took my pills on an empty stomach."

Dane helps him to his feet. "When's physical therapy?"

"Never o'clock. That's halfway between that shit sucks and I'd rather die than go back. I know what you're thinking... how am I going to thrive at the Paralympic Games if I don't go to physical therapy? Steroids and PEDs."

"We'll revisit." Dane throws out a puke saturated paper towel. "How's the girl?" Dane notices his bite. "Holy shit, did you go in there and she bit you?"

"No, this bite is old. My *Twilight* book club had a reunion. Reggie still thinks he's Edward."

Dane rolls his eyes, "Anyway, the two big dudes will be at a bar in Weho tonight. Lakers' game, they never miss."

"Groovy," Colin points with his thumb. "I was just about to check on the girl. Okay to go in or do you want to cover me?"

"You tell me."

Colin gives him the middle finger.

"Be careful, she's like what, a buck-ten."

Colin checks the monitor to make sure she isn't poised for another attack and he enters the room. She's fast asleep, in the fetal position with her back facing the door. She rouses as the door creaks open. Colin needs to channel his undercover days when he could convince a criminal that they could trust him. He's barely balancing a breakfast tray with his one arm. Alissa sits up; her hair is messy and she has bed creases all over her face. "Good morning sunshine." Colin pauses. "Whoa, do you need a brush or something? Paper bag?"

Alissa is not amused. "Ha ha. Excuse me. Are your dark cycles darker?"

"Actually its eyeliner. It's never too late to go emo."

"Emo?"

Colin dramatically drops his head, grabs his shirt with thumb and forefinger, "I keep forgetting this shirt is older than you."

"I like Metallica."

"Finally, there's hope for you yet."

"What's that supposed to mean?"

"Well, you seem pretty lame."

She hits him playfully, "You wouldn't know lame if it bit you on the neck. So, you gonna feed me or what?"

Colin looks down at the tray, "Nah, I just carry trays with food around for practice."

Alissa pretends to tip it over, "You need it."

"You're pure evil."

Alissa smiles, "Do you have anything lighter?" Alissa snatches a piece of bacon and takes a bite. With bacon in her mouth, "What really happened to your eyes? Your boyfriend hit you?"

The last remnants of the shiners still remains from when Richard's men tuned him up. "It's actually for an acting role. The same one we had you audition for."

"Hilarious."

"Almost as funny as your homophobic domestic abuse boyfriend comment from thirty seconds ago." Colin had left the door open; his dog scampers in and jumps on Alissa's lap.

"Oh my goodness, is this your puppy?"

"What puppy?"

Alissa rolls her eyes.

Colin pets her, "She's a mini Goldendoodle."

"She's so cute." Charlie licks Alissa's face and she giggles. "I used to have a dog, Hunter. My dad gave her away when my mom died."

"Yeah that guy sucks."

"Was your dad perfect?"

CHAPTER 14

"Not at all. He was disappointed I never became a Wolverine like him."

"Michigan?" Alissa asks excitedly.

"Yeah, he went there and played QB behind Don Moorhead."

Alissa points to herself. "I'm going to go to Michigan. I might try and walk on to the volleyball team."

"No way. That's great. I played a little volleyball. Used to go to Hermosa and try to qualify for the AFV event." He points to his missing arm, "I used to be pretty good, not a great leaper."

"I've been to a couple of those."

"You ever compete?"

"No, would just go and watch. Indoor and beach volleyball are completely different."

"Totally. With one you end up with sand up your ass; the other, floor burns just about everywhere." Dane enters the room holding a bag. Colin gets up and walks over to Dane as Alissa continues to play with Charlie.

"You had Wingate buy this stuff, yeah?"

"Yep." Colin grabs the bag and winks at Dane as he exits. He turns to Alissa, "Hey, it's pretty boring down here, so I got some books and movies so you have something to do."

"Any chance of me getting my phone?"

"Zero."

She looks through the bag, "Wow, I love this series of books and these are some of my favorite movies."

"I know what's up."

She playfully rolls her eyes, "I just didn't think you would know what I like."

"Unfortunately, you can fill this house with things you don't know."

"You did not."

"Oh I did," Colin smiles at her. She returns the smile. "So, I'll let Charlie keep you company, you are under sixty years old, so I'm assuming you know how the TV and DVD player works."

137

She nods.

As he leaves, Colin adds, "And those books are super easy to use. Nothing to turn on. You just open them, and when you're done the page on the right, you turn it to the next set of pages."

She gives him the middle finger.

Chapter 15

Now practically morning, Richard stares out his office window. On his desk is a paperweight Alissa made him in preschool. He keeps his pens and pencils in a cup she made him in first grade. She signed the cup, under her Picasso-esque doodle of an elephant, with her little kid handwriting with one of the 's' backwards. Richard's eyes are red and puffy; he's been crying. He can't even remember the last time he cried. He's in such shock; he can't believe this is happening. Jeff casually plops down on one the chairs facing Richard, letting out a deep breath, and he places his feet up on the edge of the desk. Richard glares at his trendy, expensive shoes on his very expensive desk, bubbling inside, doing everything he can to not blow a gasket. Normally when Jeff places his feet on his desk, he lets it slide, but everything that bugs him about his brother is magnified under the circumstances.

"What a night! I could use a cold one."

Richard looks him directly in the eyes, dripping pure contempt, and says nothing.

"Rich, what's with you? You have a cold or something? You have allergies? Try Claritin. It's like a miracle." Jeff has never seen his brother cry, therefore assuming he has been crying is like assuming a glutton won't choose the all-you-can-eat buffet.

Richard asks him, serious as a heart attack, "Where's Alissa?"

Jeff answers while giving Richard an expressive, 'why you asking me' face. "How should I know? Sleeping?" He ends it with a shrug. "It's like the middle of the night? Top of the morning? Call her on her cell, no? When did I become the idea guy?"

Richard collects himself, places his hand over his brow and turns to Vincent who is in the corner of the room. With just a look, Vince is in his ear, like Richard used mental telepathy. He whispers to him, and then he turns to his brother. "Give me your keys." Richard places his hand out like it's a command not a request.

"Why?" Jeff's tone is defiant. "What the fuck is up with you? You're acting like a dick."

Richard gets sterner. "Give me your keys. Now!"

Jeff's tone does a 180, going from defiant to high and whiny like a teenager still scared of his father. "Richey. What is it?"

Richard doesn't repeat himself and within a second, Jeff is reaching into his pocket, fumbling around for his keys. He's so nervous he can't free his hand from his pocket. He pulls the keys out and tosses them onto his brother's desk. Richard grabs the keys, squeezing them in his hand. He hands them over to Vincent who exits the room. Richard opens a drawer in his desk, dials his voicemail, and hands the phone to Jeff. "Explain this, if you can."

Jeff listens to Alissa's voice alluding to Jeff's inappropriate behavior. "What the fuck is that?" Jeff stands up and backs up haphazardly. Richard's loyal men keep the exits blocked. "Richey, I don't know what's going on here but I didn't do anything. This is some sort of ploy for attention. This is fucked up."

"Goddammit Jeff! You were spotted having sex in your car with a teenager. The cops brought you in with a teenager and Harvey showed Alissa's picture to them and they identified her."

Jeff begins to cry. "This is bullshit. I'd never touch my niece, ever. Get her here. She'd never be able to lie like this to our faces."

"If I could get her here, I would. And the police? Are they part of this fucking conspiracy against you?"

Timmy walks in holding a brown envelope. "Uncle Rich, this was outside." Timmy hands him the envelope and he tears it open. There are several black and white photos of Jeff with Ingrid. However, it is

CHAPTER 15

far enough away, a little grainy, and Ingrid looks enough like Alissa to make even a father believe this is his daughter. The magic of Photoshop. There are also close-ups of her tattoo. There are pictures of Jeff pushing the girl's head towards his crotch. Richard turns bright red and the vein in his head begins to pulsate like it does when he's pissed. If he was playing poker, this would be his tell. Included with the pictures is an anonymous letter from one of Alissa's friends. The forensic handwriting expert for the police captured Courtney's handwriting perfectly.

Richard reads the letter out loud. *Dear Mr. Pembroke, Alissa had me take pictures last night because she can't handle the abuse anymore. She said that if anything happened to her, leave them in the mailbox. She texted me from the trunk of her uncle's car.* Richard tosses the pictures over to Jeff and they land at his feet. He picks them up.

"This is fucking crazy. I'm being set up here. This is the girl, Ingrid. From last night. Not Alissa. I mean, they look similar, but you're an ass-clown if you can't recognize your own fucking daughter."

"And they have the exact same tattoo?"

"Alissa has a tattoo?"

"You took her to get the tongue stud and Trick took her to get the tattoo."

"She said the tongue ring was okay by you?"

"Does that sound like me? But that's neither here nor there."

"You see, she's played us all before, why can't you see it here?"

"Physical fucking evidence. Listen little brother. I can forgive you. You have some bad wiring or a hormone imbalance. We'll get you help. Therapy? Whatever. Just tell me where she is."

"I don't know. You've got to believe me that I didn't do this."

Vincent walks in with Alissa's iPhone and her necklace. "These were in the trunk."

Jeff throws his hands up, "You've got to be shitting me."

Vincent whispers in Richards ear, "The Luminol is showing blood and there's some hair ripped out by the roots."

"This is my girl. You killed her? You knew she would tell me and you killed her."

Jeff places his hands on his head. "Christ. I didn't do this but I'm fucked."

"The police checked your car. If they found something they wouldn't have let you go." Richard covers his eyes with his hands. "What am I going to do with you?"

Jeff looks at Richard with tears in his eyes. His sadness turns to disdain. Richard instructs Vincent to call Benny. Jeff's heart falls into his stomach. He's aware what Benny's services mean for him. Benny primarily disposes of bodies. Piney grabs Jeff's arm to pull him out of his chair, and Jeff jerks it away, stands up, and straightens out his jacket. Piney waves him out of the room and they walk outside to the cars.

He is about to get into the back seat, but his escorts won't let him open the door and point towards the trunk with their heads. Jeff shakes his head, 'no,' and they grab him and drag him to the back of the car. They try to force him into the trunk, but he resists like a cat refusing to get into its travel bag. He fights to stay out of the confined space, but too many hands are forcing him in. They shut the trunk on his fingers. He screams in agony, then screams more as he tries to free his fingers from the trunk's tight clutch. He holds his fist full of broken fingers tight to his chest.

Benny is waiting at one of Richard's many warehouses, leaning up against his van, smoking. The caravan of cars pull up. He blows the smoke out that was in his lungs, drops the cigarette, and steps on it. He walks by Richard who doesn't even acknowledge him. Benny goes right up to Vincent.

"Yo, Vince, how you feeling? You hear from the doctor yet?"

Vincent barely looks at Benny as he answers. "I'm okay. The doc didn't get the results yet. It's only been like a day."

"Who's getting offed?"

"You're not going to believe it."

CHAPTER 15

Piney and Corky open the trunk and pull Jeff out who tried to kill himself while en route with the prong of his belt. He created some puncture wounds in his neck and drew some blood, but not enough to be fatal.

Piney looks at him, shaking his head. "Take it like a man, gov. You're being pathetic."

"Fuck you, you limey faggot. I never cared for your fat ass."

"Yeah yeah."

"And you, you stuttering prick." He mocks his stutter, "You're like a reeeetard." Jeff goes limp like a little kid in the mall throwing a tantrum; they have no problem dragging him inside. In a corner of the warehouse they have a steel chair set up, bolted to the ground. Around it, the floor is discolored and stained. Years of spilling blood in this area and bleaching it has made it look perpetually grimy. They violently force him into the chair, securing his arms with handcuffs.

Richard is in the office collecting his thoughts and contemplating his next set of actions. If his day-to-day is like a normal chess match, this curve ball has made the game speed chess. He's at a crossroads and needs to act swiftly but factor in the long-term ripple of his actions. As far as he's concerned, his life will never be the same. His child is dead. He just stares at a picture of Alissa when she was twelve. He can hardly believe he'll never see her again. He's searching his soul trying to find a teeny, tiny scrap of emotion or logic to justify giving his brother a stay of execution. He can't imagine a reality where he won't be disgusted by the sight of him. If merely exiled, the thought of him out there would drive him mad. He slides his hands into black leather gloves, singularly focused on ending his brother.

Jeff is having a hard time staying conscious. His neck wounds and shattered hand have impacted his nervous system. The adrenaline released from fear and injury is wearing off. The warehouse is eerily quiet as each henchman is standing in complete silence. The office door shuts and footsteps echo, getting louder as Richard slowly approaches Jeff, whose neck and front of his shirt is covered in blood.

He speaks as he approaches his brother, "People overuse the word 'surreal.' I'm about to be that guy though. This is fucking surreal."

"Blah, blah, blah. Are you going to drone on about something before you kill me? Just fucking skip the harangue. You're the only one in this whole place that likes the sound of your voice. Trust me." As Jeff speaks, blood drool drips from his lips. "This is a set-up, but you're so dumb, you can't even see how tidy this whole scenario played out."

Fury takes hold of Richard and he slams him in the face. Jeff screams in agony as his head flies back, practically breaking his neck. "I'd believe this was a set-up if her voice wasn't on my phone. If her blood wasn't in your car. Her hair and necklace. There are fucking pictures. I know you like them young. I've made shit go away before."

Jeff grunts through blood bubbles.

"I've been looking after you forever and there was a time when I may not have believed all this physical evidence, but after the thing with Laura. Fucking Laura, my Laura. It takes two to tango and that's why you didn't find yourself fish food back then. You're a sneaky fuck that clearly cares less about me than I you. And Alissa looks exactly like her you sick prick. Fool me once shame on me, but fool me twice..." Richard smashes him again.

"Stop!" Jeff gets Richard to pause. He wiggles his nose, "I have an itch on my nose."

Richard shakes his head, then punches him again.

"Got it. Thanks."

"I'll make it quick if you tell me where her body is?"

"Let me see. After I fucked her in the ass, I buried her where you buried that guy's wife. The innocent guy with the one arm because of your 'act now, ask questions later' policy."

Richard hits him again. "Pain is so uniquely individual. Everyone has their own threshold. I'm shocked you're handling this so well." Richard hits him several more times in a row. "Obviously, I've always thought you were soft." Jeff is as close to unconscious as possible without being completely out. Richard stops for a moment. "For the first time, I sorta respect you." Richard pauses in between each punch to speak. After each thought, he slams Jeff in the face. "Pop thought you were a pussy, too."

Richard hits him again. "He would joke that you were the daughter he never knew he wanted." Richard throws another punch. "I always defended you like a schmuck." Jeff's blood is flying everywhere. He's becoming completely unrecognizable with each smashing blow to the face; a bloody mess of meat. Richard has blood on his clothes, in his eyes, and all over his face. He hits him and hits him and hits him. At this point, Richard is beating on the dead.

He finally stops. He's huffing and puffing like he just went fifteen rounds with Rocky Marciano. He throws up, wiping his bloody face with his even bloodier hands. He turns his back and walks out of the warehouse. All his men follow him except Benny who snakes to his truck, grabs his gear, and a camera. Normally, he takes pictures of the dead as an insurance policy. Tonight, he's taking pictures for Dane and Colin.

Benny lays down plastic a few feet from the chair and drags the body over. He's not only unfazed by the whole twisted ritual, he hums the theme song to *The Muppets* while he works. He pulls out a power saw and cuts Jeff into more manageable pieces. The hot blade sears the flesh just enough to create a faint smell of meat cooking. He removes the hands and teeth. He shatters the jaw to make it the most annoying puzzle to recreate. He methodically separates all the parts placing them in different plastic bags; none too heavy or too full. After loading the bags into his van, he returns to the blood pool and uses food grade hydrogen peroxide on the stains. The blood bubbles and turns white. He mops up and also bleaches the whole area. Jeff has just added to the rich tapestry that is this floor. He drives to the water, uses his little powerboat, and dumps the weighted bags overboard.

Benny learned how to get rid of bodies from his father who grew up in Hell's Kitchen. Back in the day they called cutting up the body and dumping the pieces into the water, 'doin' the Houdini.' The infamous

Eddie Cummisky learned how to be a butcher in jail. When he got out, he implemented his training into a side business and may have been the first to butcher a body and dump the pieces into the river. Eddie mentored Benny's uncle George who passed the knowledge onto Benny. However, Benny added a little ritual to this proven technique. At his place, Benny has a fish tank with two piranhas, Mork and Mindy. He would bring the victims' hands home and feed them to the needle-toothed, flesh-eating fish. Benny enters his son's room and wakes him, as it's now morning. "Hey, buddy, wake up."

Benny's son stirs and he looks up at his dad. "What? Is mom out of jail?"

"No, champ. I was thinking that we can go to the toy store, if you would like."

"Yeah."

Every time Benny cleans up one of Richard's messes, his son gets a toy.

**

Benny's son, Billy, quietly stares, with big, innocent, sad eyes, on the way to the toy store, absorbing the different visuals that define LA. One minute there are Palm Trees, then store fronts, maybe new apartment buildings, billboards for new movies and shows. He gently uses his finger to invisibly draw on the window, clearly having an internal dialogue. He's extremely reserved for his age, due in most to being exposed to the shit that inevitably happened to his junkie mom and low-life criminal dad. Kids like this always eventually find themselves at a fork in the road; that place in time where their nightmare of a childhood fuels the fire to greater things or extinguishes it completely, thwarting ambition, creating more societal drains. Billy is a few years away from this precipice. It will present itself, quickly and steeply, and it will test his mettle.

In the meantime, he'll get a toy to temporarily distract him from a life

CHAPTER 15

no one wants for their child. He has no inkling that all the possessions he's fond of are linked to a dead body. This is a macabre truth he'll never know. They enter the store, Benny's hand on Billy's head. His eyes light up and this is one of the few things that makes Benny smile. For all his faults, he genuinely loves his son. He just doesn't have the inner strength to fight gravity. The pull of the world has just been too much and when he was at his fork in the road, was so damaged, the path was as deep as a trench and his feet were on tracks; his destiny had been solidified.

Benny passes the counter and brushes by the female employee who has her coat on. She's talking to the other employee on shift who's crouched behind the counter picking up something or filing paperwork under the desk.

"Hey, I'm gonna take my lunch. This place is dead."

The employee behind the counter flirts with his clearly uninterested co-worker. "Really? I'll be here all alone?"

"For an hour. You'll survive." She's eager to meet her boyfriend for a quickie. She exits the store.

The crouching employee stands up. Benny is standing next to his son, looking at the different toys. He nonchalantly glances in the direction of the checkout. He looks away and reads the back of the action figure he's holding. As he's reading about the kung fu grip or real battle noises, Benny cocks his head to the side and he squints. The visual sent to him moments ago has been processed and reevaluated.

Benny recognizes this punk. Not long ago, Benny spent two weeks in the slammer for child support, right before his ex-wife was locked up. This little shit, who got pulled in on a small-time possession charge, had seen too many movies and shanked Benny as a ploy to keep people from messing with him. Benny was sitting by himself, reading, when this numbskull stabbed him with a sharpened toothbrush nearly a dozen times for no good reason. Benny was clearly dumbfounded; he was literally just chilling in jail like he does every time he's short on scratch for his kid's care. For him, it's a walk in the park. This type of violence doesn't happen with this type of temporary jail time. Benny slipped out of this predicament like he does most but not without a punctured lung. He couldn't smoke for two months without excruciating pain because of this idiot. When this kid realizes who was in the store, a wave of fear crashes over him, washing all color from his face.

Benny acknowledges his enemy with a cocky nod and kneels down to his son's level, "Hey champ, start checking out whatever you want. Pick out a few things." Benny struts over and even though in some circles, he's low on the totem pole and a bit of bitch, your average person would see him coming and go the other way. When you have something to lose, getting tangled up with someone who at the very least looks like they have nothing to lose and may literally have nothing to lose, is foolish.

The punk throws his hands up as he talks, "Hey, bro, sorry about the... you know. That was just my bad. Total bad call."

"Bad call? Your bad? You punctured my lung, you fucking retard."

"I was just super worried about being raped. You know what they say about jail, man. I thought no one would fuck with me if I laid out some dude."

"You were brought in for possession, probation bro, and if you killed me you'd get 5-10 easy. And I'm going to fuck with you now." Benny grabs him by the scruff of his neck. He leads him to the back of the store into the storeroom.

Billy is mesmerized by the volume of toys at his fingertips and pays no attention to the ruckus. The way his parents would fight, he can tune anything out.

The punk's voice reverts back to when he was thirteen. "Hey, man, I said I'm sorry."

Benny doesn't say anything, but he grabs a PlayStation, pauses, places it down softly, then picks up an Xbox. He smashes the punk in the face repeatedly with the gaming system until the kid falls to the ground. The carpet is thin and cheap. The concrete below is cold and

CHAPTER 15

hard. Benny spots a box cutter and with no hesitation, he sloppily cuts the lad's neck. This young man's eyes were never so big as he attempts to stop the blood flow with his own hands. He's gurgling and unable to talk; slowly bleeding to death with shock frozen on his distorted face. Benny, calm as a virgin surrounded by eunuchs, strolls out the front door, gets his van, and parks it behind the store. Benny cuts the carpet around the punk's body, with the box cutter, wraps him up, and drags him out. Benny enters the store and loads up a few bags with toys. When whoever returns to the store, there will be some stolen toys, a swatch of carpet missing, and an employee with a record in the wind. They drive home so Benny can get rid of the body. His son is so preoccupied with his new action figure he doesn't even notice the lump in the back.

* * *

Under the wrong circumstances, being predictable and locked into a routine could be a dangerous way to exist. While easier and much more comfortable for the majority, if a target, the adherence to a set schedule makes things all too easy for those plotting. Robbers and burglars love when they can set their clocks to a mark's schedule. Joel and Fred, Richard's gigantic henchmen, watch every Lakers game in the same bar without fail. Since they held Colin still while Richard ruined his suit, these two meat heads are now on the chopping block, and they don't even know it.

Fred takes a swig of his beer, "You think I'm over-training or under-training my lats?"

Joel places his right hand under Fred's left arm and feels the overly muscular protuberance. "This shit is solid."

"I want those wings, bro."

"I get it. Where are you in your cycle?"

"I'm 6 weeks into Stanozolol."

"Dosage?"

"30 mg daily."

"Try 30 mg of Methandrostenolone daily next. Stano is good for lean muscle gains, but switch it up for a cycle for some mass."

"Good call, bro. Will do." Fred downs half of his beer.

Joel points at a table with two twins who look like strippers. "Check those bitches out."

"Remember last weekend you were supposed to line up some vaginas for us? That's what I'm talking about. Those cows you found did the trick, but bro, that's the shit." Fred gets up and walks over to the equally artificial looking women. "Ladies, my friend and I were wondering if you wanted to join us for the second half of the game?"

Ironically, the women's very cliché outward appearance caught their eye, now the women size up the two muscular anomalies like they're livestock. Between the four of them perhaps they've gotten through a total of two books, and one may have just had pictures.

"We'd love to, but we have a shift in twenty minutes down the street."

While she talks, the other one scribbles a number on a piece of paper. "But I think you should call us whenever you want." She hands the number to Fred and the girls walk out of the bar. Fred and Joel pound the remainder of their beers. Several beers later, the game is winding down.

"I have to take a piss," Fred slurs at Joel.

"Me too. Let's roll towards the pisser."

They stumble towards the bathroom, noticeably inebriated. The sheer volume of booze necessary to get these two monsters drunk covers a nice chunk of the bar's overhead.

Fred places his arm around Joel. "You're the man."

"That was awesome getting those twins' numbers."

"Were they twins? For sure?"

"They may just have the same doctor."

They each assume the position in front of a urinal. Dane enters and he has a gun with a silencer in each hand. He pushes the barrels into

CHAPTER 15

the back of each beast's head. Colin watches from right behind Dane. He has a gun, but he's strictly there for show. If the tables turned and this got out of control, he'd be as useful as a noodle-dick in a house full of nymphos.

"What the fuck?" Shock and irritation twistedly exit Joel's giant mouth, unable to believe someone is crazy enough to touch him while he's draining his spaghetti.

"Don't move. Don't even shake you wank. Or I will paint the walls with your brains."

Colin quips, "Not enough for two coats."

Fred starts to turns his head, "I'm gonna..."

Dane fires a round without blinking into the wall to the side of his head. "I told you. I won't hesitate, even for a second." There's silence for what seems like eternity. Dane rolls his eyes. "Okay. Let's move. If you say a fucking word out there, I will kill you both. Pinky swear."

Joel recognizes Colin. "You!"

Pointing to himself, "I know right?!" Tucking his gun into his pants, "I've really missed you guys. It's been so long. When was the last time we were all together? Wait, I got it. Was it Cinco de Mayo? No. Was it the day I got my first boner? Nah. It was that time you were sucking the Kool-Aid out of Richard's dick and decided it would be a good idea to hold me down while he chopped off my arm. Boy, are you going to regret that." Colin pulls out a pair of cuffs from his fanny pack, and the two monsters each place a cuff on one of their humongous wrists. "Good thing these are adjustable."

"After you." Dane waves them ahead. They lead them outside and place them into the back of a police cruiser. Patrons notice them escorting the two behemoths but this crowd just doesn't care. They fall into two groups; alcoholics and sketchy members of society that avoid police. The former is strictly concerned with pickling their livers and keeping the shakes away. The latter knows how to turn a blind eye.

As they drive, Colin may occupy the space that's the passenger seat, but he's somewhere else completely. He has a connection, albeit one he'd rather not have, with those involved the night everything was taken from him. When he's around one or in this case two of them, the normal consummation with revenge is magnified exponentially and it oozes from his pores. He can feel it emanating off him like mist from a swamp. He stares out of the window seeing that night in black and white, like it's happening in real time. As Betty is gunned down, this hollow pain centers in his chest, stealing his breath. He grits his teeth and fights off this weakness, with pinpointed rage.

They stealthily pull up to one of Richard's warehouses. Benny gave them the heads-up that the coast would be clear. The brothers are met by a few loyal guys who sit Fred and Joel down in the middle of the warehouse, encouraging them to stay put with their Mossberg shotguns. Neither has uttered a word since leaving the bar bathroom. Eventually, Fred speaks, "You realize who you're fucking with?!" His voice echoes in this cavernous warehouse.

Dane, calm as can be, replies, "You're boss should've asked himself that before he fucked with us. Before long he's going to wish he did his homework."

Joel spits violently on the ground, "Richard is going to get you for this. Payback."

"I really doubt it," Colin responds, "Besides, we have a running tab and I've been ordering all the expensive shit. SkyMall, bitches."

"How's your dead wife?" Fred's tone oozes cancer.

Colin nods with pursed lips, "You got me. That hurt."

Joel speaks with a quiver in his voice, "We were just following orders."

"Oh, really?" Colin addresses his men sarcastically, "Everybody! They were just following orders. Hey, pack all this shit up. We need to let 'em go. Someone told them to do it. Totally fine."

Dane holds a bottle of water in one hand and a big pile of pills in the other. "Freddy, take these."

Fred's voice cracks. "Is this poison?"

CHAPTER 15

"It's not poison. Scout's honor." Fred hesitates and off Dane's look one of the men pumps his shotgun. "That'll kill you quicker than these." He hands the water bottle to Joel and also a handful of pills. "I hope you aren't worried about germs." Joel takes the pills. Dane goes into a bag. He pulls out two syringes that have been conveniently prefilled by Dr. Phil and walks over to Fred.

He begins to panic like a little kid who is about to receive a flu shot for the first time. "Whoa. What's with the big needle? I hate needles. What gauge is that?" He is squirming, trying to avoid the inevitable.

"Seriously?" Dane plunges the needle into his giant arm.

Joel screams out, exasperated, "Now what?"

Colin shakes his head, "So, *The Bachelorette.* That was crazy last night, yeah? I thought she was going to pick Adrian, but she picked Ethan. Terrible. I give it two months. Ethan has had his walls up, not taking the journey seriously, and he says 'I love you' to get into the Fantasy Suite? Baller move but come on, marriage?"

Dane replies matter-of-factly, "I think they're going to make it. Ethan was there for the right reasons."

"He did show a vulnerable side." He addresses the captives, "So, fellas, you'll battle to the death and the winner walks out. Sound good?"

Fred indignantly spews profanity, "No fuckin' way."

Joel spits on the ground again and growls, "This is horseshit."

Dane chimes in, "Oh boy. You're not going to cooperate huh?" He turns to Colin, "I guess we can just shoot 'em both?"

"How close do we have to be to literally blow their heads off with one of the Mossbergs?"

"Like clear off?"

"No head. Like dating a Jewish chick."

Dane laughs, "Two feet. They have pretty big necks, but I think we can decapitate them point blank. We do have a million rounds we can just pump and dump until there's nothing left."

"That sounds awesome. It'll be like an experiment. I love science."

Fred and Joel look at each other and within a minute, they're squaring off, facing each other, prepared to kill one another. They begin by circling each other, like two animals, with their fists coiled and ready, as they each wait for an opening. They simultaneously jump in. Joel grabs at Fred's slick head as Fred lands a kidney punch that bounces off Joel like it didn't even happen. The incentive of life versus death has turned them from brothers to adversaries.

Over the next sixty seconds, there's a barrage of face punches as they each take turns smashing one another. These two men conduct, with their fists, the orchestra that's the soundtrack to this battle. Queue symbols. Queue drums. Enter horns.

Fred absorbs a wallop to the side of his head. The blow impacts his balance and his left leg buckles like a termite-infested foundation, landing him on one knee. He scans the ground, panicked, knowing full well that a similar blow will more than likely put his lights out. Joel winds up but before he can make contact and possibly render his friend unconscious, Fred clumsily grabs a pipe just within his peripheral vision. He wields this weapon of convenience and haphazardly swings it, smashing Joel in the face and shattering his nose. Joel grabs his face, also scanning the ground for a weapon. He eyes an equally brutalizing pipe and they rush each other, full force, each taking pipe blow after pipe blow. Eventually, they're both lying on the ground paralyzed with broken bones, open gashes, and bruises. They're moaning, but still alive. Queue strings, light and airy. Feel the violins' sweet squeal as friction forces melody into the air. Paganini would be proud.

"That was amazing. I would clap if I could. Guys, round of applause." Dane and all the men clap. Colin continues, "I could only imagine what Richard did to his brother, but at least I got to see this."

Dane turns to Colin, "They're really bleeding a fuck load."

"Right?! Look at all that blood. Well, fellas, let's have a good news, bad news moment. Good news, I really don't feel like killing you. Bad news is we gave you guys a shit ton of anticoagulants to prevent your blood from clotting. And those injections were way too much heparin

CHAPTER 15

which does the same thing, only faster. You guys will bleed out like a couple of inbred royals very soon. You can also insert your own tampon joke here."

Fred begins to unintentionally blow blood bubbles as his lungs fill up. He gurgles out a last, "Fuck!" The two monsters of men bleed to death.

Chapter 16

Benny has found himself at a place in life where all his dreams are nightmares. He can't remember a time when he had one of those lovely dreams where he meets the perfect girl and she loves him, or he's been given the gift of flight. Each so real he almost can't believe it didn't actually happen. At some point, life made these occurrences so few and far between that they just stopped happening. Worse than that, he can't decide which is worse: the haunting nightmares that torture his sleep or his disheartening reality upon waking. A half bottle of liquor puts him one place each night, and the other half gets him through the day.

He was somewhere in between this morning when his phone began ringing. He's not sure how many times it had rung before it actually woke him up. His dark circles look like black eyes. His greasy hair is messy and his crusty lips mark his dark sheets as he covers his head with a pillow. He lays there and can't decide whether or not to answer. The sheer volume of continuous calling motivates him to move his ass and see who desperately needs something from him. He's positive it's not someone reaching out to his benefit.

His bedroom is disgusting, with empty bottles, wrappers from food, and crushed cigarette packs and butts dropped anywhere, often a few feet from a paper grocery bag he uses as a trash can. A few nearly-full Gatorade bottles full of dark brown urine are peppered throughout the room. He moves greasy pizza boxes around, trying to find his phone. Tattered sheets cover the windows and his light fixtures lack bulbs. He'll move the last remaining bulb around his place until it finally burns out. Then he's annoyed when he has to use a flashlight to see anything after sundown. He eventually answers the phone. It's Vincent.

"Benny, I need you to come to my place immediately."

"Six calls, huh? I'm in the middle of something." Vincent has already hung up and Benny continues to talk for his own benefit. "But, I'll be right there. It must be important."

His hand shakes, clearly rattled but also in need of a drink. He grabs the bottle of Jameson he opened last night and downs the rest. "Hair of the dog." Bad guys are predators and they live nocturnally, preying on the weak. It's easier to get away with illegal endeavors in the absence of light. The cover of darkness is a criminal's best friend. Broad daylight and crime can be risky and only to be used if absolutely necessary. Vincent summoning him at this hour is undoubtedly suspicious.

Benny mumbles to himself, "Fucking Vincent. What a dick. He thinks I'm so fucking dumb I'll go to him so he can just cap me like a bitch. Fuck that." Benny formulates a plan in case he's right and shit goes pear-shaped. His plan is about as complicated as just keeping his eyes open. He isn't much of a chess player and not only lacks foresight, but doesn't learn from his bad moves in hindsight. He hops in his van, turns the key and heads over to what he thinks is his end. He has his gun and his knife that he'd rather have and not need, than need and not have, but additionally a grenade. He hides it in his inside jacket pocket. If he's going down, it's with a bang.

He turns on the radio and the station is having a contest for tickets to a concert. Benny didn't hear who is performing or where, but he heard the movie quotation and he knows the actor and the movie. If he's lucky he can take his son to see somebody, for free. He dials the number and gets a busy signal. He dials again. Busy signal again. He rinses and repeats and repeats and repeats. He tells himself if he doesn't get through in three more tries, he'll quit. Three tries become five tries and five tries become ten tries. Ten tries becomes a new three, the last three tries. Next thing he knows, he's in front of Vincent's house. He hangs up his phone and rationalizes that he didn't even know what he was trying to win. They could be for something queer and why waste luck on winning something queer? He cautiously approaches the house with his right hand in his inside pocket, finger in the grenade's pin, and his left hand on his gun. Not before long, he finds himself at the front door. It's cracked open. He shouts Vincent's name, entering cautiously, heart racing, convinced he's going to be killed. Vincent is sitting on the stairs in his robe with his head in his hands.

"What's going on? Are you okay?" Feigning concern, he sits down next to him.

Vincent begins to speak but nothing will come out. His mouth is dry, his heart is pounding and he's got that tickle in the back of throat like the first time asking a girl out.

"Vince, what is it?"

He takes a deep breath, that barely makes it mid-chest, struggling to wrangle up words. "The doctor... called... this morning."

"And?"

"I went over there. He insisted on telling me in person. I knew that wasn't a good sign."

"Telling you what?"

"I have Creutzfeld Jakob Disease."

"Fuck. What is that? You get that from a broad?"

"It's a rare, incurable brain disease. It's over."

"No antibiotics or chemotherapy? Nothing? That can't be right."

"Incurable. No medicine. Nothing. The symptoms are dementia, memory loss, hallucinations. My brain is going to turn to mush."

"There's nothing you can do?"

"Two options. Let it happen or..." Vincent gestures the throat slash.

"Fuck. That's terrible."

"I have to keep this a secret from Richard until I decide what to do. You know how he is... but I needed to tell someone."

Benny mimes zipping his lips and throwing away the key. "Your secret is safe."

CHAPTER 16

"Hey, man. I appreciate you helping me find that doctor. Even though this is the last thing I wanted to hear, knowing now is better than finding myself wandering a Whole Foods in my underwear, fucking confused. I got nobody and I got some stuff. So, I'm going to leave my stuff to Billy."

"My Billy?" Benny is dumbfounded by this gesture.

"Yeah."

"I mean, that's nice and all, but I don't get it."

"There's nothing to get. You're the only guy I work with who has a kid, maybe he can be better than us. Having money is better than not. No?"

"Of course. Yeah. Thank you."

"Let me get dressed, we need to meet Piney."

"Yeah, sure." Benny has this off-feeling in his gut. His intuition has never been a strong quality, hence him finding himself in one fucked situation after another. Yet in this rare instance, he's very suspicious of Vincent's motives. Maybe it's because he's not accustomed to generosity. It just doesn't sit right, that he'd single out his kid of all people. It's too out of character. All this thinking is giving him a headache.

Vincent yells from his bedroom. "Benny, I'll be ready in a minute."

Benny shouts back in the direction of Vincent's voice. "No rush! What do you think Piney wants?"

"He said something happened in one of the warehouses."

"No shit."

* * *

The wine cellar is magnificent. A specialist was brought in to craft the perfect room that would be both stunning and functional. The finest dark grain wood was brought in to create something out of the Renaissance where artisans slaved over every ornate detail. Throughout the years, Richard accumulated hundreds of rare bottles of wine, whiskey, and other spirits. He would open a bottle here and there on special occasions to commemorate something good. He sits here now, half thinking about having taken his own brother's life and half imagining the last moments his daughter drew breath before her flame was snuffed out. He knows the exact moment, the very punch, that escorted Jeff from living to dead. He felt it. He also felt a tiny piece of himself turn black, never to be the same again. He looks down at his bruised hands, knowing full well they should feel like throbbing, hot pain, but he feels nothing. He stumbles to his scotches and grabs the Macallan Fine and Rare 1937 given to him by a warlord for whom he brokered a massive arms deal. It was bottled in 1974 at thirty-seven years old and cost about as much as a Lexus ES. He grabs one of his crystal glasses, blows any dust he can't see out of it, and pours generously, like a few thousand bucks worth. He drinks it in one giant gulp and pours another. As he brings the glass to his lips, Piney bursts in sweating and wheezing.

He places his hands on his knees, trying to catch his breath. "You're not going to believe what happened last night."

"What the fuck are you talking about? Goddammit, how out of breath are you? I need you to be tip-top and this is fucking weak."

"I know, boss. I'll do better. The wifey has been making me wear my Fitbit and watch my diet. I didn't get like this overnight so it'll take a minute."

"Alright. I get it. But what the fuck are you carrying on about?"

"Last night, Fred and Joel beat each other to death at the warehouse off Figueroa."

"What? Like I need this shit." Richard pauses. "Call Vincent and Benny. We'll need to get rid of the bodies."

"They're en route, but the police are already there. One of those gorillas called the police before kicking off."

"Fuck!" Richard pounds his glass of whiskey and throws it against the wall, sending glass shards everywhere.

CHAPTER 16

* * *

Benny chews on his nasty cuticles and dirty nails as Vincent drives, sitting in silence for most of the car ride. He assumes Benny's awkwardness stems from the news he's terminal. He's actually still wrapping his brain around Vincent leaving Billy all his worldly possessions. He hasn't been on the receiving end of kindness, nearly ever in his life. When he was younger, innocent and maybe ignorant of life's running joke, his misery, his hopes had been elevated a handful of times. Each time he was like Charlie Brown about to kick the football, when at the last moment Lucy pulls the ball out from under him, him tripping and falling, the butt of this reoccurring cruelty.

Benny becomes aware that he may be coming off weird, and breaks the silence. "Hey, Vince, when it happens, you want me to get rid of your body or you want some sort of funeral?"

"I'm thinking cremation. No fuss, no muss."

"You think you gonna tap out or run out the clock?"

"Tap out for sure. I don't need to squeeze out bad time."

"Right on. Like a boss. I have a couple grenades if you want to just kapow!"

"Seems painful. Where'd you get a grenade?"

"Army surplus."

"Shut the fuck up. They sell live grenades to anyone?"

"It wasn't live. It's a little old but they don't go bad. I had to buy the powder online, firing pin, some other bullshit. Super easy to assemble."

"Fucking A, man. That's why Isis and al Qaeda are able to operate. No offense, but you, a criminal like me, have a few live grenades with no effort."

"Oh it's fucked, but if sand niggers are going to have an arsenal, so is this guy."

They are on the scene that's already a cluster-fuck. Marked and unmarked police cruisers surround the warehouse. Fire and EMS are also in the mix.

"Holy shit, look at this mess. Richard is not going to like this at all," Vincent remarks to Benny.

"Tell me about it. The good news is the cops don't look like they're working too hard."

"They don't give a shit about this one. To be honest, I liked both guys, but whatever. They're 'roided out hard and probably killed each other over whose one-inch dick is barely bigger."

Inside, Richard stands over the bodies with his hands on his hips, completely baffled. There is a sea of blood surrounding the two men and other than their physiques, the two slabs of meat are unrecognizable. Richard changes his position uncomfortably and scratches his head. "Jesus Christ. What's this about? These guys were like brothers, no? Steroids do this?"

Piney shrugs. "Rage is a thing with their... supplementation, so it seems plausible."

"What the fuck were they doing here, though? This makes no sense. Rage like this is not premeditated. If they got into an argument it would have happened on the spot, in the moment; fucking bar, Olive Garden, whatever, right? And how'd they get here, no cars outside?"

"Seems very dodgy."

Vincent and Benny walk in and make a beeline towards Richard. He turns to them. "Vince, what do you make of this?"

"I'm not sure. It seems completely out of left field."

Richard whispers to Vincent, "Vince, you hear from the doctor?"

"Healthy as a horse and like Ted Williams, twice as long."

Richard smiles and playfully hits his chest. He turns, noticing Detective Ferina walking into the warehouse, clearly being guided in his direction by both cops standing around and Benny.

Ferina points at Richard, "Richard Pembroke?"

Richard places his hand out, "Yes. Detective?"

Ferina aggressively grabs Richards hand like he's read in self-help books to establish dominance. "Ferina. Detective Ferina."

CHAPTER 16

"It's a shame to meet under such circumstances."

"Agreed."

Ferina kneels down and looks at the bodies. "What do we have here?"

"It seems like some sort of male bonding shenanigans gone awry. Unfortunately, both guys may have been abusing performance enhancing drugs."

Ferina smiles, "These guys? You think so?"

"I suppose that's the sorta detail a detective will pick up on at first glance."

"I've been to Gold's in Venice so I've seen some shit, and these guys are built a little too well for it to be just raw eggs and hard work alone."

"Fair enough."

"It seems open and shut."

"It does to me, too." Richard pulls out a business card. "Detective, if you come up with something else, I'd appreciate a call."

Ferina snatches the card and looks at it. "Will do. I'll have the coroner grab the bodies and I can have a clean-up crew here this afternoon."

"Thank you. I'll handle the clean-up. Save the city some money."

Ferina dials on his cell phone as he turns away.

Richard finally acknowledges Benny, "Clean this up once they move the bodies. Thanks." The 'thanks' was pinned on so curtly it sounded obnoxious.

"On it, boss!" Benny is seething inside. He gets rid of bodies and cleans crime scenes, hiding their existence. This mess is no secret and any maid can clean this up, and the police offered to handle. This is a waste of his talent and skill set. Not after long, he finds himself the only one there. The police packed up and all his coworkers have hit the road. He vacillates wildly between peeved at Richard and suspicious of Vincent. Each makes him scrub harder, nearly rubbing his own skin off through rubber gloves. Once finished, he decides to visit his ex in jail to satisfy his curiosity and potentially confirm his suspicions.

THREE GRAVES

* * *

The whiff of incarceration strikes Benny directly in his olfactory system, connecting the familiar odors with memories behind bars. It sends shivers down his spine. The concrete and metal, with banal, cheap, and easy to clean paint visually reinforces those memories. A trip to the dining hall and a spoonful of whatever slop is on the menu would be the trifecta. Fortunately, they don't offer dining privileges to visitors. He walks the long hall with his escort, unnerved that he's even there. With each step, he regrets not putting forth the effort to quell his rarely present inquisitiveness. Benny's ex-wife is naturally surprised to see him as they don't speak, let alone visit each other. Years of hard living have made her look older than her years. Missing teeth from meth or crack or both, with dark circles, distract from her sunken and overly wrinkled face that even Botox can't fix. She's a bad combination of overly thin with loose skin over her entire body that makes her look like a wax figurine placed too close to a flame. Benny can barely remember a time when she was attractive. For his own mental health, he hopes his own substance abuse didn't mask this monster making her an acceptable sexual partner. He scans the recesses of his mind searching for a visual where she may have been cute. Then he thinks, if he's right and Vincent has been with Lola, then she had to have been decent.

The guard escorts Lola, "Mrs. Arnold, you have five minutes."

"Ex-Mrs. Arnold! This guy never takes more than two minutes if you know what I mean," she smiles, looking like a Jack-O-Lantern. She sits down and picks up the phone receiver. "What are you doing here?" She asks with disdain.

"That's a lot of attitude. Good thing you have plenty of real estate in that mouth. Dentist is British?"

"Ha-fucking-ha."

"You look well rested."

"Fuck you."

CHAPTER 16

"Don't be mad, you know I'd give you blood...to watch you bleed."

"What do you want?"

"Time travel to be real."

"Benny, you're the worst thing that has ever happened to me."

"I think the same thing about you. You going to ask about your kid or talk about yourself more?"

"How's Billy?" Lola looks down, embarrassed.

"Billy's fine. He misses you. I tell him, 'wait until you really know her before you put that out there.'"

"Nice. You're such a dick."

"Well, you're a piece of shit. He doesn't remember you placing him under a laundry basket with heavy shit on top while you go score."

"I have a disease." She's dead serious.

"Just one?" Benny rolls his eyes.

"You could have brought him."

Benny snickers, "The way you look, he'd lose his lunch if it ever crosses his mind that he sucked your tit for all those months."

Lola is fed up with this visit. "Why are you here?"

"Did you ever fuck Vincent?" Benny looks her right in the eyes.

Contorting her face, partially sincere, mostly stalling. "Vincent who?"

"Vincent, I work with." Benny leans in.

"Why?" Both her hands up questioning.

"Is he Billy's dad?"

Lola looks down again.

Benny slams the table. "Answer me!"

Lola shrugs her shoulders. "Maybe."

Benny mocks her shrug. "Maybe? He may have entered your cooze with his love nob, but you're not sure? Because he's so small or you're so stretched out? And no condom?" He shakes his head at his own statement, "Never mind the last question, I forgot who I'm talking to for a second."

Lola stands up, getting aggressive, "Fuck you. He traded me drugs for sex. And we sure as shit never had any money, so I used whatever currency I had."

The guard takes a step forward, Lola settles down and sits.

Benny presses his lips together tightly, his expression cold yet calm, like a corpse in a coffin. He stands slowly, processing his emotions, turning his back even slower. Suddenly the volume is turned down all the way like a muted television. He doesn't hear the buzzing of fluorescent lights flickering on their last legs, the chatter of other visitors, hard footsteps on a harder floor, and especially whatever Lola is saying to keep him from walking out.

His own lack of intelligence is fucking with him as he can't decide whether he's happy he knows the truth, erasing the ambivalence of Vincent's undoing, or he's sad the one thing he was proud of in his life isn't his to be proud of. By the time he exits the building, this calm comes over him, the sunlight hits his face and a pseudo-euphoric feeling enters his body. He attributes it to there being no better feeling than walking out of a prison. It's more likely the truth that no one wants to lose, but once its lost, there's a small window of relief before the loss is registered and the pressure of winning is no longer relevant. There's a satisfaction to being helpless in this particular instance, but that too passes being replaced with whatever damage the loss incurred.

* * *

Dane sits with his feet up on his desk, on his phone. He's killing time at the police station, with his ear to the ground. So much has been going on with the plan and all the moving parts, just knowing how to not get caught won't protect against a fluke witness in the wrong place at the wrong time. Or new video surveillance. Or a rogue fingerprint from taking a glove off to scratch an itch. A group of uniformed guys walk by, one of the guys speaks to Dane, "Yo, D, you want to come to Silver Reign? My next ex-wife, Candy, is dancing."

Dane whips his feet down, sits up, and gently tosses his phone on

CHAPTER 16

his desk, "Strip Club? Nah, not for me. Titty bars are like feeding dogs peanut butter. They think they're happy but they're mostly frustrated."

The group laughs, and continues out.

Dane's phone rings and he answers it. "Hey. Good. Not a peep. Wait. Call you back." Dane sees Ferina off in the distance, walking his way.

Ferina is walking like he just had the most satisfying bowel movement, floating on cloud nine, with a shit-eating grin. He beelines to Dane and antagonizes him. "What a good fucking day. God has got my back."

Dane raises an eyebrow. "Totally. With that face, he owes you one."

Ferina mocks laughter, "You were up next on the board, but MIA so I caught a double today and closed the case."

Dane nods his head, "The two guys that killed each other? Good police work. I'm pretty sure Scotland Yard called to pick your brain on the Jack the Ripper case."

Ferina's getting pissy, "You're just jealous because you weren't here. Where were you?"

Dane raises his eyebrows. "That's private. Between me and your wife."

"Real funny. What are you, like twelve?"

"Don't worry, she climaxed like six times. I know you don't take her to 'O Town', so she's good for now. You're welcome."

Ferina can't think of a response. Several police officers have gathered around to hear Dane rib Ferina. Dane continues, "Those pilates classes... money well spent, she looks great, and is very bendy. Sorry about the lamp though, we were trying some Cirque du Soleil shit and she slipped."

Ferina turns bright red. He lunges at Dane, but alas, all the police officers gathered in the area hold him back, protecting Dane like he's their king.

Dane quips as he exits, "Let me know if you want me to play catch with the kids. I don't want any of my boys throwing like sissies."

The police officers holding Ferina back release him once Dane is out of sight. Ferina pulls Richard's card out of his pocket. He repeatedly turns it over and over, staring into space. "Fuck it." He violently whips out his phone and dials.

* * *

Ferina stands outside Richard's compound, with his arms out, two armed guards frisking him. They take his service weapon and he reaches down to his ankle holster grabbing his back-up piece. "I have a can opener on my key-chain, you want that too?"

Only one of the guards acknowledges the remark, and barely. "Follow me." They walk him into the house and sit him outside Richard's office. Uneasy about his motives here as well as the intense nature of being cleared to enter, Ferina takes a deep breath and leans back. He begins to take in his surroundings and really looks around. As the second hand advances ever so slightly, conversely his impression increases exponentially. The piano he can see off in the distance, a Victorian-style Steinway from the early 1900s, is a work of art. The various paintings tastefully scattered about are museum quality and maybe one or two were confiscated by the Nazis during WWII and found their way here via dark channels. Even the functional furniture doesn't look like any Ferina has ever seen at a store or online. He smirks, "Fucking guy lives like a king." He pulls out his phone, a minute ago in awe, now just bitter that his Ikea furniture looks like some middle-aged cop hastily put it together on a day off after a hellish day in the Swedish superstore. He looks on Facebook to kill time, and tells himself if his wife's sister posts one more 'love yourself' post, he's blocking her from his feed.

Vincent exits Richards office with apparatus. "Detective. Stand up."

"This again," Ferina rolls his eyes and holds his arms out.

Vincent waving the apparatus head to toe, is sweeping him for bugs and recording devices. He places his hand out, "Phone, please."

CHAPTER 16

Ferina hands it over, "No long distance calls."

Vincent places the phone in his own pocket, "Okay, follow me." He opens the door and escorts Ferina into Richard's office, pointing to one of two seats across from Richard who is wrapping up a phone call. He hangs up after ten seconds of a cryptic conversation. "My apologies, Detective, I hope I didn't keep you waiting too long."

"Nah. Besides the place is very visually stimulating."

"Thank you. Has there been more developments in the crazy case at my warehouse?"

"No. That case is considered closed. They clearly killed each other. Unfortunately, when everyone involved is dead, we don't really focus on the 'why.'"

Richard leans back, now curious why this detective is here if not for official police business as far as he can tell. "What can I do for you, Detective?"

Ferina can't help but sound a bit insulted. His pride jumps the gun, even though he does want something. "I'm not going to jerk you off."

"Good. Because I haven't had a hand job in over thirty years, and I find them about as exciting as making out with my sister."

Ferina leans back, folding his hands as he speaks. "Not to come off as a dick, but I know you're a criminal. Everybody does, but good luck getting anything to stick. I'm not judging you. I look around this place and I wonder what wrong turn did I take? I have this cocksucker that I need taken out. Fucking killed. I can't deal with him anymore."

"Let me guess, some low-life got away with something vile, and since the criminal justice system is a shit show, you want to go all vigilante and wipe him out."

"Not exactly. I want you take out a colleague of mine. Dane Graves. Detective Dane Graves."

"Detective? Well, I didn't expect that at all." He leans back and whispers to Vincent, "Why does that name sound familiar?"

Vincent whispers back, "Colin Graves' brother."

Richard continues the whisper-fest, "No shit." He exhales deeply and directs his next comment right into Ferina's pupils. "Sorry. No can do."

Ferina is shocked. "What? Why not? Do you recommend someone else I can use?"

"Do I look like Yelp? And no. In fact, I'm advising you to cease this vendetta or face consequences."

This is the last thing Ferina anticipated. "Mr. Pembroke. I could understand your declining but let me contract this out elsewhere."

Richard becomes overly stern, like Ferina is his responsibility. "He's not to be touched. If I find out that he is, your wife and kids will need a mortician. I promise you that. Stay on your side of the law." Richard points towards the door, "Good day."

Ferina stands up, "Okay. Okay. I got it. I swear on my family, I won't do anything."

"That's more like it."

Ferina places out his hand, "Let's just pretend this never happened, okay?"

Richard shakes his hand, "Absolutely, and thank you for handling the warehouse situation so promptly and discreetly."

Ferina walks out.

Richard nods to Vincent, "That family has gone through hell. It's the least I could do, yeah?"

Vincent non-verbally agrees with the gesture.

Chapter 17

Colin sits in a practically empty diner at nearly midnight, now fully bearded wearing his sunglasses and a flat cap hat. He looks at his watch, a Rolex Submariner. The string of bells on the door rings and Deputy Commissioner Alvarez walks in, dressed incognito in street clothes. He notices that the only people working are an elderly waitress and a couple of Mexican cooks in the back. He scurries to Colin's table and shuffles into the booth. "Col, how's it going?"

"Besides this itchy as hell beard that keeps reminding me what I ate the day before, I'm in deep, like up in a bitches' guts deep." Alvarez shakes his head. Colin continues, "That was probably a little graphic, I've been hanging twenty-four-seven with idiots and it's seeping into my brain like BPA."

"I've been there." Alvarez changes the subject, "Have you seen Wally? He's been MIA for nearly six weeks."

"Not since the intro. Do you think he went back to college?"

Alvarez thinks about it. "He's either in the wind or the gang got him?"

Colin takes a sip from his beer, a Pabst Blue Ribbon in a can, "He is a genius, so being in wind with an immunity deal sounds about right, but Georgie can't get a hold of him either."

"Do I need to pull you out? If Georgie is suspicious of Wally, it could spill onto you."

"No way. I got Georgie wrapped around my finger. He'll carry my books to class like I'm the prettiest girl in school, and not only do I not have to give it up, I can fuck all his friends."

"Good. Well, truthfully, we hated making a deal with Wally so either way, if we never see him again, he did his part and you're in." Alvarez notices his watch, "Rolex?"

Colin holds his watch up, "This old thing? A bunch of loot came in from a lame smash and grab last week. This was a present. If I don't wear it, I look like a dick. And it goes with everything."

"This all seems as good as we expected."

"Better. You could never get Big Georgie because he was smart as hell. This guy is full-on retard. Actually, retards roll their eyes around this guy. And he's crazy. He'll fly off the handle if his orange chicken doesn't have bell peppers. He shot his own dog yesterday because of John Wick." Alvarez makes an 'I don't follow face,' and Colin continues, "Because he didn't want his enemies to be able to get to him through his dog."

"Jesus Christ."

"This guy is going to single-handedly undo everything his father built and he'll flip on everyone faster than Mary Lou Retton after freebasing a box of Wheaties."

"Good work. Keep at it and we'll meet in a couple weeks."

Colin holds up his wrist, "You want one of these? I can make it happen."

Alvarez smiles, shaking his head 'no.' He shows him his own Rolex, gets up and walks out. Colin waits a second and follows suit.

He walks home to his undercover apartment. As he approaches, he senses someone behind him, and turns quickly pulling his gun. "Jesus Christ, Dane!" He puts his gun away, "I'm deep UC, you'll get me killed or worse, kicked out of my criminal fantasy football league." Dane moves under a street light, and Colin can see his face is a mess, bruises and cuts, like he's been tuned up. "Did you cut yourself shaving?"

"I know I'm not supposed to reach out when you're under but..." He collapses; Colin gets him upstairs and on his couch. Colin gets an ice pack situated with loose ice from his freezer, a plastic grocery bag, and

CHAPTER 17

a towel. Dane holds the cold compress to his face, wincing as he talks, "Boris Amalov."

"Boris Amalov, huh? That's probably one of the worst things I've heard today. And apparently the baby panda at the zoo died this morning."

"Bai Sheng?"

"Yes, Bai Sheng, got electrocuted or something terrible. Amalov?"

"I'm into him for some cash."

"You did not gamble with fucking Amalov, that's too fucking stupid. New Coke stupid. The Russian mob is crazy enough, but that heaping pile of evil is a cannibal... yes he fucking eats people, and the Russians hate him because he's married to an Armenian witch."

"I've done some dumb things recently. Jess is gone."

"Jess? Your wife? The smartest, coolest, prettiest girl around? Well, besides my Betty. What in the ass did you do?"

"You know, there was this girl."

"Oh my God, my brother is a less talented Tiger Woods." Colin shakes it off, "One problem at a time. How much you owe Amalov?"

"$200 K."

"Wow. I was not expecting it to be that high. Amazing. You're clearly shitty at games of chance. You know even if you pay him, he owns you now. He's fucking crazy and will make you do things for him as a detective. Once you're into him, there is no getting out. It's like trying to cancel the gym."

"I don't know what to do."

Colin thinks. "Okay, you've been around him a bit, right? Tons of cash lying around yeah?"

"Tons. My 200K is a drop."

"Good. I have a plan. It'll take some finesse, but I'll get you out of this."

* * *

Dane smiles, "She's into you. No doubt."

"I think I'd be more flattered if 'us' being a thing wasn't statutory rape."

Dane shrugs, "She's barely a minor. R. Kelly married Aaliyah when she was fifteen."

"That's the first time someone used R. Kelly behavior to strengthen their argument. He tends to be in the 'what not to do' category; like don't urinate on your underage sexual partner or intentionally give someone a sexually transmitted disease."

"Well, we kidnapped her and are holding her against her will and by the time this is over, we'll have some murders under our belt... pretending to be into a minor is not something to worry about."

"If she's even into me. She may be one of those gals who exclusively likes douche bags. Versus a gal that needs douche bags. Hashtag feminine hygiene."

"Trust me. I'm never wrong when it comes to this type of shit."

Colin and Dane decide to call an audible. Not unlike the quarterback who changes the play on the fly at the line of scrimmage when he sees how the defense lined up, the brothers didn't anticipate Alissa's crush on Colin. With each interaction she's more comfortable and clearly enjoys when he checks in on her. He's charming and clever, and because his pre-frontal cortex is fully developed and hers is not, he's more capable of acting rational while she's susceptible to beguilement. Changing up the plan is always risky but may yield the greatest reward.

Colin enters Alissa's room, holding a big bag from In-N- Out. She's watching television, petting Charlie, who is turning out to be a nice prop. Alissa mutes the television and Charlie's tail begins to wag. "Whatcha got there?"

"Bowling ball." Colin smiles, "Double-double animal style with your name on it. And fries well done."

"No way! That's my order. How'd you know?"

"I went to a psychic. The Amazing Marie. I figured it was easier than asking you and I got to speak to George Washington for a couple

CHAPTER 17

minutes. Between you and me, he was sorta racist. And it only cost a hundred bucks." She laughs, he continues, "And it happens to be my order so..." She posts her food on Instagram.

"Are you going to have some too?" She moves over to make space so he can sit next to her.

"No, I got two double doubles and two fries for a gal that's maybe 105 pounds."

"You're a pain in the ass, aren't you?"

"From a purely protological standpoint, no, but otherwise, yes." Colin sits and they begin eating, "You lived out here your whole life; you over actors and musicians, famous people?"

Alissa thinks, "Yeah, after a while it's like who cares? But me and my friends bumped into Ryan Gosling. And he is super cute and super cool. He took a picture with us."

"Oh, he is dreamy. Between his stint in *The Mickey Mouse Club* and *Young Hercules*." He fans his face and pulls out a Southern belle accent, "I do declare." He clears his throat, "So no Beiber for you?"

"Ugh, no. That guys sucks."

"Thank you!" Colin places his hand up, she gives him a high five, "He reminds me of this lesbian I went to high school with."

"I also cannot stand Kanye."

"I get it. It's because you hate black people."

Alissa nearly chokes on her food and playfully hits him, "No I don't! That's awful."

"No, I can tell."

"That's horrible."

"Was it you that was telling me you're the prettiest girl in your class?"

Alissa responds, embarrassed, "I would never..."

"No, I recall you bragging about how attractive you are. I was a little put off, I'm like 'this gal is really into herself.'"

"Oh boy."

"I'm sure you look like your mother."

"I might. My father doesn't let me look at pictures of her and she's slowly fading from my memory. I can still kinda picture her, but not so much."

Colin shifts gears, "I get it. It hasn't been that long and I'm having trouble picturing someone I recently lost. It's like I saw her every day and my brain was like 'you'll see her tomorrow', so I'm not going to put the effort into remembering. Then one day, it's like all I can see is this blurry version of her."

"No. I know. Me too."

"So, your dad... well, he's a cancerous growth on the planet's anus, so..."

She interjects but cannot finish, "Wha..." She gets choked up.

Colin places his hand on her shoulder, "You're a smart girl and have to know, somewhere deep down, he's awful and needs to be removed."

She begins to panic, "Are you going to kill him?"

"Actually, I was thinking tickle fight, but that's a good suggestion."

"Is what you told us in the studio true?"

"Yes. Absolutely. All the *Golden Girls* were in porn... after the show was canceled. It's horrifyingly erotic." Alissa rolls her eyes, and Colin continues, "Yes. He killed my wife and chopped off my arm, because he thought I was someone else. He's lost his mind. He killed your Uncle Jeff."

"What? When? Why?" Alissa thinks for a second. "Did it have to do with what I said in the audition?"

"Absolutely not. He's crazy and always has been." Colin pulls out the police file on Alissa's mother and he hands it to her. "He killed your mother, Laura. He shot her and left her in a trunk at the airport."

Alissa shakes her head and starts to lose it. "No, she died in a car accident."

"From a very skewed point of view, being shot in the trunk of a car is a car accident."

Alissa opens the folder, on top is a picture of her mother, with lifeless eyes and a bullet hole through her head. She begins to cry, throws her

CHAPTER 17

arms around him and buries her face in his chest. He kisses the top of her head then tucks her into the bed and places Charlie under her arm.

He locks the door behind him and walks up the stairs towards his bathroom. At the top of the stairs, his breathing is labored and he feels like he's having a heart attack. His head is spinning and he's broken into a cold sweat. The simple act of walking on an incline has placed a stress on his cardiovascular system to the point of full body fatigue. Everything that's been numbing his pain is rotting his insides. He needs to be sharp to win this battle, and he's losing his edge. He flushes all painkillers down the toilet. He dumps all of the booze down the drain. He takes the clothes hanging off his treadmill and dusts that bad boy off. He walks at a pretty good clip, careful not to burn himself out. He calls Dane and asks for a ride to physical therapy.

* * *

Colin doesn't want to bump into crazy John, the long-distance runner, or any other nuts for that matter. He sneaks in, scanning the area so he's prepared to get away from anyone he'd prefer not converse with. He's so focused on not getting trapped that he turns around, nearly knocking over a sixty-year-old lady standing in his blind spot. She is thin, very pale, with long straight brown hair, but gray roots. "Excuse me. I didn't see you there."

"No worries. My name is Margaret, what's yours?"

He frantically looks in the direction of the front door, like a little kid dropped off the first day of school, and sees Dane pull away. "Fuck." He collects himself and turns to Margaret, "Mags, nice to meet you, my name is Pablo... Escobar."

"Pleasure, Pablo. I just got my hair cut. Same guy that cuts Eddie Van Halen's hair. I used to be into the whole rock and roll scene, really into coke and stuff. I almost had sex with Jimmy Page."

"Sorry, Mags. Almost is for horseshoes and hand grenades."

"Lately I've been disabled by parasites."

"Disabled? Really?" He looks at his missing arm. "What's that like?"

She's gravely serious as she speaks. "It's terrible. Tiny microorganisms that live in my system have made it difficult for me to do almost everything."

"I know, right, like tie your shoes, cut an apple, mime being trapped in an invisible box."

"I was in bed for a month after my last detox."

"Detox? Now you're speaking my language. Codeine? You hooked on that purple drank, Mags? And a real month, or like February?"

"No, a health cleanse. Lemon cleanse. Apple cider vinegar."

"Bummer, I was just beginning to think we were going to click. Sid and Nancy style."

She just continues, ignoring his comment, "I was detoxifying my system. I killed the parasites too quickly for my body to get rid of them through my colon. The colonics helped but I'd get sores all over my body as the dead parasites were being expelled through my pores."

"Yikes. I have to say, I don't enjoy the feeling of have stuff funneled up my ass... even warm water." She's wearing rubber gloves. "Nice gloves. Isotoner?"

"Thanks. No, these are nitrile glove, I have a latex allergy."

"You're killing me, Mags. No latex," whispering, "How are we going to practice safe s-e-x? We can go raw dog, but I wouldn't want to slip one past the goalie."

"Oh I've gone through menopause. I can't have children."

"Well, my day's looking up."

"I've been wearing the wrong bras my entire life."

"I've been wearing the wrong heart on my sleeve."

"I finally went and was fitted properly by these specialists showcased on Oprah back in the day."

"Oprah and I had a thing. Every day at 1pm."

"You ever eat at Ave?"

He shakes his head as he answers, "No, but I met a hipster mixologist

CHAPTER 17

that works there. Bitchin' facial hair, loves wearing suit vests with T-shirts."

She gets a possessed look in her eye as she continues, "They have the best Bananas Foster."

"Underrated dessert. Like the Topher Grace of desserts."

"You have to bring your own bananas though."

"Of course you do. Duh."

"The bananas they use are too ripe."

"And let's face it, restaurant bananas are used by drunken employees as dildos. I saw a whole thing on 20-20."

"I didn't see that one."

"Well, Mags, this has been great, but I need to get to work. This PT isn't going to do itself."

"The therapist sent me over to get you. We're grouped up with Bob over there. Follow me." Bob limps over to meet them halfway. He has big, capped teeth and crazy eyes. Bob invades Colin's personal space and nods in his direction, as he has no arms.

"Bobby, what the fuck? No arms? I thought I had it rough. You born this lucky or just end up being this lucky?"

He begins to speak with a minor stutter. "I worked for the electric company. Some birds were harassing me while I was fixing a box and lost my concentration. I ended up being electrocuted so badly I needed my arms amputated. The shock traveled down my spine. Along the way, it fried the nerve bundles in my pelvis. I'll never be able to feel my toes again. Even today I wake up all mixed up. How about you? What's your deal?"

"Holy shit. Me? Very run of the mill, a drug lord mistook me for a rival. He executed my wife and chopped my arm off with an axe." Bob just blinks.

Joyce, the therapist comes over to them. She has a young face and petite stature. She points to the ground as she speaks condescendingly. "Colin, we're going to start off with some stretching, so have a seat on the floor."

Colin feigns meekness, "This floor, now? Stretchy?"

Joyce nods, "Yes."

"I like stretchy. I feel it in my wiener."

Joyce tells them all to touch their toes. Bob just points his chin in the direction of his feet.

Margaret turns to Colin, "My brother died of SIDS when I was three. I don't remember him because my parents didn't take any pictures because they didn't think he was going to die."

And touch the left foot.

Margaret continues, "When my parents died, my sister and I were supposed to split everything into equal shares. However, my sister convinced my mother as she lay dying to split the inheritance among the grandchildren. My sister had five children to my one. It's not my fault she couldn't keep her legs closed."

And touch the right foot.

Margaret carries on without stopping for breath, "I was struck with chronic fatigue syndrome and against my better judgment hired my niece to run my pillow business for me. I make pillows that say funny things, like, 'I had to get rid of the kids, the dog was allergic.' So, my niece embezzled a boatload of money by not paying taxes for five years. She skipped town and moved into a house owned by my sister and myself."

Down to the middle.

"My sister was supposed to rent the place out, but my niece was staying there practically for free. My niece's husband was cheating on my niece with her best friend. My niece was cheating on her husband with her husband's twin brother."

Do not bounce when stretching; steady pressure.

Colin shakes off this harangue like a dog that fell off the bed trying to lick his own balls. He struggles to get to his feet in an attempt to flee. Joyce, instead of helping him up, helps him back down. "Hold on Colin, you need to do some band work with your legs."

"Bathroom?" He's clearly unconvincing.

CHAPTER 17

Her tone ascends to a new condescending level. "The session is going to be over in a few minutes, it would be good for you to try and hold it." Joyce even adds the little affirmative head nod as she speaks to him. Joyce goes over to help Margaret, and Bob wiggles over to Colin.

Bob speaks, out of breath from the effort. "I bet it was a shock when you lost your arm?"

Colin makes a questioning face, "Really? Pun?"

Bob seems oblivious, "I mean, I was shocked. It took me a long time to take charge of my life. I needed something to jolt me back to reality. I started singing as my outlet."

"Are you doing that on purpose?"

"What?"

"Never mind, I need to bolt." Colin walks outside.

Dane is waiting in front of the building and opens the door for him. "Col, how'd it go?"

"It was like getting your dick stuck in your zipper, mostly horrible with some confused arousal."

"It couldn't have been that bad."

Colins shoots him a look and Dane switches gears, "We're going to the laundromat from here. Benny is there now and our guy is there as we speak."

It hasn't been that long since Colin dumped out all his pills, so he's just about at the cusp of the withdrawal window, merely feeling just a little off. He senses the storm coming, though. His temperature is askew. His heart rate has been fluctuating for no reason. His temples are throbbing. However, he's going to lie to Dane and tell him he's good to go, because he wants this guy.

Dane parks in the back alley outside the laundromat, "Alright, I'll call Benny in a minute, he's sussing out the situation. I'll get the ball rolling, clear the room, then you come in?"

"So you have all the fun?"

Dane smiles, "That's sorta how I operate. Let's get ready." He gets out of the car and goes to the trunk.

Colin reaches for the door handle. Seeing double, he flubs, and rests his sweaty head against the window. Aware that in his state this could cause problems, he feebly finds the handle, opens the door and wobbles out. He places his hand in between the car door and the car, using his body to shut the door on his hand. He discreetly yelps. Dane getting weapons ready in the trunk hears him and runs over.

"Hey, what happened?"

Colin gasps, "Little help."

Dane unlatches the door, "Jesus Christ, are you okay?"

Colin is barely able to speak, "I'm good, I don't think its broken, I've been drinking my milk."

Dane goes into the trunk and grabs the first aid kit. "I think we need to call this and go home."

"No way, wrap it up, my trigger finger is fine. Besides, I'm back-up, you're clearing the room."

Dane is shaking his head. "You sure?"

"Absolutely, I actually feel great right now." He intentionally shut his hand in the door. The brain has a gating mechanism for pain, registering the most severe and blocking out the rest. The oncoming detox symptoms will take a backseat for now and he'll use pain to organize his endorphins. And for now, when he feels it coming on, he'll just bang his hand against something hard.

Chapter 18

Drug dealers can be as shrewd as any auspicious legitimate businessmen. Richard owns tremendous amounts of property and has many businesses that operate fully within the law. Benny is milling around one of Richard's fronts; a laundromat. Richard not only accounts for the cash he receives, he accounts for a percentage of his drug money. This is a classic laundering technique. Dirty clothes in, clean clothes out, same with his cash. Benny pretends to do some laundry and makes his way to the back to do some recon.

The back is an alternate universe compared to the front. If they weren't connected and enclosed by the same four walls, it would be easy to think it's two different places. The front of the laundromat has a couple of old ladies and illegals that fold clothes and chat with the customers. They all know it's in their best interests to mind their own business. Richard pays them well and they know it.

However, in the back, there's a superabundance of illegal activities occurring day in and day out. Drugs are being measured, bills are being counted, weapons are in plain sight, and some of the hired guns are hanging out playing cards. At any given time, there can be as many as a half dozen henchmen taking care of these activities and watching the place. This area is relatively soundproof, with thick cement walls and other noise dampening materials as this has been a scene of violence on many occasions. Petey was on the guest list the night Betty was killed. His curly hair and long, thin face gives him a distinctive look. He keeps an axe in his car because he thinks it's bad ass. Richard knew about Petey's proclivity for this prop, because he'd bust his chops from time to time. So he was quite aware that if he ever needed an axe, Petey had one.

Benny enters the back of the place and nobody flinches. Only people who should be there walk through the doors. He interrupts Petey who is talking to Lil' Mike, one of Richard's lower-end guys, who appears much younger with his dead straight hair and chiseled face. Benny decides to interject, "How you guys doing? You know after Monday and Tuesday, even the week says W.T.F. Am I right?"

Nobody really acknowledges him except for Petey who considers Benny good for a laugh. "Benny, what'ya doing here?" He turns to Lil' Mike, "You call for a clean-up?" No one answers his rhetorical question. "If you want, I can take a shit on the floor and you can clean that up."

"Petey, I had this crazy dream last night that you died. What do you think that means?"

Petey loses a little color from his face but plays it off. "I ain't gonna die, me and Timmy are going to pick up some hooker snatch from here. If I'm gonna die, it's gonna be from fuckin'. And there ain't no better way to go."

Benny's cell phone rings and Dane is on the other side of the line. He pretends he's talking to Billy for the peanut gallery. "Hey, champ. I'm doing a wash. Yeah, Uncle Petey is here. So are five of daddy's friends. I know you don't feel good. I'll check the wash right now. It should be done." Benny hangs up.

Petey can't keep his mouth shut. "You're one poor excuse for a human being. If you were my dad, I'd kill myself."

Benny ignores him. "See ya, fellas. Pete, we're the same age. How could I be your dad?" He walks to the front of the building to get his laundry.

Petey laughs at the ribbing he aimed at Benny and the other guys join in. Within minutes of Benny leaving for the front, the back door flies open. Dane enters with a shotgun and he pulls the trigger in the direction of the first of five guys he aims to kill. This unlucky, soon-

CHAPTER 18

to-be-stiff, with his bleach blond hair and slight build doesn't even have time to stand. The propulsion from the blast throws him into the back wall, spraying it with his blood.

The noise from the washers and dryers in the front, combined with the dampened acoustics of the back, muffle the sound completely. Benny stands there chit-chatting with the help; knowing full well what's going on a few feet away, in complete disbelief that it's undetectable by the human ear.

Dane points his weapon at the second guy who sports hipster looks and a gawky build. He catches a tight pattern of buck in his face, practically tearing it off. By this time, most of the henchmen have stood up and Petey reaches for his weapon on the table. Dane sees this, as Petey is the focus of this massacre. Firing into Petey's hand accomplishes two things: he neutralizes him as a threat and Petey passes out. Dane will worry about him when the room is cleared.

Dane pumps the shotgun and fires into possibly Richard's only Indian henchman, whose thick black hair and dark eyebrows supports the stereotype. He was retained for his mathematical prowess and tends to mostly bookkeep. Three down, two to go.

The fourth guy, exuding British formality and arrogance, gets a shot off, winging Dane's shoulder. He'll be spending eternity wishing he had better aim because Dane didn't even panic. He simply returned the favor, shooting this posh tosser in the testicles. He flies to the ground holding his junk, bellowing in agony. Lil' Mike took cover immediately and he now uses this opportunity to stand, while Dane's focus is on the newly falsetto on the ground. Lil' Mike hesitates for one second.

Colin enters, hand bandaged, to see this coward about to shoot his brother in the back and places a bullet between his eyes. Dane fires two times into the wounded man on the ground, putting him down for good. He turns to his brother and non-verbally thanks him for having his back. Dane walks over to Petey and drags him out of the building by his hair. Petey slides on the smooth floor, but once his almost lifeless body gets to the door the friction force increases, leaving Dane with a fistful of hair. The ripping out of his hair rouses him; he's utterly confused, unaware of his current location. Dane grabs him by the collar and violently drags him to the dumpster outside of the building.

Colin hustles to the car to get the duct tape. He's light headed and pauses for a second before reaching into the car. He's breaking out in a cold sweat. His vision is blurry and he could easily puke. There's a knot in his esophagus. He takes a deep breath and lightly smacks his hand against the car, sending pain signals to his brain. His brain registers the pain, placing his withdrawal temporarily in the backseat. He grabs the tape, makes his way back, and hands it to Dane. Tearing tape is tough with two arms. With one arm, Colin has a better chance of tearing a hole in the space-time continuum. Dane tapes Petey's hands, feet, and mouth.

Dane grabs Petey's keys from his pocket and hands them to Colin who presses the lock button and a car directly behind them chirps. Colin walks over to it and pops the trunk, spotting the axe immediately. He wields it, choking up on the grip, sinking the blade into the center of Petey's chest. The tape muffles his screams. Dane picks him up and throws him into the dumpster. Colin grabs a gas can from their trunk, pouring it all over Petey. Dane goes into the laundromat with an empty duffel bag. Colin lights a dollar bill, dropping the burning currency on Petey's accelerant-covered body. The flames rapidly spread. Dane comes out with a full bag of contraband. They smell Petey burning as they walk towards the car.

* * *

Dane drops Colin off at home, then doubles back to the crime scene to play cop. Colin looks like shit. His face is pale, his eyes are red, and he looks green. He's both cold and sweaty. He'd give his left nut for one of the pills he flushed down the toilet. He rifles through his medicine cabinet like a junkie, but he can't find anything stronger than aspirin. He throws the bottle down, frustrated, and pulls out his phone. He spastically paces around his house trying to rationalize procuring narcotics. He has Dr. Phil on speed dial and with every chain pharmacy practically within walking distance he has access to a party at the touch of a button. As he's about to press the call button he looks up at the monitor.

Alissa is watching television with Charlie on her lap. He decides to work on her as a distraction to his withdrawal. Getting her on board to do what he needs will exponentially magnify Richard destruction. Upon entering, both girls jump up and run over to Colin. Alissa runs over and gives him a big hug. Then she notices his pale hue. Alissa is concerned, "Colin, are you alright?"

"I'll never be fluent in sign language. So that sucks."

She playfully hits him, "I mean it, you look sick." She notices his bandaged hand, "And what happened to your hand?"

"Sick like, 'that outfit is sick' or like, 'you look diseased?'"

"The latter. And your hand?"

"Shut it in the car door. I was taking painkillers like tic-tacs. I stopped cold turkey. I'm in that fun little withdrawal stage. It's like every symptom you can have and its antithesis at the same time. I'm excessively hungry but have no appetite, congested yet my nose is runny. I'm a walking paradox. Like Kim Kardashian. Completely untalented, doesn't do anything, but gets paid a shit ton for just being her." He catches his breath. "Withdrawal is like gravity. I get it but I'd need Bill Nye to really explain it to me. Bottom line, my brain wants the yummy-yum-yums and is making me feel as horrendous as possible until I cave in. Little does my brain know, I refuse to negotiate with terrorists. Or the cable company."

Alissa hugs him. Colin has her under his spell. Some people gravitate towards those they feel they can fix. "I'll help you. I can do it. One of my friends got hooked on heroine and I helped her get through it."

They spend the next two hours in the bathroom. She sits there and keeps him company while he violently vomits. Then his eyes started tearing like his pipes froze, exploded, and then thawed. She started to tell him everything about her. She told him about her favorite birthday party when she was a kid. She always wanted a brother or a sister. Then Colin got the runny nose from hell. Alissa didn't care. She just distracted him with conversation. She never learned to ride a bike; her first concert. She misses her dog. She went to Disney World when she was eight. Then the sweating and nausea escalated, and massive goose bumps covered his body. He sat there stunned by her constant chatter without breathing. In between throwing up, they leaned against the wall, and she leaned against his shoulder. He held her hand and he told her embarrassing stories to make her laugh. She'll grow up quick, at least after all the dust settles, and never be the same and doesn't even realize it.

* * *

"What the fuck?" Richard pulls up to the laundromat in one of his Mercedes Benz. The scene is a massive shit show with law enforcement everywhere and police tape liberally roping off the entire surrounding area. The neighboring businesses, mostly strip mall nail salons, ethnic food, or massage places are not thrilled with the disruptive police presence. Tons of lookie-loos gather, pointing their phones at the scene trying to get footage of something gruesome. Timmy is sitting in the back of an ambulance with a blanket over his shoulders and his face is covered with soot. His eyes are red and he's been crying. Richard walks over to him as he asks the EMT for some oxygen. He questions Timmy as he hyperventilates. "What the fuck happened?"

Timmy speaks through the oxygen mask, taking huge hits periodically. "Uncle Rich, I don't know. I was waiting for Petey. After he was done, we were going to party."

Richard is getting impatient, "Okay. Cut to what the fuck happened."

"I was in the bathroom taking a shit and I'm in there not ten minutes when I hear the first shot, and nearly get hit through the wall with a bullet. It scared me half to death. I was almost killed."

CHAPTER 18

Richard shrugs his shoulders. "Then what?"

Timmy takes a huge hit of oxygen. "I laid on the ground and covered my head with my hands and waited until it was quiet for like twenty minutes."

"You didn't join in? Try and help our people?"

"No way, man. I left my gun on the table out there. Who takes their gun into the bathroom, right? Besides it sounded like fuckin' war, man. I froze. I came out, everyone was dead and the dumpster was on fire. They cooked Petey." Timmy starts to cry.

Richard places his hand on his shoulder. "You hear any voices? Accents? Anything we can use?"

"I'm sorry, Uncle Rich, it was just guns. No talking. I mean, Benny was doing laundry earlier. Maybe he saw something?"

Vincent comes out of the back door.

Richard whispers to Vincent, "Is everything gone?"

Vincent nods affirmatively.

Richard asks, "How much?"

Vincent whispers in his ear.

Richard brings his fist to mouth and clenches his jaw. "Somebody just shoved a fire-hose up my ass and turned the water on. Find out if it was the Domiguez crew." Richard is infuriated by this apparent robbery and potential power play. His blood is hot, and he feels a tingle in his testicles. Just the thought of unleashing holy hell reaffirming he's the alpha dog has spiked his testosterone.

Vincent walks away like a man on a mission. Richard turns to Timmy and just pats him on the head. He turns abruptly and heads to his car, nearly bumping into Dane who's there in a professional capacity. "Excuse me."

Dane pulls out a pad and a pen, "No problem. I'm actually looking for you. The owner of the property. I'm lead on this case."

Richard places out his hand, "Richard Pembroke, nice to meet you."

Dane shakes his hand, "Nice to meet you too, Mr. Pembroke. I'm Detective Graves. You can call me Dane."

Richard recognizes the name from his conversation with Ferina. Playing dumb, "Graves? Did I read about your brother in the paper?"

"Yeah, unfortunate. Wrong place, wrong time. My sister-in-law was a great person. The kids miss her the most."

Richard looks upset. "Kids? She was a mother?"

"Not yet, she happened to be pregnant. But she volunteered at a hospital for kids with cancer."

Richard feels mortified and changes the subject, "Enough about that unpleasantness, let's focus on this unpleasantness. I do own this laundromat in title only. My brother, Jeff, who recently both committed a pedophilic act as well as disappeared, was running this business."

"My goodness, Jeff Pembroke, yeah? I was working the night he was brought in. Poor girl. She was pretty upset, and he was bragging to the officers on the scene."

Richard, furious inside, hides his rage, "Yeah he disappeared the next day, I'm guessing somewhere non-extradition like that prick Polanski."

"Well I hope the girl is okay. Once she slipped out, we had nothing to hold him on. As you know."

"Yeah, very unfortunate."

Dane changes the subject, "I'll be totally transparent with you. The scene is clearly wrought with markers of illegal activity. Drug packaging paraphernalia. Drug residue. Triple beam scales. Weapons. Money counting machines."

Richards places his hands on his head, "This is all crazy. My brother clearly had problems. Well, has problems. I had no idea about any of this. I assure you that I'll personally conduct an internal investigation."

Dane nods affirmatively, "Internal investigation... sounds good."

Richard pulls out a business card. "I'll get to the bottom of this. If my brother is indeed a mastermind here, I will insist he turns himself into the authorities, post haste. I've had a private investigator trying to locate him since he disappeared. If you need anything from me, don't hesitate. I mean it. The boys in blue are all we have to prevent the wolves from our doors."

"I appreciate you being so forthcoming. You'll keep me in the loop, yeah?"

"I certainly will."

As they turn their separate ways, Richard pauses and looks back at Dane. "Detective Graves, don't ask me what I know, but I'd watch that Detective Ferina."

"Yeah?"

"I hear things, and he's got a hard-on for you."

Dane points to his own face, "Must be the bone structure, I'm told I'm quite handsome; I don't see it, but thanks for the heads-up."

Richard chuckles, "Both you guys are."

Dane looks confused. "Both?"

"You and your brother."

"Oh yeah. Yup. Good genes, I guess."

They part ways, Richard feeling good that he gave Dane the heads-up about Ferina and convinced that his damage control played well. Dane is fully aware of all Richard's inconsistencies that peppered their conversation, including him knowing what Colin looks like, only confirming that their assault on him is taking its toll.

Chapter 19

Richard has Vincent set up a meeting with the Dominguez Crew. He suspects their involvement in the laundromat debacle, but needs to be political as some of their territories overlap, and no one wants a war. Santiago Salazar is their boss and his rise to power started when Dane disappeared his brother for killing Jude, and has been exponential. His potential for wickedness was never in question. When he was a kid, he drew pictures that disturbed his teachers. His abuela thought he was possessed and had him exorcised. This didn't faze the little monster that grew up into a big monster. He's always been willing to do that which would give others pause; his strength comes from his ability to live with the person staring back at him, no matter how shadowy the reflection. He's all grown up and twisted, with a goatee and a shaved head. His tattoos read more like a cautionary tale to those unlucky enough to lay their eyes on him. With the exception of his newest ink: his infant son holding a Glock.

Richard's arrogance has always been a double-edged sword; more times than not, serving him favorably as an attitude of superiority coupled with equal ability is a recipe for victory. However, when underestimation of an adversary is the result of presumptuous assumptions, this is a recipe for disaster. Richard considers Santiago impulsive and foolish, therefore really no threat. He likens him to wild dog, and while his unpredictability will frighten most, these types burn twice as hot for half as long. Santiago sits at the table, eager to feed his guests. He lounges in his intentionally giant chair; his throne. Salazar speaks, "You know what they call Mexican Food in Mexico? Food." The low

CHAPTER 19

hum of everyone politely chuckling at his corny joke fills the tense room. "Richard, what do you think? Authentic."

Richard picks at his dish, more in the mood to discuss business rather than eat, "It's delicious. I appreciate the hospitality."

"De nada, we have been cohabitating without problems, so I was happy to sit down. Your men seem to be enjoying the food." Piney and Corky are devouring everything in front of them, almost taking off their own fingertips as they lick their fingers.

Richard gives his men a stern look, "Excuse them, their manners evaporate around food. Those Fitbits are for show."

"It's cool ese, I take it as a compliment."

"You mentioned our peace."

"Yes, yes, yes nuestro paz. Hold on one sec. You ever notice tacos, enchiladas and burritos are basically all the same thing? Like a tortilla, with meat of some sort, cheese, vegetables. Maybe salsa, sour cream, or guacamole? Same shit, what the fuck?" Salazar's men laugh.

Richard sits stone-faced, "That's a broad generalization."

Santiago is insulted, "You see, all the same. All the ingredients are the same, with a slightly different flare. You see, right?"

Richard shakes his head, "If you have to explain a joke, it's really not that funny. Of course I get it. Chicken Franchase, chicken piccatta, and chicken scampi are all chicken in a sauce, but the way they are cooked and the flavors added is what makes them different. You referred to it as flare. You see the flare is why the joke is 'meh.'" Richard shrugs his shoulders.

Santiago is visibly annoyed. "Tough crowd."

"I'm just saying avoid open mic nights and stick to murder and rape."

Santiago pushes his plate away, "Fuck you!"

"There's the guy I came to see. You wouldn't know what happened at my laundromat two days ago, would you?"

"Concrete in one of your washers?"

"I wish. Someone went in there guns blazing, didn't stop until everyone was dead, and stole from me."

Salazar smiles, "I get why you would come here, that takes some big balls, cajones grandes, but I don't need to steal from you. Your shit is shit. I'm hooked up with the Juarez Cartel."

"I knew you were crazy, but I didn't think you had a death wish. They'll have your head first, fuck up."

"I guess I can't fuck up then. But what I hear, you've been fucking up like it's your job."

"I'm business as usual."

"The streets talk, ese. And your house is in disarray. You're slipping, papi. You used to be numero uno. I have a front row seat. I just need to sit back and relax, then step into your shoes once you're gone."

Richard nods condescendingly, but visibly irked, "Is that a fact?"

"If you make it to old age, I predict that you'll be the type of old man that argues until he's blue in the face that with age comes experience and wisdom." Richard squints, trying to figure out where this is going, "Then, when you slip and get duped, it'll be because you're too old and confused. You can't have it both ways, homie."

Richard stands up and all of his guys follow suit. Piney grabs a tortilla from the plate next to him. "Well, this was fun. If I find out it was you, you've been warned."

Salazar leans back, "It wasn't me. But I take it as a compliment, because my balls are big enough to shatter a bitch's chin."

Richard smiles, "You've always been a poet."

They shake hands and Richard exits, whispering to Vincent, "It wasn't them. Who the fuck did this?"

Vincent shrugs.

"We need to get the word out, we're paying for any information."

Vincent nods, "On it boss."

* * *

The mental roller coaster that's the life of an actor is enough to drive

CHAPTER 19

most people mad and that's why at some point or another, every actor implodes to a certain extent. For many, it manifests as that come-to-Jesus moment they realize if they don't snuff out their own dream and move on, they'll get stuck in no-man's-land. This applies to those who fail. For others, success ebbs and flows and the in-between times where no one cares is like silence in a room full of people. Silence in an empty room can be peaceful, the inverse is terrifying. Each time an actor dons a persona, they lose a piece of themselves, until one day they don't know which way is up. And yet, money and fame will always be the siren's call to create unlimited supply for limited demand. Mick springs out of bed as he's feeling the upswing of a booking. His manager let him know yesterday about a guest role on NCIS that has the potential to recur. He's so excited he barely slept and couldn't wait to start the day. He heads to the park for his daily run and isn't deterred by his previous run-in with a corpse.

He enters the park, and his eyes lock onto a beautiful girl decked out in athletic garb. She's stretching and he's drawn to her like a heat-seeking missile. His confidence happens to be through the roof, either from his new job, working with the police, or the testosterone booster that he's just begun in hopes of adding a few pounds of muscle while cutting some fat. He struts up to her like he's ten feet tall. "Pre-stretch or post-stretch?"

She checks him out. "Pre-stretch. Nice whistle."

He grabs the bright orange whistle hanging from his neck, "Oh, my rape whistle, thank you. It works for most occasions, like a little black dress."

She's flirting, "Preemptive or reactive?"

"If you're asking me if I've been raped, only mentally, by Criss Angel." She laughs as Mick continues, "We should run together."

"Is that so? You think you can keep up?"

"The good news, if I can't, I'll have the best view in the park, if you know what I mean." He shakes his head, "Girl that pony tail is tight." He helps her to her feet and they begin jogging. He decides to shatter the anonymity. "By the way, my name is Mick."

"Nice to meet you, Mick, my name is May."

"My favorite day, month, and way to express possibility."

"Well doesn't that work out."

All of a sudden, May stops. She points towards some brush a little into the park. "What's that?"

Mick moves in ahead of her. "It's a headless corpse."

She screams, grabs his whistle and blows. She notices Mick is barely reacting. "Why aren't you freaking out?"

"Don't worry, I've seen this before. I consult with the police." Mickey pulls out his cell phone. "I'm gonna call the detective that I've been working with."

She points towards the headless body. "What's that tattoo?"

Mick squints as his phone rings Dane. "Naturally, it's baby holding a gun. I'm horrifyingly okay with it. The artist is quite talented."

Dane answers and Mickey talks into the phone. "Dane, you're not going to believe this."

* * *

Not everyone is so effervescent and eager to tackle the world today. Vincent woke up on the wrong side of bed and has been obsessing over his death sentence. Like the skin of a popcorn kernel stuck deeply between his teeth, he can't stop tonguing it, knowing full well that dislodging it is futile. Last night pushed him over the edge. He got several bottles of whiskey, downing as much as he could as quickly as possible. He attempted to drink himself into oblivion, to no avail. He passed out before he could poison himself. His punishment for failure is a blinding headache and wicked nausea.

In his massively depressed state, he decides to go gently into that good night. He sees Richard's ship is sinking and it's only a matter of time before he'll be pulled down, too. Between this inevitability and his prognosis, raging against the dying of the light seems exhausting.

CHAPTER 19

He feels things slipping from his control and just as the first time Superman felt pain, this is a feeling he's never felt, and it's scary. He always had his work and his mind and both are cloaked in impending decline.

He almost has too many options. A gun in his mouth isn't something he ever wants to experience. He's not into the idea of pills, sitting in a garage with the car on, or jumping off a building. There's something respectable and reserved about a good old-fashioned hanging. He'll leave a note because he doesn't want any confusion. He has enough pride to make it perfectly clear this is his choice. Richard's lawyer, Harvey, has his will so Benny's kid, who he knows is his kid, will have a trust. He'll live comfortably and no one but Billy can touch the lion share until he turns eighteen.

He goes on YouTube, rope in hand, finding the perfect noose tutorial. The video is titled, "Knot of the Week: The Hangman's Noose." He skips the ad about a website-building service before the video after five seconds of course. Even the hot model hawking the service couldn't get him to sit through the whole thing. The host of the video, part tactical guru and part doomsday prepper, opens with a disclaimer of the legality of using the hangman's knot, especially during a hate crime. After that unpleasantness, Vincent creates his noose, overhand style. It reminds him of the summer when he was ten and he made a lanyard bracelet for a girl at camp, Mia, that he had a crush on. He makes his way to his living room and ties his perfectly knotted noose to the ceiling fan. He grabs some handcuffs and stands on a stool, tightens the noose around his neck, and cuffs his hands behind his back. His head is still pounding from the hangover. He takes a deep breath, kicks the stool away, and begins dangling. His preexisting nausea, combined with the pressure around his neck, makes him gag. However, the vomit leaks out sporadically because he's constricting the windpipe. It drips down his chin, as it's mostly liquid. He turns bright red, trying not to struggle, but survival mode has kicked in. He's glad he's cuffed behind his back, because if his arms were free, his lizard brain wouldn't let him go through with it.

Benny wakes this same morning with venom in his veins. He's angry his ex not only slept with Vincent while they were married and he got her hooked on harder drugs, but that the both of them were content hiding the truth. He's been fixated, like a bloodhound on a scent, talking to himself through a clenched jaw about murdering them both. His wife would have to wait, because the odds of him getting to her while she's in lockdown are slim. He could probably pay some bull-dike to shank her, but he wants to cut her body into tiny pieces and feed her to the fish himself. He knows that his future is unpredictable; he may not be able to look in her eyes as he escorts her soul to hell. He doesn't have to wait to kill Vincent. The hint of ambition that periodically rears its head has fueled a fire; he decides then and there, he'll seize the moment. He drives over to Vincent's house with the intent of killing him.

As Benny pulls up, he violently throws his van into park. He quickly checks his gun, pats his inside jacket pocket feeling his grenade. He slides out of the car, and walks across the street with his gun tight against his right leg. He speed walks up to the front door and pauses. He takes a deep breath, lifts his leg to kick in the door, pauses again, then checks the door knob. The door is unlocked; he quietly enters, gun drawn. He turns the corner to see Vincent still struggling to breath with his hands behind his back. Benny closes the door behind him. He sees Benny and sometime between kicking the chair out and his arrival, Vincent has changed his mind. This may be the first time Benny has been a sight for sore eyes. Vincent tries to speak as he chokes, "Benny, get me the chair." Benny shakes his head.

Vincent is both scared and shocked. "Please."

"Fuck you. You got my ex hooked on stuff worse than she was on. And my kid ain't my kid. You sleazy motherfucker."

Vincent struggles and right before his number is punched, the ceiling fan breaks and he falls to the ground. He's bright red, out of breath, coughing, and struggling to inhale.

CHAPTER 19

Pure wickedness manifests across Benny's face. He grabs one of Vincent's pillows and sits on him. "You're healthy, by the way. The whole doctor thing was a scam. Same with Jeff. I've been helping Graves get Richard." Vincent's eyes bulge as Benny begins to lower the pillow to his face. The air Vincent breathes now is the sweetest he's ever taken in. As the pillow touches his face he begins to panic. He kicks his feet, but Benny is determined to Burke him.

Benny hears the chirp of a car door locking from out front. The voices in the distance appear to be approaching, gradually getting louder and louder. Benny is stuck in no-man's-land. He can't stop killing Vincent nor can he be caught killing him. Benny pushes harder, the lactic acid building up in his arms, and he feels the fatigue and burn start to set in. He nervously checks the door, then his hands on the pillow, like he's watching a tennis match. He whisper screams, "Die, you prick." Benny is sweating profusely, red with effort; random strands of his hair stick to his face. There's a knock on the door. He doesn't answer and continues pushing, using the full weight of his body. There is another knock. Like turning off a switch, Vincent stops kicking. Benny pushes for an additional ten seconds for good measure. He pulls the pillow away; Vincent's face is frozen in a terrified state. He collects himself, taking deep breaths, then moves the hair out of his face. He stands up, exhausted, and tosses the pillow on the sofa. It lands a second before Piney and Corky force the door open. It takes a moment for everyone's eyes to register who's who, and in that time they all draw their guns.

Piney looks surprised, "Oh bollocks, it's you." He lowers his gun and notices Vincent's body, "Jesus Christ, mate, what's with Vince?"

Benny tucks his gun into his pants and feigns sorrow, "Dude, this is seriously fucked up. He took himself out."

"H-h-how d-d-doo you know?" Corky stutters.

Benny walks over to the table. "Check out this note."

Piney follows him suspiciously and grabs the note out of his sweaty hands. He eyes the contents, moving his lips as he reads because hearing them softly may make sense of this madness. "Jesus Christ. Vince says right here that he hung himself because of a terminal disease." Piney places the note down and looks at Benny, "Why you all sweaty, mate? You didn't try to fuck him did ya?"

"Fuck you. CPR. That shit is exhausting."

Piney shakes his head, "Shame." He changes gears, "Well, we came over here to get Vince, so we can all get you."

Benny knows deep down he's screwed. "Me? What makes me so special? Something need tidying up?" He chuckles in the hope his nonchalant demeanor makes him seem less suspicious.

Piney senses this and matter-of-factly assures Benny he shouldn't think anything of the request. "Boss has to ask you something. Maybe about a body you got rid of?"

"No problem." Benny knows they're exchanging bullshit. "I'll follow you guys."

Corky cuts him off. "N-n-nah. Y-you come with us."

Benny plays it as cool as possible, "Sure. What about Vince?"

Piney pulls out his phone and dials. "Hi, I need to report an emergency situation. A friend of mine is suicidal and he's not picking up his phone. Fifteen Bridlemere." Piney hangs up the phone and winks at Benny, who begrudgingly walks to what he believes is his end.

Chapter 20

Colin and Alissa fell asleep on the bathroom floor at some point during his detox. He stirs once his neck tells his brain this current position will eventually negatively impact his cervical spine. He wakes feeling much better both mentally and physically. As the hours since his last pill grows, so too will his strength and the feeling of normalcy. He also turned a corner with regard to his captive and feels her Stockholm Syndrome is in full effect. He rouses her gently. She mutters incoherently, barely awake, her hair over to one side. "I need to get up, but I want you to sleep." She nods in agreement, not forming actual words but just noises. He helps her to her feet and guides her to her room. He tucks her in, she points to her forehead, and he gently kisses it.

He turns away, his ego boosted, as no human doesn't get a shot of confidence when they gain an admirer. Once he met Betty, while still admired by women because he drips charisma, outside opinions mattered little as he obtained his personal holy grail – the woman of his dreams loved him. The one person in all his years that could take his breath away. He had always thought that notion was hyperbole or romantic gobbledygook, until it happened to him.

On autopilot, lost in his own head, he locks the door and struts upstairs. He turns the corner at the top to a shocking blow that jerks him out of his daydream. His mind processes the sensation and determines the butt of a shotgun striking him squarely. He grabs his face with his hand, "Motherfucker." Colin looks up to see Miles, "Whoa, you're albino as fuck. California the best place you can live?

How much you spend on sunscreen?"

Miles smacks him, "You know why we're here."

"Okay, if I order six boxes of Samoas, will you get that new bike?"

Miles punches him in the face. "Shut the fuck up!"

Timmy grabs Miles' shoulder, "Easy, pal, we need him in one piece."

Colin turns to Timmy, "You tell 'em, future Mr. Deadbeat dad." He whispers to Timmy, "I'm a Belieber too."

Miles grabs Colin's bandaged hand and he screams in pain. He takes a second to collect his breath, "Oh man, am I going to enjoy killing you."

Miles winds up and Timmy grabs his arm. "Relax, man. The boss was specific."

"Bruce Springsteen talked about me? Cool." Colin looks right at Timmy, "I'll also enjoy killing you. The pleasure of each will be fungible."

Timmy releases Miles' arm. Miles pauses, thinks, then smashes Colin in the head with the shotgun, knocking him out cold. They drag him out of the house and place him into the trunk of their car.

***

Dane lies in bed, looking up at the ceiling fan, drenched in his and Ingrid's sweat. He's quiet, thinking about something, maybe nothing.

Ingrid quivers, "I can't close my legs."

Dane turns his head, smirking. "I'm gonna need them open in a minute or two, so don't waste any energy closing up shop."

She shakes her head, "I don't think so. If we go again, you'll kill me."

"I can think of at least a dozen worse ways to go."

"Oh, is that so?"

"Actually, it may be the best way to go."

Ingrid kisses him, "In that case, put me out of my misery."

Dane's cellphone rings. He half-heartedly glances in the direction

CHAPTER 20

of the night table on his side of the bed.

"Saved by the bell." Ingrid raises her eyebrows and bites her lip.

"I have to take this." Dane picks up the phone. "Yeah." Dane stands up, "Sit tight, Mick, I'll be there in a few."

Ingrid whines in jest, "Do you really have to go?"

He waves his fingers towards her as he speaks, "You're gonna come with me."

"To a crime scene?" She shakes her head, "I don't think so."

"There's a coffee place right by there. You'll hang there. I'll check out the scene and then back here."

"Oh, back here, huh?"

"Yeah."

Dane texts Colin. "Col, I have to check out a scene by the park. Meet me at Higher Ground Coffee."

* * *

If the first scene was a shit show, this second scene is a special type of shit show; like Nickelback opening for Jon Lovitz while naked midgets wrestle for meth. Legitimate media and stringers are itching for the scoop, like overdue crack heads, as two decapitations are exponentially more newsworthy than one, and each subsequent decapitation will cause spontaneous orgasms from the head honchos at each news outlet. The police presence is substantial and they have the area roped off, so the camera crews can't get footage of the decapitated drug lord lying face-down in the park. They are cock-blocking best they can, like the ugly chick who goes out with her hot and loose friend that everyone gravitates towards because they can smell her desperate necessity for attention.

Mick is standing by the out-of-shape coroner who is patiently smoking as he waits for Dane to get on site. "Did you check the liver temp?"

The coroner coughs, "Yup."

Mick places his hand out, "Dude, my name is Mick. Nice to meet you. I was at the other scene too." The coroner places the cigarette in his mouth and shakes Mick's hand without introducing himself. "How do you determine the time of death based on temperature? What's, there like an equation?" Mick crosses his arms and leans in for an answer.

The coroner takes one last puff of his cigarette. He licks his fingers and puts the cigarette out with his moist digits. He then places the ciggie in his pocket as to not contaminate the crime scene. "Okay buddy, I'll tell ya." He's very dry and speaks deliberately. His tone can come off condescending, but since he's a functioning alcoholic, he's really just trying to hide his well-known secret. "After the demise of the deceased, the temperature will drop one and half to two degrees per hour for the first, let's say, approximately twelve hours. Now this isn't exact because the surrounding temperature and the amount of clothing are significant factors. For example, I had one case where the guy died of hyperthermia."

Mickey excitedly questions what he believes is an enigma. "He froze?"

"No, hypothermia is when the body temperature drops below what's required for proper metabolism. Hyperthermia is when the heat regulation within one's body malfunctions and body temperature increases beyond a point of no return. This can be caused from many things from too much sun to various medicines to drugs to chemical weapons. My point is, the temperature didn't drop each hour from 98.6 but rather from a higher temperature, skewing the time of death."

Dane makes his way through the police tape. He casually walks up to the coroner and taps him on the back.

"How's my second favorite medical examiner?"

"Fuck you. Quincy ain't got nothing on me."

"But the ladies loved him." Dane places his hand out to shake Mick's. "You may want to invest in a treadmill."

"No shit."

The Captain joins the pow-wow. "Any leads on the other decap?"

Dane guides him out of earshot of Mick and the coroner. "Not yet, Cap. We'll see what turns up at this scene, but we may want to call in the BSU."

The Captain is a little annoyed, "The Feds? Are you thinking serial killer?"

"Cap, I don't know what to think."

"I haven't slept in months. Between the murders of the chief and deputy chief and these two brutal decapitations, and no leads, we look incompetent."

Dane places his hand on the Captain's shoulder, "What happened to Scully and Alvarez was professional. It's like a ghost took them out. This is different. We can't identify the first body, but we know who this is."

"Well, that's the best news I've heard all day."

Dane points, "This is Santiago Salazar."

"Salazar, eh? You have history with this clown. Is this going to be a thing?"

"His brother. And nope. Not a thing. The other decap could also be a major hitter. My gut tells me it's a boss, like Salazar."

"That's good. Two dead criminals doesn't keep people up at night." He waves over the coroner, "Do you know the murder weapon at least? I'm sure it's not a guillotine."

The coroner walks over and chimes in, "Upon initial examination, the wounds are consistent. They were made with something extremely sharp, like a samurai sword or one of those Ginsu knives." He snickers at his own joke, "Something sharp as hell."

The Captain and Dane walk out of earshot again. "Dane, see what you can do. We can't have this get out as a serial killer. Find out who the first decap was so that we can release a statement that it's criminals killing criminals. Also, come up with something, anything, in reference to the chief and deputy chief."

Dane nods. "On it. With regard to the other thing, cyber found some money in off-shore accounts of both the chief and deputy chief. Could take a while to trace, but it looks like pay-offs. Could be Russians or somebody with deep pockets doing something illegal."

"Fuck me. If that gets confirmed, we need to squash it. And check with CI's if any top-ranking guys are in the wind. Could be our first decap."

"Will do." Dane pats the Captain on the shoulder as he turns away.

The Captain moves over to the police tape border where the press is eager to get a statement. He holds his hands up and speaks clearly in the direction of the recording devices. "We're unsure of the situation here. It looks to be an accident of sorts. Other than that, I have no comment." The press doesn't buy what the Captain is selling and they follow him to his car. The Captain has been playing this game for years and gives them nothing.

Dane turns to Mick, "Thanks for giving me a call."

"No problem."

"I'm gonna grab some coffee across the way, you want to tag along?"

Mick shakes his head with a smile, "I can't. I have a hot little thing waiting for me." He sticks out his fist and Mick pounds it. Dane leaves the scene and walks towards the coffee place. Ingrid sits outside, wearing shades and sipping her small latte with skim milk, playing on her phone. She sees him approaching, and can't help but smile. Between the sun and the way he carries himself, he just looks like a leading man. She's giddy and cutely waves at him. He smiles and returns the gesture, closing in.

She stands and begins to walk towards him, as even this minor distance is too much at the moment.

In Dane's peripheral vision he notices an El Camino suspiciously bearing down on his position. He moves quickly towards Ingrid and once he can see the driver, Piney, he knows he's in trouble. On the passenger side, Warren is hanging out of the window. Black and in his late twenties, Warren is monstrously muscular. He has a shotgun. Dane pushes Ingrid out of the way and she falls to the ground. Dane catches the full force of the shotgun blast in his center mass. He

CHAPTER 20

also catches some stray buck in the face due to the spray pattern of the gun. The momentum of the blast throws him through the coffee shop's storefront window, with him landing inside. A person's natural reaction to gunfire is to turn away from it, cover your face and head, and duck down. Ingrid does exactly this, revealing the temporary tattoo, fading but still recognizable, to the street. Piney sees the familiar pattern.

Piney screams, "Warren, grab the girl, mate."

He gets out of the car, grabs Ingrid, sees Dane's lifeless body ten paces away in the coffee shop. The police from the park are suddenly on the scene. He places the girl over his shoulder and forces her into the car.

"Hurry, mate!!" Piney looks out of the windows as the cops approach. "Come on, we need to split."

Warren stays calm, "Okay, okay." He fires a shotgun blast at the cops and they take cover. He gets in, with Ingrid sitting in the middle between he and Piney. "Hit it." They speed off. "Cop is dead."

Piney smiles, "Lovely." He slams on the gas and they speed off.

A uniformed officer kneels before Dane who opens his blood filled eyes and whispers, "Get the coroner and a body bag." He winks at the uniformed officer. Before he was shot, he noticed Corky across the street hanging by the newspaper stand and he knows the value of his death. He wants Corky to report back that the job was done. The coroner pulls up, examines Dane, and they place him in the body bag. Dane's vest caught most of buck, but needs his death to look legitimate. He gets taken to the morgue and has the coroner take a few pictures of him on the table. Other than Colin, the police were the only ones who knew he was working the scene. Somebody is crooked. "If anyone asks where my body is, say it was released to the funeral home." The coroner nods and Dane sneaks out of the morgue and is driven to Dr. Phil's office for stitches.

* * *

In this town, clientele can be anywhere on the spectrum from normal to fancy depending on the situation. Not only is Dr. Phil good, he's known to be very loose when it comes to most things. He enters the room sucking on a lollipop. His patient, a movie producer named Abe Bregman has that old school producer mentality. He dresses trendy, dyes his hair, and is married to a much younger woman. He's schmoozy when he needs to be, difficult the rest of the time. He's vile and truly feels people love him for his winning personality, not because of his place on the food chain. He sits nervously on the deli paper waiting for the verdict. "Doc, what's wrong with my prick?"

Dr. Phil pulls the lollipop out of his mouth to answer. "Well, Abe, you have an STD, my friend."

Abe places his hands over his face. "Fuck! My wife is going to fucking kill me."

"I've had it. No big deal." Dr. Phil puts his hand up, "Maybe you got it from her?"

"Nah. I got wasted at this benefit and fucked this dumb bitch actress. She's been around the block. It was like fuckin' a bucket of water. Just terrible. And laid there like a dead fish."

Dr. Phil shakes his head, "That's too bad."

"Doc, what am I going to do?"

"You need one injection. That's it. Like a tetanus shot, only one single dose of a strong antibiotic."

"One shot?" Abe places his hand over his chin. "My wife and I had sex last night. She's in the waiting room. Would you tell her that I have something else and give her the shot saying I'm contagious?"

"Yeah. I can do that. You get me tickets to Beyoncé?"

"Done."

Abe exits the room and Dr. Phil takes a bottle of pills out of his pocket and downs a few of them. He's back in a minute with his wife, Debra, who is extremely attractive. She places her hand out to shake and Dr. Phil kisses it.

"Mademoiselle. The pleasure is all mine."

CHAPTER 20

"Hiya Dr. Philla... Dr. Philla..."

"Call me Dr. Phil, my lady."

"My husband said that you wanted to see me."

"Your husband has a bacterial infection in his lungs and sinuses. He's very contagious. I want you to take an antibiotic injection as a precaution."

Debra shrugs her shoulders. "I feel fine."

Abe grabs his wife's shoulders. "Hun, I felt fine too."

"Mrs. Bregman, this is a super bug and if your husband didn't come in when he did, it may have killed him."

Debra looks down, shocked her husband may have died. Abe looks at Dr. Phil like he's laying it on a little thick. Dr. Phil shrugs his shoulders at Abe. Debra is oblivious to their exchange.

Debra sighs, "I don't want to die. I'll take the shot."

Dr. Phil had the needle ready and gives her a shot before she knew it was coming.

She jumps a little. "Hey." She rubs her arm.

"I call that a sneak attack. It's over before you can feel it. Abe, your turn."

Dr. Phil gives Abe the shot and when it is over, he shakes the doctor's hand and winks at him. "My assistant will messenger those tickets over later today."

Dr. Phil smiles, "I hope she sings 'Single Ladies.'"

Debra turns to Abe, "Is he going to Beyoncé too?"

"Too? No. I'll tell you about it later."

Dr. Phil exits the room and his nurse tells him a patient is waiting in Room 2. "I thought I was done for the day?" His nurse shrugs. He enters Room 2 to find Dane lying down holding a rag to his face. His shirt is saturated with blood and tattered from bullets. "Dane, my goodness, were you shot in the face?"

"Just a little. I need you to pull some buck out and sew me up."

"Yeah. You want a few belts of something to loosen you up?"

"Just Novocain today doc, I need to be lucid."

Dr. Phil washes his hands and gets to work. Dane stares into space, contemplating his next move and doesn't make a peep. He suspected something was fishy when his brother didn't get back to him. As soon as he's cleaned up, he'll need to find out if he's in possession of his only leverage... Alissa.

Chapter 21

Benny had a feeling today wasn't going to be his day. No day has ever been his day, but on the scale of barely shitty to as shitty as possible, today is the Lance Armstrong of shitty days. He felt it when he woke up, ignoring that feeling in the back of his brain. Ignoring the organ that functions as the coordinating center of intellectual activity has been one of his pastimes, and perhaps the reason why there's a direct correlation between his biggest fuck-ups and not listening to that inner voice that keeps most people out of serious trouble. He was completely fixated on Vincent and is just grateful he prioritized paying him a visit before it was too late. Richard was waiting for him to arrive at one of his warehouses. Benny looks at the men milling around; this herd has been thinned out. Richard barely notices Benny one hundred percent of the time, but he immediately approaches him and grabs his shoulders.

Richard smiles, "Benedict, how've you been?"

Benny responds calmly, "I've been pretty good. I tried tapas for the first time. You ever have tapas?"

Richard's tone is fake. "I love tapas. But, I have not been well. Did you hear about the laundromat thing?"

Benny nods, "Yeah. Crazy. Fucking hoodlums."

They're verbally dancing, but Richard is leading. "Yeah, hoodlums. Timmy tells me you were doing laundry there that day."

Benny counters with a natural turn, "Was it that day? Maybe. I feel like I'm always doing laundry. Kids are dirty man."

"Tell me about it." Richard pauses, realizing he's now childless.

"Seems a little far from your place?" A reverse fleckeryll from Richard.

"I don't want to get anyone in trouble, but the girls there do it for me and they don't charge me."

Richard hesitates. "That's nice of them." He gestures to Timmy, taking the cross-body lead. Billy is brought into Benny's line of sight. "This is your boy, right Benny?"

Benny nods and says nothing.

Richard continues, "He looks a little like Vince. Piney, doesn't he look like Vince?"

"I'd say there's a resemblance."

"Piney phoned to tell me that Vince killed himself and you were there all sweaty and agitated."

Benny can barely speak. "Vince was sick and depressed. I was trying to revive him." He places his hand towards his inside pocket.

"Easy mate." Piney cocks his gun.

Benny backs off and Richard continues without losing his train of thought. "I'm going to tell you what I think. I know that my problems started after you tipped me off about an up-and-comer. Then retracted your tip. It could be karma but I doubt it. I want you to tell me everything you know, or I'll slit this boy's neck. I'll cut him up while he's breathing."

Billy's lip begins to quiver but he holds back tears. Benny waves his hand at him, "Relax, kiddo. I'll handle this." He directs the conversation towards Richard. "If you spare the boy, I'll tell you everything. But you promise me, nothing happens to him. He's just a kid."

Richard nods, "You tell me what I want to hear and the boy lives." Benny proceeds to tell Richard about Colin and Dane. This causes the chain of events ending up in Colin being snatched from his house, Richard seeing Dane's text, and Dane being shot in broad daylight. However, he leaves out just enough, knowing that he's a goner and Richard still needs to suffer even though he's holding most of the cards.

CHAPTER 21

* * *

Richard paces around his office within the warehouse, attempting to figure out his next move. The last of his inner circle stand watching their leader exude nervous energy. "I have a plan for Benny, but I don't know what to do with our one-armed friend. I'm at a crossroads. A bullet to the brain doesn't seem fitting, considering our history. I'm opening up the floor. Any suggestions?"

Corky decides to take a chance and impress his boss. "B-b-boss, you know those *Saw* m-m-movies?"

Richard shakes his head. "Vaguely. I'm not really into the horror genre. I did like *Insidious 4* though. And *The Taking of Deborah Logan*. And *Escape Room*."

Corky continues before he loses his train of thought, "I was thinking, that m-m-maybe you hand-c-c-cuff his good arm to the w-w-wall and give him a s-s-saw. You could l-l-let him go if he ch-chops off his own arm." Everyone in the room picks up on the flaw in the plan, but each commends Corky's diabolical thought process.

Richard is also proud of Corky but can't help himself. "Corks, how would he hack his arm off?"

Corky looks at one of his arms and pantomimes chopping with the other. After a little too long, his eyes bug out. "Yeah, th-that's n-n-not possible with this guy."

Richard jumps in before Corky gets dejected. "Don't worry, Corks, you're an inspiration. Follow me." He exits the office with them all in tow.

Colin sits in a chair off in a corner with a hood over his head. His leg shackles are bolted to the floor. He perks up when he hears footsteps coming his way, getting louder as the distance is quickly covered. Miles rips the hood off his head and Colin's eyes take a second to adjust. "You guys may have a mold problem? You don't happen to have an antihistamine?" Colin lifting his feet, "Leg shackles on tap? Kinky. Those look police issue. eBay?"

Miles to Richard, "I told you, fucking smart ass."

Colin addresses Miles, "I'm sorta a wisenheimer, not to be confused with a Weimaraner which is an awesome dog, but something completely different."

Miles punches him. Richard says his name softly, "Miles." He collects himself, walks away, and takes deep breaths.

Colin points with his head, "That guy's more unpredictable than two retards playing ping-pong. And equally adorable."

Richard pulls up a chair and sits across from Colin, "Do you have any bad habits you would like to break?"

"I need to answer your question with a question. Is having a monomaniacal obsession to collect every Precious Moments Figurine a bad habit or just a nice hobby?"

Richard turns to his men pointing at Colin, "I do like this guy. Under other circumstances I think we would get along swimmingly. He's been busy."

"I have. You cleared my dance card so I've had tons of free time. I'm thinking about investing in an alpaca farm. Is taking up knitting too aggressive?"

"I'm not sure what's the fair way to deal with you. I get it. I fucked up hard on this one and you have every right to be angry."

"Angry is a grounded teenage daughter on prom night." Colin says smugly, "Not something you have to worry about."

Richard bites his lower lip, "How do I punish someone for reacting exactly how I'd react? Seems hypocritical to blame all this on you."

"Love your use of the word hypocritical. You play Words With Friends? We should battle. I'm not sure 'Za' is really a word. Short for pizza? Debatable."

"Well, we both fucked up. Machiavelli wrote, 'Never do an enemy a small injury.' I was guilty of this first, now you. If you aim at the king, you better make sure he's dead." Richard stands up. "I had your brother killed. I have his whore girlfriend under lock and key. Clever stand-in for my daughter. She's going to be on the next boat to Russia.

CHAPTER 21

They'll pump her full of drugs, and charge five bucks a ride. If she thought being a whore here was rough, she ain't seen nothing yet. Those Russian motherfuckers are despicable pigs." Richard kneels in front of him, "You've been beaten. I have you locked down, you're a cripple, and no one is coming to save you. I would love to test your mettle."

"You challenging me to a game of roshambo?" He turns to Timmy, "And not rock-scissor-paper, this guy knows what I'm talking about, right K-Fed?" He whispers, "Urban dictionary."

Richard ignores him, "Quickly or with maximum pain and suffering?"

"Names of your sex tapes?"

"Miles!" Richard cries angrily.

Miles steps ups and punches Colin in the face. "Was your mother a five pound bag of flour?"

Richard turns away, "Fuck this guy. Let's get Benny situated. I'll kill him in a minute."

Piney whispers to Richard, "Benny's kid slipped away."

Richard shakes his head, "Whatever. Fuck it. I'm not going to hurt a kid and hopefully he's picked up by social services. It's his only chance."

The other guys have their attention aimed at a big vat up against the wall facing Colin. It's been slowly filling with water. Timmy and Miles are dumping ice into it. Corky enters the room, pushing Benny who has bruises all over his face. Benny is whimpering and mouths to Colin, "I'm sorry." Colin rolls his eyes.

Richard addresses Benny directly, pointing his finger at him. "Benny, are you familiar with Dante Alighieri?"

"That dealer who works Wilshire over by Bristol Farms?"

Richard shakes his head, "No."

"Pimp? Sandler's buddy? I think I have his skateboard."

"Shut the fuck up! Of course you don't know. He was a poet. He wrote *The Inferno*."

"I love that movie. Newman and McQueen. Awesome."

Piney can't help but interject, "That's *Towering Inferno*, mate. Let the boss finish his thought."

"Thank you. Dante wrote *The Inferno* about Hell. There are several circles or places in Hell, and each type of person is relegated to a circle based on what they did in life. Do you know where he placed snitches?"

"Purgatory? That's what that show *Lost* was about, right?"

Richard's pesky forehead vein begins to dance. "Jesus Christ, shut the fuck up."

"I get chatty when I'm nervous."

Richard shakes his head. "Anyway, he placed them in the lowest point of Hell and made them stand in ice water up to their waist for eternity. Not murderers. Not thieves. Not rapists. According to him, snitches deserved the worst afterlife."

Benny nods. "You ever think this Dante was maybe a murdering, thieving rapist and just not a snitch? It's his story, right? He can write whatever he wanted? Sounds like fake news to me."

Richard throws his hands up, "Fuck this guy. Get him in the vat, he'll freeze to death in under an hour."

The henchmen grab Benny and they force him into the water. They shackle his arms above his head. They rip his shirt off and splash ice cold water on his exposed skin.

Richard turns to Colin, placing the gun against his head. "I'm thinking like a Band-Aid."

Colin replies to him calmly, "Spoiler alert. She's not dead."

Richard releases the hammer into the safety position, "Who's not dead?" He lowers his gun.

"Amelia Earhart... Alissa silly."

Richard turns to Timmy and Miles, "You searched his house?"

They look at each other and nod affirmatively. Richard gets close to Colin's face, "Where is she?"

"Someplace you'll never find her, if you kill me. And if you don't think we had a contingency if you got to me or my brother, you'd be wrong."

Richard's phone rings. He looks at the caller ID: LAPD. He answers the phone and after a brief back and forth hangs up.

Piney looks concerned, "Boss, you okay?"

Richard sounds relieved. "The police have Alissa, apparently she's safe." He turns to Colin, "If she's hurt, I swear..." He then addresses his men, "Everyone, come with me, let's get her. Miles, you watch this prick," pointing to Colin. "Depending on Alissa's account of his treatment of her, we either shoot him and throw him in a hole or torture him for a week. And Miles, don't touch him until we're back. The police fucked up once already, I'm not doing anything until she's in pocket."

Miles nods and give Colin a look like he's lucky Richard said something. The group exits. The few windows up high have been painted over, blocking nearly all outside scintillation. Colin observes the light from the outside sneak inside as they leave, but as the door closes it's devoured by the warehouse's caliginosity, creating a gray dusk. Miles pulls out a pack of cigarettes, places one in his mouth and heads outside. "You ladies stay put."

Colin smirks, "You really shouldn't smoke those... they'll end up killing you."

"Fuck you."

Benny begins to scream and Colin shushes him. "You know, in this light, your eyes really pop."

Freezing to death, he speaks through erratic breaths, "Colin man, they said they were going to kill my boy. I had to talk."

"Oh that. It's okay. If I wasn't bolted to the floor, I'd come over and give you a tight fist bump."

His teeth are chattering as he speaks. "I'm freezing. Figure something out before he gets back. Dane is dead, man. They shot him. He won't be here."

Colin is not counting on being rescued and watching Benny freeze to death is giving him a chill. He grabs the necklace his mother made him promise to wear since his grandfather's murder. Is it an emaciated Jew nailed to a cross with a crown of thorns? Nope. Jesus can save somebody else today. He can help a football player catch the game-winning touchdown or someone win a Grammy.

His grandfather was handcuffed with his own cuffs and murdered. Colin's mother decided to make her sons' necklaces from police-issue handcuff keys. Colin takes his key and places it into the keyhole of the first shackle and it pops open. He attempts to do the same thing for his other foot, but much to his dismay he can't; either because of the angle or his lack of flexibility. His face gets flushed. He begins to sweat. He twists his arm and struggles to line up the key. He drops the key on the ground. "Fuck." It's just out of reach. Colin looks over at Benny who, even though he's freezing to death, finds this amusing. All of a sudden he hears the door squeak open. Colin begins to panic as his cockiness has been absorbed by his discomfort. His throat is closing; his easy escape is being botched by his inability to reach the key. He stretches harder than he ever has, like his life depends on it. Sweat is dripping into his eyes. He takes a deep breath, collects himself, and stretches every fiber to find any slack. He reaches it just barely.

Miles walks over to the tank and notices that Colin is not in the chair. "What the fuck?" He turns towards his blind side a hair too slow.

He brains him with a pipe; Miles is out cold and Colin whispers in his ear, "Told ya I'd enjoy killing you... and that smoke break you just took is the reason I have the opportunity." He hustles to the office and rifles through the drawers, finding a gun. He spots his phone and grabs it on his way out. He places the muzzle of the gun in that little divot behind Miles' ear lobe. He pulls the trigger and the bullet doesn't exit, but it rattles around in Miles' head just enough to scramble his brains. He shoots him a couple more times for good measure.

Benny is pleading, barely able to talk, "Colin, please let me out of here."

"Sorry chief, end of the line."

"Go into my inside jacket pocket..."

CHAPTER 21

Colin obliges Benny and finds the grenade. "Awesome, you shouldn't have. I guess it is my half birthday." Benny's body is shutting down. Colin places the grenade in his pocket. "Goodbye, Benny." As he walks out, he calls Dane praying that the coroner doesn't pick up his phone.

"Yo," Dane's salutation when he knows it's Colin. "You okay?"

"Yup, idiots shot me in my vest."

"Alissa is at the police station."

"Nope. That was me. I had the desk sergeant call, hoping that when Richard came to the station, we could tail him back to wherever he had you."

"He is going to be pissed when he gets there and Alissa's not."

"Yup. Clerical error."

"I'm at Dr. Phil's. Get over here ASAP."

"I thought your vest caught the bullet."

"Shotgun spray. Caught most of it."

"Got it. Be right there."

Colin runs out, finally feeling like he's got some strength back. He's even maneuvering with one arm like he's been doing it for years. He hops into Miles' ride, a beat-up classic muscle car. He turns the key and the engine sputters. He pumps the gas a few times, turns the key, and it roars on. He heads directly to Dr. Phil's office. He hasn't driven since having both his arms, but he's crushing it. He parks out front of the doctor's office and runs in.

Dane is sitting in reception. His shirt is bullet-ridden and his face has scattered bruising and small pockets of stitches randomly throughout.

Colin smiles, "Finally, I get to be the good-looking one."

"If you say so."

The two brothers embrace. Colin pulls out his keys and his cellphone, and begins juggling them with his one hand, "Look at this... this is more entertaining than a clown on fire, yeah?"

"I told ya. Once you get the hang of this, you'll be better than most, handy-capable."

THREE GRAVES

* * *

They beeline to Colin's house to make sure their main asset is still under lock and key. Dane enters the house cautiously, gun drawn, in case Richard decides to check out the place once he's turned away at the police station. There's no sign of life. He clears all the upstairs rooms, and Colin heads to the basement. He stands in front of the door for a moment, taking a deep breath before entering. As his hand approaches the knob, it shakes a little and he's reminded of his withdrawal. He's improved, but not better. The adrenaline released by his brush with death temporarily masked his body's yearning for painkillers. He takes a deeper breath. His heart starts to flutter and he becomes lightheaded. He gently taps his injured hand on the bannister, and the pain shoots up his arm to his brain. It relaxes him. He opens the door and enters the room. Alissa is sitting with Charlie, visibly annoyed.

"Lis, do you believe in alien abduction? The truth is out there." Alissa crosses her arms, clearly pissed. "How 'bout just abduction? This albino fuck and an aborted Eminem kidnapped me this morning and your asshat of a father tried to kill me."

Alissa pops up and her demeanor shifts. She runs over to him and gives him a hug. "What happened?"

"I'll tell you later. We need to grab some stuff and get the fuck outta here."

Alissa begins to cry. "I'm so sorry. I hate him."

"He is a total dick." He hugs her. She cares more about him now than her own father. He looks down at his pants. "Could you help me undo my belt?"

She turns her head to the side confused, "I thought you said we have to leave immediately."

Colin realizes the optics and her interpretation. "Whoa. Nope. Not what I mean. I'm too much of a feminist to talk to a lady that forwardly. I've had to pee for like five hours. My belt is stuck and my zipper is broken."

She undoes his belt, "Good, because I'm too much of a lady to be talked to that way. But you are cute."

He deflects, "I do have all my teeth."

She playfully hit his arm.

"I'm going to pee. You grab anything you want to take with, starting with Charlie."

Dane and Colin pack up some gear, guns, and cash. They head over to their new base of operation.

Chapter 22

Mick sits in the bar of the Beverly Hills Hotel. He continually checks his phone and shifts in his seat. His neuroses only appear when he's anxious. He's able to reel them in most of the time and is a decent actor, because he's always acting. His persona is an amalgamation of traits and qualities he accumulated over his life from studying both real and fictional people. The source of his anxiety comes from his uncertainty of how to act in a given situation. Since nothing is natural, he must analyze the hell out of everything, adapt and adjust on the fly based on social cues. It's exhausting. He has a big meeting with a low-budget movie producer. He's cautiously optimistic as this producer has been known to cast unknowns that become stars. He sits visibly unnerved by his first meeting as a potential headliner, shaking his left foot excessively, practically rattling the little circular table.

He notices the producer immediately from having googled Greg Dancer. Greg is heavyset and has a shaved head. He's wearing a black bedazzled T-shirt with a skull, but not an expensive trendy shirt, rather the Target version. The shirt looks stiff and the skull looks itchy. His jeans are ripped and covered with paint stains and other marks, but not designer. An overzealous Asian kid in a sweatshop didn't distress these jeans. Instead they were the end result of manual labor. More likely the holes and stains are from when he changed his own tire, fixed his own toilet, or painted his own apartment.

Mick stands up and places his hand out. "Mr. Dancer, nice to meet you, my name is Mick."

CHAPTER 22

Greg has an unlit cigar in his mouth, and he adjusts it as he shakes Mick's hand, "Pleasure to meet you, Mick. Call me Greg."

"Not to sound like a total kiss ass, but I'd like to say, I'm a big fan of *Now We Die* and *Never More*. Those are my favorites. *Enough Too Late* and *Unable to Forward* were excellent, but your vision matured like Drew Barrymore from *E.T.* to *Poison Ivy*."

"You know, it's nice to have your work appreciated. Thank you, Mick. I liken my career to the life cycle of a bug. Larvae to adulthood, if you will."

The waitress comes over, "Sir, I'd just like to remind you that there's no smoking."

Greg nods, "I don't smoke 'em. They're terrible for you."

"Can I get you guys anything?" She asks with her pen poised above her tiny little notepad.

Mick answers meekly, placing his hand up, "I'll have a Coke."

Greg shifts around his cigar. "I'll have a vodka tonic. Well please."

The waitress walks away from the table and Greg leans in. "Mick, I could've had us meet at Chow's. Do you know why I didn't?"

Mickey shrugs. "It's hard to get in?"

"Nah, I'm tight with one of the bus boys. I can get in any time I want. 11 a.m. and 2 p.m. are easier, but if I needed 1 p.m., with enough notice, shouldn't be a problem. But, this is the place. You may see your Rob Schneiders or your Josh Brolins eating there, but here's where the action is."

"I love Brolin. Worked out next to him at Gold's in Venice. He just did bicep curls and was wearing all red Studio Beats by Dre like a boss."

Greg points at Mick with his cigar as he speaks. "What does the VP of Development at Paramount look like?" Mick shrugs his shoulders. "You don't know, but he's right there behind you." Mick looks at the guy Greg pointed out. He won't correct Greg, but saw him check in for the real estate conference. He doesn't work at Paramount and is from Idaho.

"That gal gets things done. That guy over there is who you want reading your script or handling your head shot. The room is full of ballers."

The waitress comes back with the order. "Here ya guys go. Can I get you anything else?"

Greg looks her in the face, "You have any bagel chips?"

The waitress shakes her head as she speaks, "No sir, I don't think we do."

"It's cool. You positive? Never mind. Do you need to check? You know what, no worries. It's okay. If you see some back there let me know. Any flavor but garlic."

Mick politely tells the waitress, "I'm good." She walks away.

Greg is animated as he speaks. "You see what I did there?"

Mick looks confused, "Tried to order Bagel Chips from a fancy hotel?"

Greg continues, "She will remember me forever. I just branded her with my mark. Not in a sexual way. My strange request will occasionally pop into her head and her mental hard drive will bring my picture up. And that's what it's all about. The more people you touch, the more meaning your existence will have. I make films because every pair of eyes that will have seen my work will have my brand burned into their hard-wiring."

Mick is assessing the situation and needs to start acting like this guy is both awesome and profound if he wants that part. "Yeah, man, you're totally on to something. Fucking A. Genius."

Greg continues, "You know Mickey Rourke?"

"No. I mean. I know who he is. I don't know him. Do you?"

Greg takes a sip of his drink. "You guys have the same first name."

"How do you like that... We totally do."

Greg nods his head affirmatively, "That's cool. Me and Rourke have been trying to link up professionally for about a decade. Each time I'm busy, he's free and vice versa."

"So you do know him?"

"We go to the same dentist."

CHAPTER 22

Mick wants to get down to business. "I'm excited about your next project."

"Me too. Me too. Here's my pitch to you. I want you. I saw the CSI and the commercial with the kangaroo. I like what you do."

Mick smiles, "I appreciate that."

Greg sipping his drink, "Was that kangaroo real?"

"CGI."

"No kidding. It looks real as shit when it punches you in the face."

"Yeah, everyone thinks it punched me in the face."

"That's acting, man. As for the film, we're gonna have to do a table read, see how you sound as the main character. Sort of like a chemistry type situation. It's how I do all my films. D'ya think you can play an adopted hit man who unknowingly has to kill his biological parents?"

"Hell, yeah. Dude, the script is tight."

"Thanks man."

Mick leans back, "I have a question for you."

"I love questions. Questions are like free presents."

"Aren't all presents free?"

"Exactly." Greg leans back and places his hand on his chin.

"If you could work with any actor, living or dead, who would it be?"

Greg strokes his chin. "I've thought about this extensively." He pauses for effect. "Elias Koteas."

Mick respects Elias Koteas big time, but is taken aback. Of any actor living or dead, he would have never guessed that answer. Mick takes the high road. "Love Koteas. He looks cool in hats. He was great in the *Traffic* mini-series."

Greg stands up, "I have to run. I'm meeting one of Anthony Quinn's kids. Not the sixty-year-old one or the child, one of the ones in the middle. He wants to be a stuntman or a camera loader. I'll throw any offspring of 'The Shark' a bone." Greg pads himself down, "I misplaced my wallet. Mick, I'll get you next time."

Mick obliges, "Sure, I got this."

"Listen, can I have a ten spot to get my car from the valet?"

"Sure." Mick is unsure why he's bankrolling this tete-a-tete but he'll write it off. Mick settles the tab with the waitress, leaves the bar area and walks over to the bathroom.

* * *

Dane parks on a side street next to the hotel. They bypass valet so they can get to their car undetected and at any given time. They also want to be as least memorable as possible to the staff. Dane grabs most of the gear, Colin carries what he can, and Alissa walks Charlie in. She has a bounce in her step and is so smitten with Colin she'd probably go anywhere with him. If he wanted to take her to a kitten torturing party, as long as he was there, she'd be down. They enter the hotel, Alissa excited like a child on vacation. Dane checks them in.

Colin turns to Alissa, "I need a tissue, hang here, I'll be right back."

"Yeah." She sits on one of the leather chairs in the lobby.

Colin walks to the bathroom. As he enters, he notices Mick immediately, just wrapping up his meeting, taking a piss, before the ride home.

Colin taps his shoulder while at the urinal, "Mick."

Mick flinches at first, as no guy expects to be touched at the urinal. Once he sees who it is, he lets his guard down, "Col, how'ya doing? How's the sting?"

Colin blows his nose, "I have to tell ya, sting operations are as unpredictable as two blind guys boxing. What brings you here?"

"Meeting with a producer. Oh, and I have a recurring role on *NCIS*."

"Good for you." Colin scratches his head, "That shows still going on, eh?"

"Yup. It's got legs like Cindy Crawford."

"Ah Cindy, brings me back." Colin walks over to the sink to wash his hand. He presses the faucet down and it turns on but upon releasing, it stops. Mick sees the frustration on his face and holds it down for him. Colin maneuvers soap onto his hand and rubs his fingers and palm together. He grabs a towel and dries off. They exit the bathroom, still talking about Cindy Crawford and how fucking charismatic Rande Gerber must be to land the quintessential woman. Dane is sitting near Alissa.

Mick is excited to see Dane, "Dane, what's up?"

"How's my favorite actor?"

"Great. Just had a bizarre meeting with a producer. It went well but the guy is fucking out there." Alissa registers who Mickey is and vice versa.

Mick turns to Alissa, "How are you?"

Alissa has no hard feelings because she thinks she's with the man of her dreams. "I'm good. Whatever your real name is."

He places his hand out, "It's Mick."

Alissa shakes his hand, "Holy shit, you're on the kangaroo commercial. I can't believe I didn't notice when we first met."

"Yup. That's me."

Alissa continues, "I knew you looked familiar, but couldn't place you. Did it hurt when that kangaroo punched you?"

"Nope. All CGI."

Dane holds up two room keys. Colin nods and turns to Alissa, "Okay then, let's get up to our rooms."

Mick's eyes wander and locks in on a guest checking out at reception, "Son of a bitch."

Dane recognizes the source of Mick's anger, "There's the SNL guy, from like the nineties."

Colin concurs, "Yeah, the liar guy. He's tan as fuck."

Mick barely separates his teeth when he talks. "That prick."

Both Dane and Colin ask what's got him so fired up. "When I first moved out here, I walked dogs and taught spin class. That asshole was watching his girlfriend's dog, a little mutt of some sort and he hired me to walk him twice a day. So he has this fucking ridiculous party, gets wasted, and literally falls on the dog, crushing him instantly. He blames me to his girlfriend, saying I walked him too long and he died of a heart attack. She sued me and I had to pay for a dog autopsy to prove he was crushed. I won but it cost me all of my dog walking business and the autopsy was like a grand... I'll be right back." Mick storms over there and stands behind him.

The comedian is at the front desk complaining he was charged for too many adult films. "I didn't order *Ass Pirates of the Caribbean*, starring Johnny Deep and Orlando Bum." He's dressed completely in tennis clothes from head to toe, like he is ready for the U.S. Open. Mick taps him on the shoulder.

The comedian turns, "What? Can't you see I'm in the middle of something?"

Mick leans in, "Do you remember me?"

"No, should I?"

Mick crosses his arms, "Does BamBam refresh your memory?"

His eyes bug out, "What the fuck? That was ages ago. You were cleared, what's your problem?"

"Like a real asshole, you never said you were sorry."

"I am sorry. What I did was fucked up. I was doing a lot of drugs back then and was in a really bad place."

Mick taken aback. "Okay then, cool."

"You still walking dogs?"

"No, I'm an actor. I just booked a recurring role on *NCIS*."

"That's great. I didn't know the show was still on." He pulls out his card and hands it to Mick. "Get in touch with me, we should work together."

Mick's tune changes, "Awesome, thanks man."

They part ways and Mickey heads back to Dane, Colin, and Alissa. "He apologized. Crazy. I'm going to bounce. Good seeing you guys and gal." Colin and Dane bid him farewell and the three walk towards the elevator and press the button.

Colin places his arm around Alissa. She smiles and buries her head in his chest. The elevator is taking forever. Colin glances at the time and blows out a deep breath.

CHAPTER 22

Dane turns and looks at him. "Col, do you want to leg it?" Colin nods and Dane opens the door to the steps, and they walk through.

*　*　*

The vein in Piney's head is about to explode as he explodes into the working girl, Sherry, who he sees this time every week. The police station debacle where Richard's hopes were dashed did not deter Piney from making his standing appointment. He needed to blow off some steam. He's so out of shape, lacking flexibility from head to toe, that his mechanical thrusting doesn't impress anyone, let alone a professional sex worker. Sherry is high-end, expensive, and works out of the Beverly Hills Hotel. She's discreet, her clientele is wealthy, and has greased enough palms that no one hassles her. She has to pretend this fat, sweaty, animal got her off, but then again, shouldn't be too hard; she's a failed actress and his ego wouldn't let him think otherwise.

"What do you think, luv, pretty impressive, eh? I'm no tosser. I feel like you lost control of your body, two maybe three times?"

"At least." Sherry has been at this long enough to lie. "Yeah baby, if you can get it up again, it'll be on the house." She knows he's a one hit wonder.

"Sorry luv, not today. I have to save some for the ball and chain."

She lies in bed, on her phone, waiting for Piney to get dressed. His hands are shaky, struggling to do up the last button on his shirt. He places his shoulder holster on loosely, and pulls out a wad of cash. He counts, stops, and slaps it on the desk. "There you go, luv, a little extra. Buy yourself something lovely."

He picks up his coat and walks out. He enters the hallway, pushes the elevator button and waits. Within a few seconds the door opens and he gets in. After his door closes, the other elevator opens, and a man in a business suit exits. He walks directly towards Sherry's room door.

The elevator hits the ground floor as soon as Colin and crew hit the stairway. Fate has determined that Piney will miss his boss's adversary by a second or two. He's fairly stuffed into this Otis coffin. He patiently waits for the older couple and the family with the three young kids to awkwardly pack up and exit the elevator.

* * *

In the hallway, Colin and Alissa part ways with Dane whose room is a few doors down. Dane grabs Charlie's leash, "I'm gonna room with my favorite niece." Alissa kneels down and pets her face, Charlie loving the attention.

Colin gets to the door and pulls out the key card. Alissa asks if she can open the door. "Are you sure you can handle the responsibility?"

She gives him the middle finger. He hands her the card, she places it in the slot, the light turns green, and she turns the handle. She practically runs into the room and hits the bathroom first. "Col, there's a sewing kit in here. And some really pretty soap. We have to bring this with us."

He closes the door, locking the top latch, and checks out the room. "Soap and thread are awesome. Definitely steal it."

Alissa runs out of the bathroom, plops down on the bed and turns the television on. "Ooh, HBO!"

He walks towards the window, moves the curtain slightly and checks out the view. He notices Piney getting into his car and wonders if it's just a coincidence. He turns to Alissa while reading the mini bar price list, "What the what? M&M's are eight bucks for a mini bag."

"Do you think they have a pool?"

"Yeah, I think so." There's a knock on the door. Colin opens the door and Dane walks in. They talk in code, "You know that limey fuck?"

Dane's following, "Yup."

"He just left."

"Here?"

Colin nods.

Dane remembers, "Ah, when we did recon, he has a standing appointment. He gets cleaned out once a week."

"Perfect."

"We're going to wait until dark for the thing with the guys. But we can do the thing with the guy now."

"Yeah, let's do the thing with the guy."

"Meet me in the lobby in ten."

Colin nods to Dane and turns his attention to Alissa. "Alright girly, I need to do some stuff. You take it easy, watch some TV. If you get hungry, eat the eight dollar M&M's and don't get too wasted. Remember you hold my hair back while I throw up, not the other way around."

"Now?" Alissa is disappointed.

"Yeah. Something now and something later. This isn't really a vacation. Pretend this room is like the basement at my house. Yup, that doesn't get any less creepy sounding."

"Can I help?"

"You're helping by staying here. We'll have some time in between. I'll be right back. Don't leave this room or open the door for anyone. Except Ed McMahon."

"Who's Ed McMahon?"

"He's a dead guy. Need to know my audience when making Publisher Clearing House jokes. Otherwise, no pay-off. Pun intended."

"What?"

"Never mind. But seriously, do not open the door for anyone." She nods. He goes over and opens the curtains up. "It's nice out."

Chapter 23

"Yup. Fuck this guy." Colin piles a handful of over-the-counter analgesics with caffeine in his mouth, picks up his water bottle and takes a sustained gulp, trying to get them all down in one massive swig. He's attempting to put a dent in his pounding headache.

Dane is driving, "Who would've thought Timmy would unwittingly pull the thread that could've unraveled our whole plan?"

"Right? I'm sure he gets tangled up in cat's cradle. He's somewhere on the spectrum between imbecile and full on fucktard."

"I'd say closer to fucktard than imbecile." Dane points out of the front windshield, "This is his building. We'll park down this side street."

The brothers walk towards the building, Dane merely a half-step ahead, "You know who I saw at Bristol Farms in West Hollywood?"

"Someone paying more for food because they can? A gay? Spongebob Squarepants?"

Dane places his hand up with an inch between his thumb and forefinger, "Mini-Me."

"No shit. I'd pay some money to see him holding a forty. Two forties."

They enter the building. Dane continues, "He's fucking tiny. Like how do all his organs and shit fit in that little body?" The concierge, an older black man, reads the paper. He lowers it as the brothers approach. Dane shows him his badge, he points to the elevator, and goes back to his paper.

CHAPTER 23

Dane continues the conversation as they enter the elevator, "Yeah, does he have normal size organs all crammed in there or proportional? If he needed a heart transplant, would mine take up his whole chest cavity or does he need like a five-year-old's heart?" The door closes and they go up to the third floor.

"I'll have to google that later. I may have to revisit his sex tape. I'm pretty sure he almost fell into the gal."

"You know, Kenny and Riva in admin have a death bet that he doesn't make it to fifty." The door opens and they walk out. Dane draws his gun.

"He doesn't look a day over four feet." Colin draws his gun and they walk towards the apartment. "That's amazing. Death bets are so cool."

"His birthday is January 1st so New Year's Eve that year, money may change hands." They are outside Timmy's door. Dane whispers, "Every time he's in rehab or the hospital, they both get super excited and check TMZ constantly. It's like a ten-year bet if he makes it."

"We need to come up with like a ten, fifteen year bet. Keep things interesting."

Dane's down with the idea, "We'll come up with something like *Trading Places*."

"Yeah, a social experiment."

Timmy sits in his apartment playing video games. His uncle finances his life as Richard loves his sister, so his disappointment of a nephew gets a free pass. His 65-inch 4K LED television is perched neatly on a nice piece of furniture holding all his game consoles. He has two gaming chairs for when Petey used to come over and they'd be up all night entering fantastical worlds where avatars embodied everything they'd never be. The only time he's ever felt in control is when he's controlling the life and death of an amalgamation of pixels held together by code, where there are no stakes. His nightmare is reality; when visiting worlds where anything is possible, being impotent in this one is worse than death.

This building is relatively high-end and not cheap. Timmy's apartment is dingy as he's barely a mannish boy. He has unopened piles of mail, with jury duty notices and parking tickets strewn about. Every surface and wall is covered in a thin layer of grime. It's never been cleaned. The light beige carpet is peppered with small and large spots from dirty shoes, spilling all types of liquid and food. He has drunken parties where people he doesn't know show up, treat the place like shit, and leave without a second thought.

Timmy is talking to his television as he plays, "Come on." He wiggles in his chair, twisting out of the way, subconsciously believing his movements will translate into the game. "Yeah, have some!" He moves his hands quickly. "I'm the man! Bring it. Bring it. Bring it." His door flies open with a kick from Dane's boot and Timmy nearly jumps out of his skin. They enter the apartment guns drawn, Colin closing the door behind them.

Timmy throws his hands up, "Don't kill me!"

Colin turns to Dane, "Well then, let's go."

Dane smiles, "Come on Timmy, you're the man."

"I'm soft, guys. Softer than fuckin' toilet tissue."

"Maybe that three-ply stuff. But the industrial 'tp', people sand wood with that shit," Colin says.

Dane poses a question to Timmy. "Do you know the difference between a schlemiel and a schlimazel?" Timmy shrugs. Dane continues, "Of course you don't. You're an idiot."

Colin chimes in, "That's kinda insulting to idiots."

"A schlemiel is the guy at a dinner party that's carrying a tray of champagne and he trips and spills it." Dane closes the gap between he and Timmy. "A schlimazel is the guy who the drinks land on." Colin checks the kitchen, visible from the living room, while Dane toys with Timmy. "Which would you rather be?"

Colin reaches the stove, "Dane, there's some pasta boiling in here."

"Timmy wants it al dente." Dane turns back to Timmy. "Well? Schlemiel or schlimazel?"

CHAPTER 23

Timmy shakes his head, making an unsure face like he was tasked with making nuclear fusion viable, "I don't know."

"It's tricky. On one side of the coin you're the drink spiller, the buffoon who in a room full of people looks like a klutz, but you're dry. On the other side, you did nothing, you're the spillee, but have a lap full of bubbly and I'm not talking about the bleach blonde hooker with the good gag reflex."

Colin shouts from the kitchen, "Love her! Gentle hands and such a soft mouth. She's a sword-swallowing goddess."

Timmy feebly attempts to talk himself out of this situation. He's better off having Helen Keller do the talking. "Um, like, I know my uncle was a little harsh, when he cut off your brother's arm."

"That's very astute." Dane purses his lips and nods, sarcastically agreeing that cutting off an arm is a little harsh.

Timmy doesn't pick up on his sarcasm. "The very next day, I swear, I suggested hush money. You know. A gesture."

Colin strains the spaghetti. "That would've made things right. We could've avoided this whole thing. Dane, can we nominate Timmy to negotiate with North Korea? He's got a knack for solving problems."

Dane seizes him by the back of his neck, dragging him into the kitchen. "Timmy, don't struggle. I'll just shoot you." He grabs his right arm and holds it against the table. Before Timmy can even flinch, Colin has separated his hand from his wrist with a cleaver. Timmy screams. Dane places a dish rag in his mouth and opens a drawer, "Everyone puts their duct tape in this drawer, god bless you Timmy." He wraps the tape around his head, with the rag in his mouth muffling his screams. Blood is spurting from his wrist. Dane covers it up with duct tape.

Colin grabs the tongs hanging above Timmy's stove and picks up as much pasta as possible. Dane pulls Timmy's pants away from his body and they drop the scolding hot pasta down his pants. He screams and falls back, knocking over chairs and hitting the ground hard. He struggles to pull the spaghetti out of his pants with his one hand and severed wrist. He practically has a heart attack. Colin grabs Timmy's keys from a hook by the door. Dane drags him out of the apartment and down the steps, Timmy thumping and banging down all three flights. They place him in the trunk of his own car.

Now dark, they drive onto Richard's property, using the clicker in Timmy's car to gain access unannounced. It's eerily quiet around the compound. They carefully sneak around to the trunk using the key to open it. Dane begins to twist on a silencer. Timmy is in and out of consciousness. Colin smacks his face to wake him up, "Wakey-wakey, eggs and bakey. I want you to be awake for this."

Dane places smelling salts under his nose, "Just like an NFL quarterback, trying to fake his way through a mid-game concussion exam. All better."

"Did I read Jim McMahon would wake up in the middle of the night confused, and would piss into his dishwasher?" Colin asks Dane.

"Dishwasher or washing machine."

"I guess he Super Bowl shuffled his way to brain trauma."

Colin leans into Timmy, "I told you, I would enjoy killing you when you came and got me at my house with Casper the fugly ghost." He places the barrel up against Timmy's rectum, "This is going to hurt." He squeezes off three bullets. Timmy moans in pain and wriggles slowly. If he wasn't confined in his tiny trunk, the pain would have made him vacillate wildly. Dane drops an envelope in the trunk and closes it.

***

After a faint beep and a click, the hotel door opens not long after Colin left with Dane. The room's entryway is a three-foot hall with the bathroom to the right, opening into the main room. From Alissa's vantage point, she cannot see who entered, and assumes its Colin, "Col, come here, I'm watching this thing on dolphins."

A soft, mid-tone, nebbish voice answers with an off-kilter cadence,

CHAPTER 23

"I'm sorry. Your friend is still out." He cracks his neck, "We'll be able to get acquainted though."

Alissa curls up towards the bed's headboard creating as much distance, without getting up, between her and this intruder. "Who the fuck are you?"

Roger is the reason the FBI has a Behavioral Science Unit. He exhibits nearly all the common characteristics attributed to those who murder for some sort of psychological gratification. His is lust. He's raped and murdered nearly a dozen girls, mostly in the Midwest. Since his motivation is sexually based, this aspect is where he obtains his pleasure; he's actually ashamed of the murder. However, for his proclivities to continue without capture, killing the victim is a prerequisite. His distaste for the killing had recently curtailed his activities, but when he saw Alissa in the lobby, he was triggered. All his victims are similar in age, height, build, and could be Alissa's sisters. His compulsion bubbled out of control, and since he's a bellhop at the hotel, he's able to get into any room. He paid his buddy at valet fifty bucks to call him when he saw Colin come back. He told him he needed to take a nap to sleep off a migraine and he was going to use Colin's room since he knew he was out.

He closes the curtains. "My name's Roger." He sits down on the edge of the bed, "You remind me of my sister. Becky. She was a good girl. She used to look out for me. My father sold her to all his friends. She was four years my senior. When I was thirteen, a gang of them got too rough. They broke her neck. Even dead, they all finished. My father made me help him get rid of her body. She was soaked and dripping in semen. It was disgusting. We cut her up, like we'd done with so many deer and buried her where no one would ever find her. My father filed a police report that she'd run away." Alissa's face is frozen with terror. She sits, paralyzed, as Roger continues, "When I got old enough, I made some chloroform, very easy to make, gathered all those men and dear old dad. I brought them to a cabin nearby. It was a life-size diorama; I set them up at the card table with cigars, beers, chips. The whole thing. Then I set the place on fire and they all burned. I dealt them all cards. Everyone had a full house. How neat is that? I mean most of the cards were burnt beyond recognition, but if anyone knew, I think they would really like that touch."

Alissa musters enough saliva to attempt to talk. She clears her throat as a giant knot materialized the second Roger started talking. "My father is Richard Pembroke."

Roger doesn't flinch. "I'm not familiar. I surely don't care."

"He's a criminal too. He kills people."

Roger pulls out his knife, "Maybe I'll pay him a visit when we're done. Tell him what happened to his little girl right before I turn him inside out."

"My boyfriend's a cop!"

Roger shakes his head, "Now you're just grasping at straws. The gimp? I wouldn't be deterred by the idea of an able-bodied cop, no way a cripple raises my pulse. Besides, I've been working law enforcement like they're circus monkeys my whole life." Alissa stands up and Roger springs forward, closes the gap, and slams her against the wall with the blade of his knife against her neck. His mouth is one inch from her face. She's terrified, wincing with her eyes closed, unable to make her vocal cords work. "This is how this works. You're going to lie on this bed and play with yourself until you climax. You'll have ten minutes. If you're successful, I'll kill you quickly and painlessly, and rape you post-mortem. If you fail or fake it, I hate fakers and goddammit I always know, so don't you even fucking try. I'll smuggle you out of here, and a dungeon will be your home for the next few days, until you bore me. I will do the most unimaginable things to you, until you beg me to kill you." He throws her on the bed, pulls her pants off. She lies there in her panties and a tank top. He pulls the desk chair over, sits in front of the bed and checks his watch. "Go."

Alissa has always been pursued, by boys and even men. She's always been shy and Richard, being both overprotective with a bodyguard always tailing her and a reputation that would scare any boy into

CHAPTER 23

thinking twice about even kissing her, she's inexperienced to say the least. Her heart is racing as she slides her right hand down her panties. She gently bites her lip, pretending she's anywhere but here.

Roger stands up, guiding his knife towards her upper thigh. Alissa wiggles as the cold back of the blade presses against her flesh, "Let me help you," he pulls up on the knife, cutting the right side of her panties then the left. The cotton Lycra mix spring off, and he grabs them, "Continue. Don't stop."

Alissa closes her eyes and does her best to get to a place nearly impossible to get to under the circumstances. Roger gets jittery as all this is exciting him as much as ever. There's a knock on the door. He pulls out his cellphone to check for a text or missed calls. He points at Alissa. "Don't say a word."

Alissa whispers, "Pause the clock."

Roger smiles and winks, "Thatta girl." He approaches the door and looks through the peephole, "Yes, can I help you?" BANG. BANG. Before he can focus, he has an eye full of lead. He flies to the ground; his heart stopped before impact with the hotel floor. The card key hits the lock, and then there's a beep. Dane hangs back in the hall. Colin enters, stepping over the body, then rushes over to the bed to calm Alissa down. She's half-naked and hysterically crying. He wraps her up in a blanket and holds her.

She whispers in his ear, "You came just in time." She repeats it over and over.

"Shhh. Breathe."

Alissa looks up, "How'd you know?"

"I left the curtains open. When we got back they were closed. You can see from outside."

"He said he had a guy valet watching for you."

"We parked on the street like before and came in the side entrance." She just hugs him as hard as she can.

This PR nightmare for a high-end hotel gets handled quickly and quietly. The manager calls in a fixer, Frankie Fracaso, a throwback in the vein of Fred Otash and Eddie Mannix from Hollywood's Golden Age. He's ex-police and famous for diffusing Hollywood scandals. Dane enlisted Frankie to change the narrative of Betty's death and Colin's crippling. Frankie is tall, handsome in a tough guy way, and just his gait suggests strong and capable. He comes onto the scene quiet, focused, but once he sees Dane and Colin, a giant smile washes over his face. He places his hand out shaking with Dane then Colin, "Jesus Christ, I should have figured the Graves boys would be at the center of this situation."

Dane shrugs, "One less rapist, yeah? It's not even Christmas."

Colin greets Frankie, "Has our President hired you yet to fix anything?"

Frankie laughs, "I wouldn't take that bloated fuck's money for anything." He changes the subject, "What are we looking at?"

Dane fills Frankie in, "Serial killer rapist from Ohio. At least a dozen unsolved out there."

Frankie leans in, "Sick fuck. I'll get this all cleaned up. We'll get you moved out of this room and down the hall."

Dane chimes in, "And I can't be involved. I'm officially dead at the moment."

"You look great for a dead guy," Frankie nodding, "No problem. I have a half a dozen cops that can use the collar and a medal."

Colin points to Dane, "This guy doesn't have any room on his jacket for another medal. It weighs like thirty pounds."

Dane agrees, "It is starting to look a bit gaudy."

Frankie puts his arms around both guys, "I got you guys and if you even need to put me on retainer, just say the word."

Colin and Alissa move down the hall to another room. While Colin transports their belongings, Alissa is lying on the bed on her side, with her back facing the door, crying. Colin enters with the last of their stuff. "This one arm shit is fun. I get to make double the amount of trips. Yay fitness." He sees Alissa crying, and sits next to her on the bed, and begins petting her head, "Hey you." She doesn't really respond. "That was 'heyy' with two 'y's, by the way. It's hard to tell when verbalized but if we were texting, you would've totally known that." She laughs a bit. "I know all that was terrifying and it's going to take a second to process, but you're safe now. Well, I mean, machines will take over the world soon and I'm not entirely convinced zombies are science fiction, but for the foreseeable future, you're safe."

Alissa laughs, "You're a dork."

"Absolutely, card-carrying dork. Not to be confused with a geek, which now means expert, but when I was a kid, it was a carnival performer whose act consisted of biting the head off of a live chicken or snake."

Alissa sits up, "What?" Her hair is smashed from laying on it.

"Yup, that was a thing," he glances at the top of her head.

Alissa touches her hair, "Is my hair all messed up?"

Colin turns his head to the side squinting, "Not messed up, exactly. I'm sure some tribes intentionally style their hair in an asymmetrical manner as such."

Alissa springs up and looks in the mirror, "Oh my god, I'm a hot mess."

Dane enters the room after a quick knock. "Col, you ready."

He stands up and turns towards Dane, "Yup."

Alissa looks at him. "Where are you going?"

"Disneyland... and you can't come."

Alissa can already tell when to ignore him, "I'm scared."

"We have an officer on the floor and if you use the lock thing, you'll be fine. And until you fix your hair, no one will rape you."

She gives him the middle finger. "Scared... for you."

"No reason for that. Dane wouldn't let anything happen to me." He looks where his missing arm should be, "This was all me. I should be fine now that he's got my back. Right, Dane?"

Dane answers calmly, "I'd say so, but only Dionne Warwick knows for sure."

"Don't mind him," Colin tells Alissa. "The psychic hotline joke was for my benefit." He kisses her head. "If you don't eat the eight dollar M&M's, I'm going to." She smiles.

* * *

Revenge is an artistic endeavor commingled with strategic precision. The paradox of structured or planned art, as some will argue creative chaos yields the most impactful results, is necessary for efficacy. And as in a bullfight, the matador must weaken the bull with carefully placed lances before he can entertain the crowd and toy with his adversary. Now that Richard is weakened, the brothers can inflict more suffering, pushing him over the escarpment. Tonight, they tie up a few loose ends. These are the finishing touches and like any masterpiece, each stroke is important from the very first to the very last. There are indirect and peripheral characters in this cast and each will get their credit. Benny gave Dane and Colin their names and each played a part, albeit some minimal. Nevertheless, like a birthday dinner where the check is split regardless of who got what... everyone pays.

Dane throws the police van into park a block away from a dive bar off of Sunset. "What a piece of shit."

Colin struggles to open the door. "Fucking latch is sticky."

Dane uses his shoulder to pop the tight door open. The door's metal lets out a groan. "Jesus Christ. Did you hear that?"

"It's nice to know pedophiles invest more in their shady vans than the department." He slams the door, and it closes with a clunk. "Who's up first?"

"The courier."

"That's right. Finn Dixon."

Dane points to the bar, "He's known as the worst gambler in the world."

"Like bet against Globetrotters? Hits on twenty? Shorts Amazon stock?"

Dane nods affirmatively, "And he pays his debts off to Richard by delivering things."

"Like anything liquid, fragile, perishable, and potentially hazardous. Apples and lithium batteries."

Dane smiles, "Something like that."

They enter. Dane spots Finn immediately and points him out to Colin. Finn sits at the bar, staring at the game. Dane takes the seat to the left of him and Colin the right. His eyes never leave the television. He quaffs his beer and points the Red Stripe bottle at the television. "Goddamn Lakers. The refs are fucking with the spread." He turns to Colin. "What do you think?"

"About the refs? Or like Isis? Cool uniforms, don't know if I can give up bacon."

Finn scrunches his face, confused. "Whatever." He stands up, and walks towards the bathroom. They follow. He pushes the door in, walks right up to an empty urinal, and begins pissing. His eyes open slowly as the hard, cold metal of Dane's gun on the back of his head and the click of the hammer jar him from his comfortable piss.

"Don't move, finish up," Dane tells him.

Finn is panicking. "I don't know what you want... I have no money."

Colin says to Finn, "Don't care about money. You're the butt-truffle with your nose so far up Pembroke's ass that you're going to die from proximity."

Dane turns him around and he finally notices Colin's missing arm, "Oh shit, it's you."

"It's nice to know that your witnessing my dismemberment hasn't been too hard on you."

"Hey man, that was brutal, I didn't know he was going to do that."

"So brutal, you forgot what I looked like until now. But I didn't forget money changing hands when he killed my wife. One of the few bets you've won, yeah?"

Finn stays quiet and Dane places his cuffs on, "Get in the fucking van. And shut your mouth."

Kurt Hilburn is their next stop as they wrangle this set of targets.

Kurt is Romani. He's the type of gypsy that gives gypsies a bad name. He's an outcast among his community; one of the few tenets they hold sacred is that it's unacceptable to fuck over family. Everyone else is fair game. Kurt has ripped off his own kin more times than either is willing to admit. He's so unscrupulous and undiscerning, he'll steal a broken wheelchair from a cripple, and has done so... more than once. He'll steal a penny just to pocket something he doesn't deserve, even if its worthless. Using Richard's name gets him in doors otherwise slammed in his face, and in return he kicks back a high percentage of his takings. Richard likes the bag of cash he brings him and is able to keep him under control because he has hard evidence he uses as leverage that, if revealed, would place Kurt in a small cell for the rest of his life.

Dane gets a text from a source privy to a drug deal going down tonight between Kurt and Japanese gangsters. They head over to a sketchy area downtown, met by a half a dozen other guys, tactically dressed with night vision and Heckler & Koch MP5A3 sub-machine guns with silencers. Dane addresses what's essentially his Seal Team 6. "Alright, boys," he holds up a photo of Kurt, "We want this guy, Kurt Hilburn, taken alive."

One of the super soldiers, built like Superman, "What is the ROE?"

Colin steps into the fray, "Glad you asked. None. In fact, just take everyone out but Hilburn. Quickly, and if it comes to pass that Hilburn needs to be put down to protect anyone in this circle, do it." The men all smile and fist pump, excited for the mission. Kurt sits slouched in his car, listening to an audio book, drinking lukewarm coffee. He looks at his watch, exhales frustrated breath as lack of punctuality is a pet peeve of his. Off in the distance, two SUVs are approaching and they park facing Kurt's car. Nearly a half dozen gangsters exit the vehicles. Kurt covers his eyes as their headlights are blinding. He exits the car, shouting to the men that just arrived, "Jesus Christ, you guys are like twenty minutes late." As he walks towards them he stops, realizing he left his gun on the passenger seat. He looks back at his car, pauses, but continues.

Hisoka Sato addresses Kurt, "Sorry Kurt, Waze took us some crazy way," they shake hands.

Kurt smiles, "Goddamn Waze." He shakes his head, "I think it's trying to kill us, having us make left hand turns across busy streets. I don't know. Rise of the machines. Right? Fucking *Terminator 2* is happening."

Hisoka continues, "I don't even want to think about it, man. It's going to be tough to work in the shadows with electronic eyes everywhere. But whatever. Let me see the stuff."

"Of course," Kurt walks to back of his car and pops the trunk, "This stuff is prime time. Pure fentanyl powder. You can do anything you want. Mix with shitty H, pill press it and sell it as oxy. Sell it straight up or use it all."

Hisoka looks suspicious, "How'd you get your hands on this China White?"

"You let me worry about the how. You're asking me about the past, when you should be right here in the present."

Hisoka gestures to one of his men. On this cue, the entire group is flanked by Dane and Colin's men, bullets flying precisely, taking out all the men in twenty seconds. During this time span, the only noise is silenced machine guns that sound like quiet blow darts and dead weight hitting the ground, then nothing. Kurt had flinched and froze, Hisoka's blood on this face.

The brothers stroll up. Dane orders one of the guys to grab the Fentanyl, one to grab the cash, and another to grab Kurt and get him on his knees before the brothers.

Kurt is shaking, "What the fuck?"

"I love killing drug dealers," Dane tells Colin. "It's like pulling weeds so better plants can grow."

Colin nods, "I know you do. I think besides scrapbooking, it's your favorite thing."

"Right? Give me some lignin-free paper and I'll dry emboss all day."

Colin turns his head to the side, looking down on Kurt, "We haven't formally met. Names Colin, you may remember me now?"

Kurt looks terrified. "I was just there, man, I had nothing to do with that. I swear."

Colin processes Kurt's testimony. "I get it," he points out the scene, dead gangsters and the drug deal, "This whole situation was good for us to lock down, and killing you is kinda the cherry on top."

Dane kneels down, "If you're wondering how we knew you were here, your brother Arthur tipped us off."

Kurt spits on the ground, "That bastard!"

They escort him to the van, cuff him and place him next to Finn. They know each other but don't dare converse. The next stop is a driver, Mike Bishop; sometimes legal driving and sometimes not. Colin and Dane sneak up to his duplex in Hollywood and can see in through the back sliding glass door. They see Bishop with his family, two little girls and pretty little wife. The girls are blonde like their mother, and they're reading in the living room. The scene looks like a Hallmark movie. Colin signals for Dane to hang back. He walks around to another window and looks inside. Everyone's shoes are neatly piled up and on the coat rack is a Carhartt jacket with 'Mike's Garage' embroidered on. Colin makes his way back to the window where Dane is crouched.

Colin whispers, "No-go on this one."

"You sure?"

"Yep. It just occurred to me, the milkshake that brings all the boys to the yard, is not an ice cream beverage is it?"

Dane shakes his head, "I got you. We only eat other monsters."

Once they had picked up the first of their current two passengers, the brothers have sat in silence, each stop, as to give those within earshot nothing. Dane parks the car in a bowling alley parking lot. Colin, about to explode from the silence, turns to the guys, "Either of you guys ever drop a nickel? Five bagger?" He looks at Finn, "This guy looks like a cranker for sure." They remain expressionless, "No? Nothing?"

Warren bowls this time every week. This massive black man sticks out like a sore thumb in most instances; within Richard's inner circle and even more so at bowling alleys. He happens to be enormous, black as night, with a voice so low it echoes from his cavernous torso like it's coming from the belly of a ship. He grabbed Ingrid and nearly killed Dane outside the coffee shop, so the brothers are going into this abduction laser focused. Richard had an affair with Warren's mother, a prostitute being run out of a high-end hotel. One of her Johns beat her to death when the boy was eight years old. Warren's father is allegedly a famous football player, hence his gifted genetics. Richard helped his grandmother financially and would take both Jeff and him bowling. Richard liked the idea of Jeff having a diverse group of friends. Some of Warren's best memories are bowling with Uncle Richard, so subconsciously it's become his main hobby.

Warren stands by the ball return waiting for his custom ball, clear with a skull suspended in the center. Warren places his hand over the air fanned out of the ball return. He blows on his right hand, calming his face and lowering his heart rate. His ball pops up and he grabs it. He walks five feet from the line, places his feet together, sporting his own shoes, not rentals. He pauses with the ball in front of his face, poised and serious. Warren takes a few steps and fires the ball down the right side of the lane with the spin and power of a professional. The ball spins into the pins perfectly and they fall with authority. He pumps his first and lets out a yelp. Warren turns and the screen above him displays his score. He's in the ninth frame with a strike in each previous.

The shoe attendant, a real low-life, walks over to Warren's lane. He's wearing a flannel shirt with the sleeves cut off, a mesh hat that says 'My Nuts Your Mouth,' and dirty jeans. "Boy, they're towing your ride out there."

"My ride?"

"Yours the black Jeep?"

"Yeah."

"Well git movin' boy. They strapping that up to the tow truck as we speak."

Warren unlaces his shoes, slips his feet into boots and takes his glove off, dropping it on his bag to run outside. He scans the parking lot and there isn't a tow truck in sight. "Fucking cracker, tryin' to ruin my perfect game."

Colin taps him on the shoulder with his gun. "Hey, big guy, I hear your voice is pretty annoying...and it's your best quality." Warren turns around and smacks the gun out of his hand like Colin was a child holding a toy. Within a second, his giant hand is around his neck. He picks Colin up by his throat and throws him on the hood of the nearest car. Dane's retractable nightstick swishes open. He smashes Warren in the back of the head. Warren turns around, unfazed. Dane strikes him again on the head, then the leg, and then the mid-section. Warren doesn't flinch. Dane does flinch when Warren grabs the nightstick and throws it. Finn and Kurt watch from the van, cracking up at the scene. Dane pulls his gun. Warren grabs his arm and twists it behind him, so as he fires the bullet shatters the glass of the correction van whizzing between Kurt and Finn. Warren punches Dane in the face and he flies to ground. Warren straddles him and begins to choke the life out of him.

Colin gets to his feet and scans the parking lot. There's a hillbilly couple walking towards the building, each with a bag. He grabs the bag out of the man's hand.

"Hey. Whatcha think you're doing?"

"I'm commandeering your bowling ball. Just stand back with your cousin-wife. Or sister-wife? You're not twins, are you?" Colin runs over and smashes Warren in the head with the ball in bag, three times, knocking him unconscious. He falls onto Dane, cutting off his oxygen. Colin feebly attempts to roll him over as he weighs a ton. Dane pushes and Colin pulls. Dane is red with asphyxiation and they eventually move the beast. He pops up, coughing and struggling to breathe. "Great. How are we going to get him into the van?"

"The same way Copperfield made the Empire State Building disappear."

Dane shakes his head, "Don't say magic."

Colin says, "Magic" at the same time as Dane.

At the last and final stop, Colin sits in a chair next to the bed at a convalescent home, pretending to read to the old man lying in the bed. "And the two princes bring peace to the land by balancing the power vacuum..." Dane just looks on as Colin closes the book, "And that's why we're bringing you with us, you geriatric, liver-spotted, goblin-looking fuck."

Dane picks up the old man, who weighs practically nothing, and places him in a wheelchair. The old man doesn't struggle; he barely has the strength to keep his head up. He says to Dane, "This place is nice. Television, board games, activities. All your friends in one place. It's like camp without the wedgies."

Dane smirks, "Not a terrible last stop."

"Not to mention all the old lady cooch you can handle." Colin wiggles his eyebrows, "Raw dog all day." He points to the old man, "This guy knows what I'm talking about."

Dane shakes his head, amused. "That's disgusting."

* * *

The coast is clear at Richard's main warehouse. Miles is still lifeless in a pile on the cold floor and Benny is still hanging there, half-submerged in water. His lower body has already begun to bloat. Dane and Colin's men meet the guys there and help escort the four captives into the warehouse. They are lined up and cuffed behind their backs, with the exception of the old man who just sits there in the wheelchair, half slumped over.

Dane and Colin place nooses around each man's neck. Colin addresses them, "I'm not going to harangue you guys with some speech. You're each a duffle bag filled with shit, so I'm going to just rip this off like a Band-Aid. This is for Richard's benefit anyway, kinda like a tableaux vivant." Kurt and Finn begin to cry. "I do hear crying will make this go quicker, so continue."

The old man clears his throat. "I like you. You got balls."

"Thanks, creepy old guy. I like you, too. Are you getting a little chubby over there?"

Dane places a hood on each of the four men. The ropes were slung over a beam and attached to the front of a forklift. Dane gets into the driver's seat and places the lift into reverse. The lift begins to beep and Dane slowly backs up. The men are raised off of the ground and the old man out of his chair. They begin to kick their feet, sans the old man who hangs lifeless, accepting his death.

Colin walks over to Dane who sits in the lift. "You still remember how to drive that thing. I'm impressed."

Dane speaks, "There are some things you learn working at Home Depot that you'll never forget. This and don't bring children there, unless you want to buy a tiny coffin."

"Wow, that just got dark."

Dane looks around the warehouse first at Benny, then Miles, and finally at the four men struggling to take their last breaths. "Uh-huh. My comment is what made it dark."

Chapter 24

Richard barely slept. The hope that his little girl was indeed still alive, then soon thereafter dashed as abruptly as the news of her initial demise, is enough to kill a person. Then, upon returning to the warehouse to find the man responsible had slithered out of his shackles, killing one of his few remaining soldiers, was a blow he was not prepared to take. He sat in a leather chair in his study all night, wondering how this all happened so quickly. He had a few fingers of a very expensive scotch in an attempt to calm his racing mind, to no avail. He reflected on the destruction of his world, pinpointing the exact moment it happened, like the asteroid that led to the extinction of the dinosaurs. He just muttered in a whispery rasp, 'Colin Graves' over and over again. His hubris and lack of due diligence had crumbled everything he had worked his whole life to build. Mistakes a younger version of himself would not have made. He dozes off for a moment, waking at first light. Strictly out of habit, he goes outside to get his paper. He's one of the few people keeping paperboys in business these days. He notices Timmy's car and shakes his head as he walks back inside. Piney is looming, keeping an eye on things.

"Timmy here?" Richard asks with a hint of suspicion.

"I don't think so, why?"

"His car is here."

"Yeah, been here since last night I think. Haven't seen him, though."

"Nowhere? Doesn't that seem odd to you? He's so annoying."

"Now that you mention it, seems quite queer."

"He hasn't asked me for anything," Richard opens the refrigerator, "Fridge is still stocked." Richard, now full of suspicion, walks back outside with Piney in tow. They approach the car cautiously and see the keys resting on top of the trunk. Richard nods to Piney, who pulls out a gun and opens it.

Piney speaks, "Son of a bitch." Timmy is in the trunk, purple with death. An envelope sits on top of him.

Richard opens the envelope. He reads the note to himself, "Dad, I'm alive and well. I know what you did to mom and I hope you die painfully for it. It looks like you lose all of your girls to other men. Alissa." Richard's blood is as hot as lava. Dead. Alive. Dead. Alive. He doesn't know how to process that his daughter has been turned against him and wishes for his demise. Both his sociopathic and psychopathic switches have been flicked. His eyes go black. "Get Ferina over here."

Richard gets dressed as he waits for Ferina. He decides to dress gangster casual; jeans, Henley, and boots with a shoulder holster. He grabs his favorite Sig Sauer from the safe and slips it into the holster. In his closet are several jackets; he pulls the leather one off the hanger. He zips his jacket, noticing the zipper possessing his logo. He smiles, remembering a time not long ago where his legitimate businesses were occupying his day to day. He heads to his study and waits on his guest to arrive.

As he sits in his chair, his thumb and forefinger pinching the bridge of his nose, he's trying to come up with a plan to get out of this quicksand he seems to have landed in. Normally, he operates like a chess master, but the board is so muddied he can't see his next move, let alone future ones. There's a knock. "Come in."

Ferina enters aggressively with his hand out, "Mr. Pembroke, to what do I owe the pleasure?"

Richard stands and they shake. He points to the chair across from his desk, "Sit. Please." They both sit and Richard continues, "Do you know what a foible is?"

Ferina squints like he didn't quite catch what Richard just said.

CHAPTER 24

"Fable?"

"Not fable, foible." He continues, "A foible is a personal weakness or character flaw. Fucking tragedies are wrought with characters displaying foibles. Usually the source of their downfall. I'm in the midst of a tragedy. I've been reflecting, trying to pinpoint my foible."

"Any luck?"

Richard shakes his head, "I'm not sure where to begin." Ferina says nothing as Richard continues, "I need you to act as my bodyguard. Colin Graves seems to have been more wily than I gave him credit."

Ferina sternly interjects, "He's crippled now and can't do shit without his brother."

"I assure you, he has somebody helping him."

Ferina shrugs his shoulders. "I don't know what you expect me to do?"

"Dane is dead per your wishes. You owe me a pound of flesh."

Ferina stands up, "Sorry pal, I remember you turning me down. No deal."

Richard smirks, like his old self toying with a field mouse, "I heard Dane Graves was killed shortly after you solicited me." He plays a recording of Ferina asking Richard to kill Dane and Richard refusing. "I'm assuming if I sent this over to your superiors, they will open an investigation into you, no?"

Ferina plops back down in his seat, "Well fuck. It seems like you have me over a barrel."

"It's really the best way to ensure cooperation. Don't worry, you get me through this, I'll make sure you're also good on the other side."

* * *

"Nope. Not giving it to you," Colin continues, sipping his coffee, as Alissa laughs. "Two packets instead of one for hot cocoa is not a special recipe, it's diabetes." They're finishing up breakfast at the hotel.

Alissa changes the subject, "Why don't we go to Mexico?"

"You know what they call diabetes in Mexico?

Alissa answers, "El diabetes?"

"El abuso de azucar."

"Random. Let's just get out of here and leave. Get a little apartment in the safest place in Mexico."

"The safest place in Mexico is not Mexico. But a small apartment sounds nice. It'll take a minute to vacuum and air condition, and no time to get to the bathroom in case you drink the water."

Alissa mockingly pantomimes laughter, "I'm serious."

"Sorry, I have to wrap this up, and I get you're ambivalent because that means killing your dad, but them's the breaks, kid."

"I'm not ambivalent; I'm worried about you. He killed my mother and his own brother. He's awful and you can't underestimate him. He's clearly evil." She hugs him, "I love you and don't want you to get hurt."

They walk back to the room, Alissa holding Colin's hand. He shakes his head, "Mexico? Really?"

"What? People escape to Mexico all the time on TV."

"When they're running from the law. And didn't you tell me when we first met that you'd been kidnapped a bunch before? You know what Mexico's main occupation is... kidnapper."

Alissa jokes, "Oh how cute, you remembered." He gets her into the room, kisses her head and tells her to use all the locks. After he leaves, she just slides her back down the door with her hands over her face, about to burst into tears.

Colin walks down the hall to Dane's room. He enters as Dane is packing up a couple of bags with various assorted weapons. "You almost ready?"

Dane nods, "You remember that terrorist thing downtown?"

"The pop-up ice cream shop or the one where you almost died?"

Dane shakes his head, "Yup, dumb question. And those were Turks that opened the ice cream shop, and I think they were legit."

Dane was working S.W.A.T back then and there was an anonymous

CHAPTER 24

call about an al-Qaeda sleeper cell in Los Angeles that had just been activated. A team was sent to this abandoned building downtown, a real rats' nest. Twelve men in body armor and helmets surrounded the building ready to breach. The second floor was accessible on two sides and was a wide-open room. Place was previously a garment manufacturer but had been empty for years. Dane led half the team up the front and another team member led the other half up the back. There were about eight terrorists in the room on the second floor. There were drugs, money, guns, and all types of contraband. Dane and the other commander conferred via radio, and both teams rushed in. Within a second, one terrorist fired an Uzi in Dane's direction.

He took a few rounds in the chest and was spun around and thrown down the stairs he had just come up. The other eleven men rushed the terrorists but couldn't subdue them before they were able to detonate an explosive device. Dane found himself in the street as the explosion filled the sky. If it weren't so tragic, the reflection off of his blue eyes would have been breathtaking.

Colin pats his shoulder, "I bet you were never so happy to have been shot."

"Tell me about it."

* * *

Dane and Colin are parked down the street from Richard's house. "You know I never liked the show."

Dane sips his coffee, "Me neither."

Colin continues, "Michael Long gets shot in the face. A billionaire saves him, gives him a new face, mind you a better one…"

"Tell that Larry Anderson."

"Right?! Larry was a handsome devil in his own right." Colin continues, "Changes his name to Michael Knight and gives him an indestructible, highly intelligent car, and it's a Pontiac?"

"You remember my first car. The Bonneville. What a piece of shit."

"Exactly, and what a misnomer. K.I.T.T. is the name of the car, no one rode around in Michael Knight."

"That we know of."

"That's gross. The Hoff did seem sorta, ya know."

Dane's peripheral caught some movement down the street.

"Look alive," Richard exits the driveway with Piney, Corky, and Ferina. As they turn the first corner, Dane pulls the car up and uses Timmy's cloned gate opener to enter. They approach Richard's house with guns drawn. The place is like Pripyat; no signs of life. All Richard's men are dead, with him, or they've called in sick until further notice. The brothers walk in and enter unopposed. Dane to Colin, "You go down, I'll go up and we'll meet in the middle."

"Devil's threesome style... hopefully our dicks don't touch." Dane runs upstairs and Colin takes the stairs down to the basement. Ingrid is on the floor, clearly drugged. Colin checks her pulse as Dane makes his way down. "She's alive, just out cold." Dane picks her up and carries her outside. They're met by a police cruiser, Dane places her in the back and sends them off.

"She'll be fine," Colin tells Dane. "Once she's up and around, you can nurse her back to health with..."

Dane cuts him off, "Don't say magic cock."

Colin says, "Magic cock" at the same time as Dane.

"Jinx!" Colin pats him on the back, "Let's put this dog down."

* * *

For the first time in as long as he can remember, Richard genuinely feels fear. It's been so long that the physical sensations compound the terror. That lump in his throat. The shallow breath that can't slip past the sternum. A hard, irregular heartbeat he feels in his neck and ears. Sweat dripping down his back and cotton in his mouth. Outside the warehouse, Piney opens the door slowly with his left hand, gun in his right. Corky and Ferina have both hands on their guns. Richard, not used to needing his gun, still has his tucked neatly in his jacket. They have no idea what's waiting for them on the other side of this door.

They slowly enter, almost as one unit. The visual hits them in the face like a shovel. Barbaric. Medieval. Miles and Benny still dead from the day before. Now, four hooded silhouettes dangle like a crib mobile. Richard covers his mouth. "What have I done?" The room spins around like it's trying to homogenize all his molecules. He throws up. Doubled over, he instructs, "Piney, get them down." He removes the first hood, the old man; his father, he sees his own resemblance to this decrepit corpse. Those dead eyes stare through him and his father's voice echoes in his head, 'I told you so.' His legs give out and he falls to his knees.

"This is not cool, man. Not fucking cool." Ferina is flummoxed out. "What have you gotten me into?"

Corky comes out of the office and throws up. Piney questions him, "What is it?"

Corky gagging, "In the fr-fr-freezer."

Richard questions him, "What? Uses your fucking words, you stuttering prick."

The door bursts open and slams into the wall. The brothers enter like specters, nearly floating in. Wrath personified, they're calm and decisive. Both are armed to the teeth; Colin is wearing several holsters and guns. Since he can't change clips, he'll just change guns a la John Woo.

Between the sound of the door and the adversarial entrance, Piney grabs his chest and falls to his knees. He's dead before one shot is fired. A massive coronary takes the first casualty. Corky, surprisingly, draws his gun the quickest and squeezes off a shot, clipping Dane's knee. Ferina fumbles then fires at Dane a second late as he falls from the shot to the knee. Ferina's bullet whizzes over his head. Dane is saved by a bullet again. Colin's first shot pierces Corky between his eyes. He fixed his stutter. Dane takes out Ferina from a kneeling position.

Richard is frozen this whole time, like in a dream, unable to move.

Colin approaches him, then Richard's brain catches up and he reaches for his gun, neatly zipped up in his jacket. He panics, trying to grab hold of the zipper. He tries to unzip. The irony of the situation presents, as it's one of his zippers. It's stuck. He can't get to his gun. Even the YKK people are laughing. Undercut the competition and get stuck in your own jacket. He tries to take his jacket off over his head. While he wrestles with himself, Colin shoots him in the gut. He falls to the ground. Colin kneels down and whispers in his ear.

* * *

Georgie is getting impatient, "So what's so important?"

"I think I have perfect childbearing hips, but no uterus, so I guess we'll never know for sure." Colin sits across from Georgie discreetly in a Chinese Restaurant.

"You crazy motherfucker."

Colin takes a bite of an egg roll, "I really hope the dog I lost last week isn't in here. Although, if he is, this is one of the best tasting egg rolls I've ever had. Oh and I have a solution to our east-side problem."

"Jesus, Vic, about time. Those fucking Russians are bleeding into our area. They're animals, man. What's the plan?"

"Amalov."

"Amalov? He's not the problem."

"He's our solution. We go in and take him out."

"Just kill Boris fucking Amalov?"

"No, I meant 'take him out' to dinner. Then maybe a hand job." Colin leans in, "After he's dead, we set up a meet with the Russians, tell them what we did and give them half the shit from the Amalov take for the east-side. Maybe forty percent or thirty? Whatever."

"Pay for our territory?"

"Yes. It's found money and by doing them a solid, they'll back off."

"But Amalov is Russian."

"They hate that guy. He's like Ari on the Bachelor... no one affiliated with the show can publicly voice an opinion about what he did to Becca for PR reasons, but no one's a fan. They're furious he's married to that Armenian witch. Not Ari... Amalov... I had a bunch of coffee today. If we did this they would be thrilled."

Georgie visibly thinks this through, then smiles, "Fuck it. Let's do it. You have a plan?"

"Do I have a plan? Is Viagra like reading glasses? Everyone needs it eventually so who cares... Of course I have a plan." He turns over the place mat and pulls out a red crayon, "What? I got here early." He explains the plan with crayon in hand, "Amalov has his main operation set-up off Alameda. I'll have a guy on the inside set off some tear gas. You, me, and the young guys go in, kill everyone inside. Except for our guy of course. Grab all his stuff. Easy breezy lemon squeezy."

"That's like some tactical shit. No old timers, eh? You ageist?"

"I'm planning on doing it during *Murder She Wrote*, you know how they get when they miss their programs. Besides, if it does go tits-up, they'll be a liability."

"I like it."

"And for my guy inside, I need some cash. He'll be paying back a debt to them to gain entrance, but we'll just get it right back."

"Yeah, no problem."

Dane stands outside Amalov's place holding a small duffel bag. The heavy-set guard outside stops him. "What the fuck you think you're doing?"

"Me and Boris are going to braid each other's hair." The guard rolls his eyes. "I have money for him, dickhead."

"Open the bag."

Dane opens the bag filled with cash. "Or you and I can go to Gap... get you some pants that fit?" The guard steps aside. Dane pats him on the shoulder, "Good choice. You may want to consider a diet, it's almost swimsuit season."

Boris Amalov is surrounded by nearly a dozen men, each covered with tattoos all very Russian looking and scary. Amalov greets Dane,

"Detective Graves, it's amazing how what was impossible days ago is now possible!"

"Yeah, totally. I had sent this Nigerian prince some money and he paid me back tenfold. Good thing I didn't delete that email."

"Okay, hand it over."

"Whoa, take it easy, I keep the bag. You know how hard this was to find? The stitching is flawless. Great for a weekend trip." Dane discreetly sends a text and quickly goes into his bag and pulls the pins on a few cans of tear gas. He drops them, places on his mask and hustles towards the bathroom.

All the entrances and exits are immediately filled with Georgie's soldiers in gas masks with AK-40's or shotguns.

They begin to clear the room. A few are casualties, but after a short period all Boris' men are dead. By this time, the tear gas has cleared and Georgie pulls his mask off and pats Colin on the back. At this point, Dane comes back into the fold and shoots Georgie in the head, then he and Colin turn on the remaining guys. They clear the room once again but now of Georgie's men. Dane takes his mask off, "Well, that worked like a charm."

Colin takes his mask off, "That was amazing. We just got rid of two major players in under five minutes. What do you say to you and me running the board? I mean, look at all this cash."

Dane is confused, "Like no more being cops?"

"Not exactly. I get out, you stay in, make sure I don't get jammed up and we just move up the food chain, then eventually, we retire rich as hell. There are like a million things I want to buy Betty... as cop, I'll be lucky to get her a shitty house in the Van Nasty. Plus, my cover is bad ass. I have contacts now up the yin-yang and tons of street cred."

Dane thinks on it. "Yeah, lets do it. But Scully and Alvarez have to go. They're the only one's that know you're 'Fitz.'"

"Yup. We need to take them out."

Dane taps his chest, "You got me out of this, I'll handle that... we'll muddy the water by opening off-shore accounts and wire some

CHAPTER 24

Russian money into them. Between this massacre and their deaths, the police, hopefully with me investigating, will just come to the sad realization they were dirty and died at the hands of Russian gangsters."

Colin puts his fist out, Dane bumps it, "To running the board..."

* * *

Richard's eyes bulge as he feels each hot bullet in his gut like a virgin being gang banged. "I'm known on the street as Vic 'Fitz' Fitzgerald. You had me, you dumb fuck. The right guy all along. I killed Sonny, Santiago, the Japs, Yakuza and now you. I'm taking over." There's the twist. Dane dances with the devil... his brother. He empties his gun into him with contempt.

* * *

Dane called the Captain and held a press conference outside the warehouse. "What we have ascertained is: Detective Ferina was working as a hit-man for Richard Pembroke. The heads of Sonny Bartucci and Santiago Salizar were in the freezer of Pembroke's warehouse. According to the coroner, the wounds are consistent with a samurai sword found at Ferina's residence. Pembroke's gang and Ferina kidnapped Ingrid Barclay yesterday. She was held hostage overnight, but was able to get a 911 call to the police. I was positioned outside his residence as surveillance due to suspicious activity. The distress call gave us probable cause to enter the house. Ingrid was able to describe a previous location, this warehouse. I sped over here. The police, under my command, arrived but unfortunately Richard, Ferina and his crew refused to be taken in and questioned in a non-violent manner. They were all killed in an ensuing shoot-out."

* * *

Max calls Dane right after his employers, Colin and Betty, were pulled into the van. Dane ran the plates and they came back to his confidential informant Benedict 'Benny' Arnold. His parents doomed him to life as a snitch. Benny lent his ride to Vincent. He was supposed to be at the execution. He was so inebriated, he blew it off. Dane tracks down Benny double time, unsure of why his brother was snatched, but positive that whatever the reason, time was of the essence. Dane finds his sleazy snitch practically passed out in a dive bar that Benny frequents. Dane storms in, grabs Benny by the scruff of his neck, and pulls him into the back alley. Then sobers him up with his fists.

Benny squints up at Dane, visibly miffed that Dane ruined his buzz. "Dane, man, what the fuck?"

Dane speaks fast and chooses his words carefully, "A van registered to you was just involved in a kidnapping. The victims are my brother and my sister-in-law. Where are they?"

"How should I know?"

Dane punches him in the stomach. "Why would somebody even feel compelled to do this?"

Benny gasps for air and places his hands up, "Shit man, this guy I work for, Richard, pays well for intel and I mentioned what I had heard about this guy, 'Fitz.'"

Dane punches him again.

Benny places his hands in front of his face, "Fuck. I hear shit man, I was just trying to get ahead."

"This is the instance that you choose to demonstrate an iota of ambition? Call him, tell him you fucked up."

"He'll fucking kill me."

"I'm going to kill you if you don't. He already knows you're a moron, maybe he won't hold it against you."

Benny fumbles with his phone as he dials. "Richard, uh, it's Benny. The guy I was telling you about turns out to not be the guy. I was misinformed." There's a pause. Benny hangs up the phone because Richard has hung up on him.

CHAPTER 24

"Where are they?"

"How should I know?"

"Call him back."

"He won't pick up, but my van has GPS. You can track that shit."

"You better pray they're fine."

Dane grabs Benny and throws him in the back of his car.

* * *

Cleaning up messes and taking care of business is second nature for Dane. He sits in an apartment in the dark. He's stereotypically dressed in all black and has a nine-millimeter Glock with a silencer. Poor stupid Max has no clue. His key hits the lock and he clumsily walks into his home holding his dinner. As he flicks on the switch, before his eyes can adjust to the light, he has a bullet lodged securely in his brain. Max was Colin's bodyguard and it's his blunder that led to Colin and Betty's abduction. While it may be debatable whether or not he could have done something, Dane decided to make this big moose pay.

* * *

Colin goes back to the hotel to spring Alissa. He opens the door and she's wearing one of the hotel robes. As he closes the door, she unties the robe and slides it off of her shoulders and it drops to the ground, revealing her naked body. "Whoa," Colin looks down at the ground, "Put the robe back on, por favor."

At first she thinks he's being shy and playful, "Come on, Col. I'm ready."

He picks up the robe, not looking at her as he covers her up, "So, this is not going to happen... you're a kid."

"Come on. I want you." She places her finger in her mouth and wiggles her right foot on her big toe.

"I'm sorry, girlie. Our story wasn't written by Shakespeare. I'm not going to fall for the daughter of my enemy under any circumstances. Our story is written by someone who can't even spell iambic pentameter and is probably some asshole that does Crossfit for fun."

"I thought you liked me."

"I do like you. I love my wife."

"She's gone."

"So am I. There's no planet that you compete with her. I told you from the beginning you were a pawn and I wasn't going to hurt you. And while I may have hurt you in a way I didn't anticipate, you'll be better off driving people your own age crazy."

"I love you."

"No you don't. You don't even know me. Not the real me."

"What am I supposed to do now?"

"I've taken over your father's business in its entirety. You'll never need money and I've convinced an old friend to keep an eye on you until you're old enough to handle things yourself. You'll be fine."

*　*　*

Tony hustles back to the states once he gets word that his brother, Trick, is dead. He finds a nice plot in a quiet cemetery and buries him. He sits by his grave, reminiscing out loud about some of the times they had as kids. Colin and Dane show up, both sharply dressed, Dane holding a folder.

Tony springs up and goes for his gun, but both Dane and Colin draw quicker, and Tony uses his thumb and forefinger to drop the gun on the ground. "What do you want?"

Colin replies calmly, "Take it easy big fella. We come here as friends."

Tony is standoffish, "You killed my boss and generally guys like me are a liability for new management."

Dane jumps in, "True, but you had nothing to do with the inciting event and in fact, we not only want to shed some light on what

CHAPTER 24

happened to your brother, we want to offer you a different role in our new organization."

"My brother killed himself for losing large on the ponies."

Dane hands him a folder, "Here are pictures lifted from video at the parking structure; your buddy Vincent left the structure earlier that day the police found your brother. Look at the time stamp."

Colin continues, "That clump of foreskin you called your boss had Vincent kill your brother for losing his daughter and made it look like a suicide as to not anger one of his best men."

Tony is furious, "That prick."

"So..." Colin tucks his gun into his pants, "As you mentioned, we are the new management, and instead of eliminating a valuable member of the team, we are offering you a different role. You go back to babysitting Alissa, super high salary with plenty of vacation days. Practically no responsibility and no chance of dying on the job or getting arrested."

Dane places his hand out, "But your job is to keep her in line. No revenge shit, you squash that nonsense. We played her hard to get Richard and she'll be pretty pissed."

Tony shakes Dane's hand, "I got this and appreciate the knowledge you just dropped on me."

Epilogue

Fifteen years flies by in a blink. Colin and Dane age like movie stars, less worse for wear than regular folks due to their massive wealth and access to the best of everything. The future is not much different. The machines didn't take over because, let's face it, they were created by less than perfect beings so the idea that artificial intelligence would be able to fill in the blanks is purely science fiction. However, medicine has taken leaps and bounds over the decade and a half, and Colin has had a fully functioning arm for the past five years. It's clunky and robotic, but works well and he can crush aluminum cans with ease.

The brother's endeavors post-Richard exploded exponentially as they went from the largest criminal presence in LA to an international crime syndicate. "Fitz" became a Keyser Söze type figure; an almost mythical anti-hero and was an amalgamation of the brothers, neither one playing the role exclusively. They insulated the entity and no one knew they were working for 'him' or dealt with 'him' directly. People either worked with Colin and Dane directly on his behalf for big deals, or their representatives for things easily handled by underlings. Their inner circle was composed of ex-military or ex-police and they paid so well that loyalty was never an issue. However, fear of crossing "Fitz" was omnipresent and since he became nearly omniscient by paying well for any intel, people would rather die than flip on him. Betraying him would place their family or loved ones at risk.

One of the main contributing factors for this unbelievable growth was Dr. Phil losing his medical license for abusing his prescription pad. He fell back into the family business: shipping. The brothers were able to move anything anywhere, domestically and internationally,

EPILOGUE

without a problem once they partnered up with Dr. Phil. If insurgents needed weapons or a zoo needed a panda, they could deliver anything. They became an unstoppable force.

About six month ago, Colin and Dane were heading home after a lovely meal, when they were jumped by a couple of tweakers. Just a random occurrence having nothing to do with how they spent their day to day. Dane was about to handle the situation when he was aided by an ex-special forces soldier, John Sage, who just happened by and took charge of the situation. Mid-twenties, handsome, capable, Colin took to the young man and brought him into the fold...

Colin enters an abandoned building in a bit of a panic. Dane's emergency text seemed dramatic, which of course was not like Dane. He enters, barely able to see, using the light on his phone to maneuver this death trap of a building. He hears Dane in the corner, breathing heavy, clearly in pain, but suppressing as much noise a possible. "Hey brother, you delivering a baby over there?" POW. Colin is hit by a bullet and spun around, thrown to the ground landing nearly next to Dane who is lying against the wall plugging his gunshot wounds with his own fingers. He turns to Dane, "Fuck, Dane, I think I owe you a dollar." Dane smiles, barely able to speak on his last legs. "Just hang in there a little longer. Can you do that for me?" Dane winks at him.

John Sage enters the frame, holding a flashlight and his rifle. "Hey boss."

"Hey, Billy Boy. I have to say, I'm pretty disappointed. Not *The Bachelor* season 53 disappointed, but pretty disappointed."

"How do you know my real name?"

"John Sage? Really? The supposed illegitimate son of Benedict Arnold? Besides *The Bachelor* and cartoons, I watch the History Channel from time to time. And we've been watching you since you slipped out of this warehouse, the day Benny was killed."

"You could've saved him... and you let him die."

"I absolutely could've saved him, just like Rose could've made room for Jack on the big piece of boat she was floating on, but she liked the idea of no romantic encumbrances and a jewel the size of her fist. Besides, he was the whole fucking reason my life was taken from me."

"You were watching me. What the fuck does that mean?"

"Well, before you overreact and shoot me because you'll want to hear the whole story... we also killed your mom, Lola. You're welcome. We had her shanked in prison."

"Why on Earth would you do that?"

"Your real father, Vincent, who Benny killed... do you see now why maybe you should've decided to ask questions first, then shoot your gun later?"

"What the fuck is happening?"

"Let me start again. Dane and I made a little wager a la *Trading Places* fifteen years ago, to make things interesting. A social experiment, nature versus nurture."

Billy starts to run his hands through his long hair, pacing and panicking.

Colin continues, "If Lola lived, she would inject your inheritance in her arm so we had some bull dyke shank her in prison. Then we found you a solid foster family; we opened doors for you that would never have been there if we hadn't inserted ourselves, albeit it from afar. Dane thought no matter what we did and what schools you went to or what toys you had, you would come looking for the people who killed who you thought was your father. I thought you weren't as far gone and would've just enjoyed getting the life your younger self had always dreamed of."

Billy points his gun at Colin, "You assholes!"

Colin turns to Dane, "You were right. Should I Venmo you the dollar?"

Dane smiles one last time and dies.

Colin smiles with his eyes wet, "See ya soon, brother."

Billy wraps his brain around all of this, "So if you knew this could happen, why did Dane let me get the drop on him?"

"For the same reason I did... Dane was dying and I've been dead for fifteen years. We were both ready to go." Colin starts to feel death's cold hand on his back. He whispers, "Come here... I'm almost out of time."

Billy moves forward, kneeling, "I can't believe I did this... I did exactly what was expected and now I'm sickened."

Colin waves him closer, and whispers in his ear. Billy's eyes bulge with fear as he looks in Colin's robotic hand at Benny's grenade, pin pulled and a second from taking them both far from here.

Colin suddenly finds himself in a glowing white room. He looks down and sees his arm is back. He feels his face; the creases and wrinkles from the past fifteen years gone. His eyes focus and before him he sees Betty standing there, as real as the last time he saw her, "You look great, by the way." She gives him the middle finger. "There it is, the money shot." He places his arms out and she jumps into them and they kiss. He looks at her, alive for the first time in as long as he can remember, "Sorry it took me a while... Dane would've been lost without me."

"Dane would be lost, or you became obsessed with *The Bachelor*?" Betty responds playfully.

"A little from column A and little from column B. And were you spying on me? I feel a little violated."

"It's a good thing you didn't remarry or even date, otherwise we wouldn't be speaking right now."

Colin wipes his brow, "Whew. I had a feeling other chicks would be a problem. I had a ton of opportunities, believe me, like Elvis opportunities. And gorgeous." Betty hits him, and he nervously laughs as he continues, "But I passed on them all. I was too sad." He gives her puppy dog eyes.

Betty hits him, "And you went to multiple Five Finger Death Punch concerts without me! I couldn't ever get you to go, I get killed and then you go with Dane?"

Colin shrugs. "They're amazing live."

"If I wasn't so happy to see you I would be very mad at you right now."

"You look great, by the way...."

Made in the USA
Middletown, DE
13 February 2021